The Moment of Truth

Shari Low

First published in 2015 by Shari Low

Author's website: www.sharilow.com

Cover design by Jim Divine
at www.jimdivine.com

ISBN-13: 978-1508501398
ISBN-10: 1508501394

To
J, C & B

Everything. Always.

<u>Personal Proposals</u>

Candlelight, champagne, a diamond ring, a promise ...
It might be the most perfect day, the unforgettable moment
you set your future with the love of your life.

Or ...

It might be a big fat cheesefest that's been done a million
times before.

Longing to ask the person of your dreams to walk down the
aisle with you?

Let us turn your special moment into a unique experience
that truly reflects your personalities.

We can help you arrange to write "Marry Me" in the sand
on a Balinese beach.

Or pop the question at 5 miles high while skydiving over the
Alps.

Or have a flash mob rap your declaration of devotion.

Make it more than an engagement ... make it a
Personal Proposal.

www.personalproposals.com

1

"If we ever meet that bloke who was our careers officer at school, remind me to kill him," Tash said. At least that's what Laney thought she said. It was difficult to hear over the noise of the wind and forty horses and their riders restlessly waiting for the command to charge.

Laney's stallion stepped to the side and she gently pulled on the reins to steady him. They were the central figures in a long line of warriors waiting just under the precipice of a Stirling hill, all of them dressed like extras from *Braveheart*. The attention to detail had been meticulous, no expense spared. The Hollywood take on the rustic Highland dress of the late thirteenth century. The wild hair. The battle equipment of a poor man's army. The heavy, excruciating itch of an ancient Scottish plaid that was right now chafing Tash's inner thighs. She swore under her breath, an expletive aimed at no one in particular. When the client had first contacted them from his office on the forty-fifth floor of a New York corporate bank, this was the last scenario she'd expected. Tash's thoughts had immediately jumped to the warm, fire-lit halls of a grand Perthshire estate. Or perhaps the glorious surroundings of a historic bedroom at Edinburgh castle. Or even, dear God make it happen, a luxury yacht floating on the glistening waters of Loch Lomond.

But no. Turns out Hal Bradeston's fiancée had a Scottish great-great-granny, a genetic connection that had elevated *Braveheart* to her favourite movie of all time. According to Hal, his beloved Diandra adored the windswept romance and epic drama of it all. No mention of the incidents involving blood, gore and accents so dodgy they sounded like Shrek impersonating Sean Connery. While on crack.

A line of horses' heads bobbed up as Millie rode into view, her flame red tresses floating in the air behind her, an ethereal vision of utter gorgeousness. Riding alongside was Hal, all twenty stone of him, on a horse that would definitely deserve an extra few carrots when this was done.

Tash was the first to react. "Holy Papa Smurf, he's wearing the blue face paint."

Laney sighed and leant closer, so that the other thirty-eight riders in the line-up wouldn't hear. "Ten grand, Tash. We're earning ten grand for this. That's ten thousand reasons to slap a smile on your cynical face and help make this perfect."

Tash's response was cut short by Millie and Hal thudding to a halt in front of them, thrilled expressions on their faces – his painted, hers not. Millie looked like a kid on Christmas morning. This was a woman who loved her job; adored every heart-thumping, romantic, windswept moment of it. She could barely contain her excitement.

"OK, she's ready. She's sitting at the table at the edge of the visitors' centre café, facing this way. This is going to be incredible!"

"Are you ready, Hal?" Laney asked, her voice calm and warm.

"Sure am. Let's do it." He had all the gung-ho confidence and attitude of one of those motivational speakers that make people walk across hot coals without a fire extinguisher on standby.

Like a true warrior going into battle, he punched the air with his fist, yelled "Freedom," and thundered off.

"Shit, he's moving. Go! Go! GO!" Laney yelled to the others, who broke the perfect line by reacting with varying degrees of speed.

The riders from the Stirling South Stables were more used to a civilised, leisurely hack than a gallop across a cold field in pursuit of a thirteenth century legend on horseback.

By the time they'd gone a hundred metres over the brow of the hill and were heading down in the direction of the William Wallace visitors' centre, they'd managed to form a cohesive group again. Millie spotted Diandra in the distance, looking around her as she waited for Hal to return from the toilet. Getting him into costume, wig and face paint had been done in five minutes, and altogether he'd been gone for nearly fifteen. The cover story of a lavatory visit caused by a dodgy haggis wasn't going to hold up for much longer.

It was a little old lady sitting at a table, defending herself against the stiff breeze with a cuppa and a ginger slice, who spotted them and pointed first. Her tea drinking chums soon followed.

Eventually, Diandra turned in the direction of the invading force. Millie just hoped the cameraman furtively recording Diandra's reaction from a few tables away was getting all this in close up.

Fifty metres. Thirty. Ten. Hal held up his fist again and the riders slowed to a stop behind him.

He dismounted from the relieved horse, and strutted towards his girlfriend, who was standing, mouth open, eyes wide with shock, trembling so much her tartan beanie hat was visibly shaking.

Sir Hal Wallace was in front of her now, and he went down on one knee, to gasps of "Aaaaaw" from the bus party of elderly tourists from Carlisle.

"Diandra," he said, voice thick with the Scottish brogue he'd been practising for weeks as he worked up to the big line from the movie. *"Ah love you. Always have. Ah want to marry you."*

Tash gave Millie a nudge. "At least his Scottish accent's better than Mel Gibson's," she hissed. "And he's yet to call her Sugartits. Always a bonus."

Millie wasn't listening. Two gigantic tears dropped down her cheeks as she watched Diandra's shock and confusion turn to joy and delight.

"Diandra Kapalskowi, will ye be ma bride?"

Millie was so caught in the moment she didn't realise she was nodding. *Say yes*, she willed. *Say yes. And please say it before Hal notices that his knee has sunk so far into the sodden mud that if he was boycotting*

4

underwear like a true Scotsman, he'd be about to feel the wrath of nature on the nethers.

"Yes," Diandra whispered, to a rousing cheer from forty costumed riders and fourteen blue-rinsed ladies in comfortable shoes.

As Sir Hal Wallace took his bride in his chubby arms and quite literally swept her off her feet, the reactions from the Proposal Planners differed wildly.

Laney pictured the cheque clearing on the balance sheet. Millie cried some more and sent up a prayer of thanks that it had all gone to plan. And Tash muttered something about Smurfs being banned from mating.

Their job was done.

2 LANEY

"Time to get the diaries out."

Laney tried her best to keep things on track, despite the fact that Cam's erection was pressing into her back and his hand had snaked around her body and was now inserting itself into the folds of her short, cream, silk robe.

Laughing, she smacked it away, and reached into the upper cupboard for two mugs.

"I have a big day today. Loads to prepare for the next month's proposals and I'm meeting with a new client. I need to be out of the door in fifteen minutes …"

"That gives me time to do it twice," her husband joked.

With the swift expertise of a barista, she slid a cup onto the tray of the coffee machine and pressed the 432 buttons required to make a skinny latte. Cam Cochrane had a thing about gadgets. Their townhouse in Bearsden, what estate agents would call an "upmarket suburb of Glasgow", was packed with them, the more convoluted and geeky the better. This was why their coffee machine rivalled the technological complexity of the Hadron Collider.

It was also why her diary was of the Luddite paper variety and his was a tablet he'd loaded with more gizmos than a flight deck – apt really, as the first time she met him her immediate thought had been Val Kilmer, *Top Gun*. The gym-defined body, the short blonde hair, the slightly arrogant expression, as if he knew something the rest of the world had yet to learn.

How many times had she watched that movie with her dad when she was a kid? At least monthly. She could recite the script pretty much verbatim and the imagery had obviously sunk into her psyche, leaving her with an irresistible attraction to blokes who looked like they could fly a jet upside down and beat their opponents in a topless game of beach volleyball. She'd married him within six months, an uncharacteristically impulsive act that she'd never regretted.

"OK," Laney said, holding out the coffee as a barrier between her erect nipples and his torso, giggling at his expression of resigned disappointment. She threw him a bone of titillation. "Here you go. Right, diaries first and no huffing."

Cam pulled a leather breakfast barstool across the slate floor, plonked himself down and sighed as he flicked to the calendar on his iPad. He browsed the screen for a few seconds. "Right. So I'm away today, in Birmingham until Sunday. Then away again on Monday, to London for a few nights. Then the following week

I'm in Manchester with Anderston Inc. We're training their middle management level to use the force."

The force.

Cam was one of a team of corporate NLP practitioners, super-sharp business consultants that worked with blue chip companies on neuro-linguistic programming, the science that trained people to focus on reaching goals and making life changes. Or something like that. It had seemed really interesting when they'd first met, but back in the first flush of lust, he could have told her that he collected stamps while trainspotting and she'd have found it fascinating, as long as he was naked. Things hadn't changed that much over the last five years. She still found him utterly irresistible – as long as she'd already had her coffee.

Attention back on her diary, she scanned the dates he'd just given her.

Laney groaned. "But you'll miss Tash's birthday party."

"Somehow, I don't think she'll be gutted." He had a point. In her very own inimitably candid style, Tash had once blurted out that she'd rather spend the night with a fungal infection than socialising with Cam. Laney didn't understand her friend's antipathy then and she still didn't now. The only explanation she had was that Tash thought NLP was, as she frequently quoted, "A load of New Age pish."

However, she wasn't going to lose sleep over it, especially since, at the last count, Tash disliked the approximate population of the whole world.

"Good point. But I'd have liked you to be there." She absent-mindedly ran her fingers through her chestnut pixie crop. Going from locks that reached halfway down her back a month ago had taken huge courage and three large glasses of cava, but now she loved it. Up and out the door in twenty minutes instead of spending an hour with a hair dryer and straighteners. Shame Cam preferred it long, but it would grow on him eventually.

"Anyway," she pressed on, flicking over the pages, "I'm in Inverness the following week – proposal on the shores of Loch Ness. Darling, we are going to be like ships passing in the night. I think we're only going to be in the same city for one or two nights this month." Sometimes it just worked out like that. But the good thing was that often the busiest times were followed by dips in their workload when they could make up for the separations by nipping away for a few days. A romantic break to Paris. A couple of nights in a gorgeous chalet in Killin on the banks of Loch Tay.

"We'll make up for it," he said, reading her mind.

Laney checked another date and frowned. "Can we make up for it the weekend after that? It's peak ovulation."

"I can make that happen," Cam assured her. With a swift, sweeping motion he pushed his iPad to the side, reached over, pulled her towards him, and undid the belt on her robe. It dropped to the floor, exposing her nakedness and he immediately leaned in to plant a series of kisses along her neck.

"But let's have …" Kiss. Kiss. "A little…" Kiss. Kiss. "Practice." Kiss. "Right now."

Laney's hands ran up the front of his rock hard pecs, then curled around his neck.

The new client might need to wait.

3 TASH

The alarm clock snapped into action, blaring out a chorus of "Oh Happy Day". Eyes still shut, Tash reached down to the side of the bed for a discarded Jimmy Choo pump, then used the sole to batter the buttons on the top of the clock until the tune stopped.

Oh. Happy. Fucking. Day. If only there was a song entitled, "Oh Happy Bugger Off And Don't Come Back Until After Noon".

The light was streaming in through the voile curtains and even the slightest effort to open her eyes was causing laser death rays to shoot directly to her brain. *Reminder to self, buy blackout blinds.* They were on the list of required furnishings she'd made when she moved into the flat. After three years, she should probably have struck a couple of them off the list by now.

With a loud groan, she levered herself up into the sitting position, then pushed back the raven hair that covered her face like a curtain. It wasn't her normal look. With her chic black bob, short fringe and bright red lipstick, she was more of a cross between an impeccably groomed Uma Thurman in *Kill Bill* and a glossy Dita Von Teese. The nightwear was a bit of a contrast though – one of half a dozen American football shirts she'd picked up on a trip to Miami last year. Today's variety was white and announced that she was affiliated with the Miami Dolphins.

A dolphin with a thundering pain at both temples. Painkillers required urgently. On a scale of bad ideas, that last mojito had dinged the bell at the top. The night had started off fairly civilised. A few drinks in Glasgow's West End with her twin brothers, Jordan and John O'Flynn, professional athletes who played rugby for the Glasgow Gore. Athletes. So they should, in theory, be clean living, disciplined specimens who treated their bodies like temples. And they did. If you were referring to the types of temples that hosted weekly drinking sessions that invariably ended with unusually large drunk men up on the bar singing songs that demanded audience participation and had an unusually high number of references to the penis. The cobbles of Ashton Lane were crossed several times as they moved from bar to bar, only stopping at the heaving Jinty McGinty's pub when the rest of the rugby team arrived. It was all downhill from there.

Without even turning to look, she reached to her left, opened the drawer in the walnut bedside table, popped two paracetamol out of the foil wrapper that immediately came to hand, reached down to the side of the bed for a bottle of water and then administered the self-prescribed pain relief.

Eight a.m. Bugger. An hour until she had to be at work. That left her enough time to jump out of bed, remove her Dolphins T-shirt and pants combo, pull on her workout gear, do five miles, home, shower, muesli, then walk five minutes from her flat in the old Post Office building in George Square to the office in Ingram Street.

Or she could lie there, smoke a cigarette in bed and watch something on TV designed to lower the intelligence of the nation.

Cigarette and a repeat of a screeching talk show won. Some woman from Ipswich was accusing the father of her six children of romancing the neighbour. If "romancing" meant shagging her in the garden hut while the missus was down the bingo.

Tash sat up and crossed her legs, putting the ashtray onto the bed in front of her. Ouch, those inner thighs still hurt. Good old USA Hal and a thoroughbred stallion called Butch had a lot to answer for.

On the TV, a fight broke out and, in her second major dilemma of the day, Tash was torn between switching it off before the screeching made her head explode and waiting to see if the betrayed partner would deck the neighbour and then tell the scrawny bloke to take a hike.

The betrayed partner crumbled. After the altercation calmed back down to minor wails and recriminations, she begged him to come back to her, tears and snot everywhere.

Tash pressed the off button and slumped back in disgust.

If she ever humiliated herself like that over a man, she'd give Laney a gun and beg her friend to shoot her.

Actually, she might do that anyway if this hangover didn't subside soon.

At her age, she should really know better. She was thirty next week – what the hell was she doing going drink for drink with twenty-four-year-old rugby players that had the constitutions of tanks?

How had she got home? A flashback made her wince. Drunk. Taxi. Chips. There may also have been a kebab. Lord, she was six kids and garden hut away from sitting next to the woman in the chic tracksuit on that talk show.

Still, no one had to know about her self-inflicted state. Laney would only give her a full-scale lecture on the risks of drinking to excess and Millie would just want details of every guy who was there and then interrogate her as to the potential mating qualities of each one of them. On one of the occasions Tash had taken her business partners to one of her brothers' rugby nights out, Laney had persuaded the coach to hire them to arrange a proposal to his girlfriend and Millie had spent the whole night trying to fix her up with a prop forward called … called … called … nope, it wasn't in there.   Blank.

She stubbed out the cigarette and put the ashtray back on the bedside table. The headache was finally calming down from apocalyptic to a raging thud. It was progress. All she needed to do now was get up, make it to the shower and then, by some biological miracle involving bloody-minded determination and tar-like coffee, get herself into a human condition before nine a.m.

Flush.

It took a moment for it to register. Yep, that had been the sound of her toilet flushing and no, she wasn't in the bathroom.

She reached for the Jimmy Choo. If she was going to get murdered by a burglar in her own home she was going to go down fighting with an eight-inch heel on an iconic shoe.

She reached for her phone, typed in 999, and let her thumb hover over the "call" button, ready to summon the cavalry to defend her against … nothing. No charging burglars. No imminent attack on her general shambolic being. Not another sound. Perhaps she'd imagined the flush. Maybe there was so much alcohol in her system that she was hallucinating. Or perhaps her senses were so heightened by the intoxicated state that the flush she'd heard actually came from Sy, the flash bloke with the Porsche that lived next door. She'd seen him yesterday morning in the hall. Tall. Gorgeous. Cheekbones from the pages of *GQ*. Wearing an impeccably tailored suit, accessorised with a silk tie, Italian shoes and a six foot model who bore a resemblance to Giselle.

"Hi."

"Fuck!" she blurted.

"Erm, no, you're fine thanks," he replied. He filled the doorway, making escape impossible, so it was just as well that, size aside, this guy had all the threatening presence of a Labradoodle - if a Labradoodle's morning outfit of choice was nothing but a pair of black jeans and a six pack.

His black floppy fringe didn't hide the sleepy eyes and as he leant against the doorway his lazy grin would, in the right circumstances, be admittedly cute.

It was … was … nope, she still couldn't get his name. In the name of the holy prop forward, why wouldn't her brain engage?

However, she was lucid enough to realise that if Millie were here right now she'd be doing a Mexican wave.

Another fuzzy flashback. Arriving home. She'd dropped her keys. Someone had picked them up. Opened the door for her. The faint whiff of a kebab. She knew it! There had definitely been a kebab.

"I saw you home last night. You invited me in. I'm just filling in the blanks to speed this up a little," he told her.

"Oh." Tash dropped the shoe. It now seemed superfluous to requirements given that he'd obviously been in her apartment all night and she was still alive, in one piece and her flat screen telly was still on the wall.

"And you slept …?"

Oh no. They hadn't. She hadn't. Had she?

"On the couch. You told me if I laid a finger on you, you'd remove my testicles with a spoon."

That sounded about right. One night drunken stands had never been her thing. One night sober stands, yes, but the combo of booze and fried carbohydrates had never been much of an aphrodisiac.

"Anyway, my intact bollocks and I are just heading off."

She attempted to avert her eyes as he shook out the T-shirt he was holding and pulled it over his head, but

somehow her focus refused to be diverted from
shoulders so defined they rippled as they moved.

Bugger.

"OK. Well, thanks. For seeing me home. And, you
know, not giving me any reason to use my spoon, erm
… erm ... erm …"

"Matt."

"Matt! I knew that." The flush creeping up her
cheeks made it clear that she actually didn't.

With another grin, he turned and headed down the
hall in the direction of the door. Tash sighed and
slouched back on the pillows. Bloody hell. What a
beamer. Still, at least he was gone.

"So I was thinking ..."

His voice invoked a surprised jolt and a strangled,
"Fuck!"

"Again, thanks, but I'm fine," he answered with a
grin as his head peeked around the door.

Tash basked in the inner heat of extreme
mortification. "Sorry, thought you were gone."

"Do you want to go out some time? For a drink?
Although maybe not as many as last night?" He was
loving this, she could tell. Found it all very amusing.

"No. Thanks. I have a boyfriend."

"You don't. I checked with your brothers."

Damn. Those two would be crap in a CIA
interrogation situation.

"I do. They just don't know about him."

One eyebrow lifted and disappeared under his fringe.
"Well, if your secret boyfriend ever isn't around, I'd like
to take you out. I'll leave my number."

He flipped a business card out of his pocket and

tossed it on to the dresser.

Only when the door banged shut did she force herself into a standing position and tentatively ease her way across the room. The card was sitting face up.

Matt Buchanan. Accountant.

An accountant. Oh dear God. It was fairly certain she'd have more in common with her fake, non-existent boyfriend than with an accountant. Not that she was stereotyping.

Twenty minutes and that tar-like coffee later, she followed in the wake of the man with the least exciting job in the world.

Carefully closing her door so it wouldn't bang, she turned left and headed for the lift. The next door neighbour's door opened at the exact moment she walked past it. Of course it would. She looked like she'd spent the night in a skip, so clearly it was going to be the day she met everyone she'd ever known.

"Hey, Toots." If Matt the Accountant was on the young side of the abacus, Sy the Flash Neighbour With The Porsche was veering towards the other. In his forties, he had the wealthy, polished exterior of someone who had life sussed. So sussed, he owned the four bedroom duplex penthouse, while she lived next door in a one bedroom flat that was yet to be adorned with blinds.

"Morning. No Giselle?"

It took him a fleeting moment before he caught on.

"Nope, she's on a shoot today. Lingerie. It's her specialty."

"Lovely," she sneered, before carrying on down the hallway, determinedly ignoring his smug, gloating face.

"Interesting bloke who delivered you home last night. Think he left his chips in the lift."

Nope, she wasn't going to rise to it. She wasn't. Definitely not. What a twat. She was well past him now and kept her eyes front and centre.

He could carry on his conversation with the back of her head.

"So. Tonight. Seven o'clock. My place. Come naked."

Again – what a twat.

The Patron Saint of Swift Escapes must have been on duty because as soon as she pressed the button for the lift, the doors swung open.

Tash stomped in, pressed ground and then watched as the doors started to close before her intensely irritating neighbour reached them. She made no move to re-open them. Instead, just as they were about to fully shut, when she could see he was just feet away and within hearing distance, she let rip with the best retort her addled state would allow.

"You are such a dick," she spat. "I'll be there at eight."

4 MILLIE

There was a distinct aroma of toast in the air when Millie opened the door to the kitchen. The plate and the pile of crumbs on the table next to it told her that he'd been there. Cue butterflies in her stomach and an irrepressible smile. When she told anyone that even after living with Leo for two years, he still had this effect on her every single day, they reacted with incredulity. Except Tash. She reacted by making vomiting gestures into the nearest bin.

Pulling her fleece robe tighter around her to block out the chill, Millie grabbed a banana from the fruit bowl and then headed through the heavy door to the main lounge area. There he was. Standing in front of the full-length mirror by the slate fireplace, rehearsing lines. Pausing in the doorway, she watched him for a few moments. Aside from the fact that he was wearing nothing but white, skinny cotton boxer shorts, he was a captivating sight.

Millie Jones had loved him from the moment she clapped eyes on him.

They'd met at a gallery when she and Tash had been on a reconnaissance mission, looking for venues for an art lover who wanted to propose by having an artist dip himself in body paint and then crawl across a huge canvas, leaving the words "Marry Me" in his wake.

Leo had been there, one of the waiting staff, passing round canapés while some pretentious sculptor gave a twenty-minute soliloquy on the artistic merit of constructing a six-foot apparition made entirely of sponge.

"They're only in here to get out of the cold," Tash had whispered, gesturing to the crowd.

Millie shushed her, face flushing in case anyone had overheard, but the noise had made Leo turn, smile, catch her eyes and that was it. Love at first sight. Truly, she knew. There was no explaining it. It wasn't necessarily his looks, although she'd always gone for the long haired, skinny vibe. It was his – oh God, she was going to sound seriously bonkers – but there was an instant familiarity there, an inherent feeling that she'd known him before and a thunderbolt connection that she'd never experienced with anyone else.

"Eeew," Tash murmured, her words barely permeating Millie's trance-like state. "What's with that guy's stringy hair? Someone ought to tell him that the other Musketeers are on the phone and they want their wet-look gel back."

Pause.

Tash tugged on her sleeve. "Would you stop leering?

C'mon, hon, let's go – if I don't get a coffee and a pecan plait in the next ten minutes I'm going to go major diva cow on someone. Millie? Millie?" she hissed.

The words seemed like they were being said in another ether, like a TV droning on in the background.

She heard them again.

"Millie, are you OK? Too hot? About to faint? You look really weird. C'mon, let's get out of h— Where are you going? Oh, Christ, she's gone rogue."

Tash's words faded into the distance behind her as Millie was drawn towards him, their gaze never breaking, until they were separated only by a large tray of bite sized vol-au-vents.

"Tuna? Chicken? Coffee somewhere else?"

His voice was hypnotic, horny and utterly irresistible. And he knew. He felt it, too.

Tash was left behind to vent her general irritation over a pecan plait in a nearby bakery. Meanwhile, Millie and Leo's cappuccinos turned into a twelve-hour encounter in which she learned that he was an actor, working in bars and on agency shifts to make cash between roles. His last major part had been in a commercial for Scotch pies and he was up for a minor role in a new sketch show.

That day ended with them wrapped in each other's arms in his studio flat, above a dry cleaners on a busy street in Glasgow city centre.

He didn't get the sketch show part, but he got Millie.

The studio had been their home for the first six months, until they'd pooled their finances – or rather, Millie raided her meagre savings – and they moved to Shawlands, in the south side of the city, and rented the flat they lived in now.

It wasn't much but Millie didn't care about money or property. Sure, it would be great to have Laney's swanky pad in Bearsden, but not if it meant being married to a guy who worked so hard he was never around. And yes, Tash's city centre pad was in a great location, but it was tiny. Millie and Leo's basement conversion in an old building might be ramshackle, might have no viable heating and might come with a fairly permanent pungent aroma, thanks to the old lady upstairs' dedication to cabbage, but when you opened the doors on a dry day it was glorious. Even more so if a pants-laden clothes horse wasn't blocking the view. Housework wasn't one of Leo's talents. But then, as he regularly pointed out, it was highly improbable that Al Pacino was a whizz with a Dyson before he got *Scarface*.

He was rehearsing for a last minute audition that was taking place that afternoon – an ensemble role, one of five brothers in a Glasgow gang flick. The actor that had originally been cast had been forced to pull out yesterday, only days before shooting started, because he'd been injured rescuing hostages from a real life siege situation. Or been attacked by a gang of gangland criminals after he foiled a bank job. Or whatever other rumour his agent was spreading. The truth was that he'd staggered out of a nightclub after too many Cheeky Vimto cocktails, and fallen down a pothole, breaking his leg in two places.

Millie felt terrible for him, but she was grateful for the opportunity it presented for Leo. The gig would give him three months' work. It wouldn't change their lives, but it would be enough for him to quit working in The Bean Counter, the city centre coffee joint frequented by stressed out secretaries and suits who were too busy barking into their mobile phones to even acknowledge the guy behind the counter.

It made Millie's heart ache. He wanted this career so badly and, if she was honest, she wanted it for him too. How many nights had they lain in bed discussing how they'd get married as soon as he'd made it and had a bit of money behind him?

Of course, she was happy to be the main breadwinner and support him in the meantime. He was a true talent. He deserved to be nurtured and encouraged.

He stopped speaking as he spotted her in the mirror and turned around to greet her with a distracted, "Morning, babe."

That was OK. He had a lot on his plate. This was an important role for him and he'd probably been up for hours, repeating his scene again and again.

Perfectionism drove him. That, and the fact that he was almost thirty, and moving from being considered for the "young hunk" roles to the single dad, lawyer, and – in this role – waster brother who had never amounted to much.

"I won't disturb you," she said, "but can I get you some more toast? Or anything else?"

Unsurprisingly, he shook his head. He never snacked between his three meals a day. That might explain why he had less than ten per cent body fat while Millie had to lie down on the bed to squeeze into her size fourteen trousers this morning,

Curvy. Voluptuous. A true hourglass figure with

thirty-eight EE boobs, a smaller waist and hips that didn't hide from anyone.

Not that Millie minded. Life was too short to deny herself great food and gorgeous wine and lovely long romantic dinners with Leo. And anyway, he loved her curves.

She retreated to the bedroom, showered and changed into her favourite yellow floaty dress. If the hippy movement made a resurgence, she was ready and waiting. Jeans did nothing for her. Jeggings had never graced the inside of her wardrobe. If she had a fashion icon, it was Stevie Nicks, circa 1977, ten years before she was even born, but forever captured by her mother who had worn a similar style until she passed away four years before. Too young. Cancer. Bloody disease. Millie flickered her eyes heavenward, her daily greeting to the parent she was sure was still up there, in a floaty Laura Ashley creation, singing "You Make Loving Fun" while decorating a mirror with glass tiles she'd discovered while back-packing in a village in Peru.

Back downstairs, she ran a paddle brush through her long red waves, then returned to her movie-psychopath-in-training.

"OK, I'll get going then." Abandoning plans to avoid interrupting him, she kissed him longingly on the lips. Aaargh, she could take him back to bed right now.

"Good luck today, my love. You'll be amazing," she promised.

"I think you might be biased, but I'll take it," he told her, his grin revealing a natural, perfect smile that had made him the face of Balls Y-fronts for a giddy year in 2008. He returned her kiss, before breaking off and turning back to the mirror, script back up at eye level.

Millie grabbed a banana and a muffin before gently closing the door.

Her ten-year-old VW Beetle was waiting for her, desperately in need of a paint job and decent music on the stereo (no, according to Tash and Laney, the greatest hits of The Backstreet Boys wasn't a classic) and headed out on to Pollokshaws Road. Sitting at the fourth set of lights on a mile long stretch she glanced to the travel agent's window on her left, as she always did. The pictures of sun-kissed beaches and turquoise seas looked incredible.

One day, she told herself. She and Leo would scuba dive through shoals of fish. Dine at sunset on a deserted beach. Sleep naked under mosquito nets. Life was going to be fabulous.

In fact, she had the best job in the world, the best friends, the best boyfriend, so life was already great. And she was absolutely confident that it would stay that way. Starting today. Today was going to be a good day.

She barely got the last word out when a loud bang was immediately followed by a violent thud that threw her forward against the steering wheel.

Seconds later her door was wrenched open and a tall, broad shape blocked the daylight. As she squinted she saw a white shirt, sleeves rolled up, black trousers, a mop of brown curly hair.

"Oh, Christ, I'm so sorry. Are you OK? Oh bugger, you're not – your nose is bleeding. I'll call an ambulance. Right now. Hang on. Shit, I dropped the phone."

There was a cracking sound as a mobile phone hit

the tarmac and bounced under her car.

The guy followed and fished it back out, then fumbled as he was trying to press the buttons.

Despite feeling like she'd been smacked in the face with a shovel, cartoon style, Millie immediately felt sorry for him.

"It's OK. I'm fine," she hurriedly explained, "but I'm not sure what happened."

"The van behind me ran into the back of my car, and shunted me into yours. I'm so sorry."

Millie's natural aversion to causing a fuss kicked in, and teamed up with her general compulsion to take care of everyone. She automatically wanted to reassure him and make that panic-stricken expression disappear.

"I'm OK. Really. And look, it's barely bleeding. I'm fine, I promise. It's just … oh, my poor car."

Turning, she saw that the back bumper of her Beetle was hanging half off. Bugger.

"Look, I'll pay for it, it was clearly my fault. Actually, it was the guy behind me, but I'll take the blame for your car, of course. Why don't you come into my office and we'll sort out the details?"

Millie shook her head. Ouch, that hurt right between the eyes.

"I'm afraid I don't have time to come to your office—"

"Sorry, I should have explained. My office is right here. I'm Guy. I own the travel agency on the corner."

5

"Hey, we were starting to worry," Laney said as the door opened and Millie appeared. Tash's eyes made it to Millie's face first.

"Jesus Christ, you got a nose job?" she blurted.

Millie shook her head and her eyes filled. "A car rear-ended me on Pollokshaws Road. Does it look bad?"

"Nope not at all," Tash replied, before adding, "if you were a cage fighter."

Laney swatted Tash with a ruler. "Thank God you don't work for the NHS. Your bedside manner would up the body count." Already out of her seat, she dived to Millie's side and put an arm around her. "Come and sit down. It just looks a bit bruised. And sore. And swollen. Did you go to hospital?

Millie shook her head. "It's fine. I just need some ice."

Laney immediately headed to the freezer in the small

kitchenette. There was a permanent stock of ice because every new client was offered champagne when they signed with the agency.

Tash took the bucket from Laney, shoved a handful of cubes into her grey leopard print scarf (a tenner from eBay, but from a distance it could pass for the six hundred pound Louis Vuitton ones that all the celebrities wore), and gently placed it on Millie's face.

"Did you get the details? What was the other driver like? Did they admit responsibility for being a slow-braking twat?"

"Ouch!" Millie wailed. "It was the guy who owns the travel agency at the lights on Pollokshaws Road and yes, he was really nice."

"Brilliant!" Tash exclaimed, pressing a little too hard on Millie's ice pack in the excitement and eliciting another yelp.

"Brilliant, how?" Laney asked.

"He hit her car and made our friend cry!" Tash explained. "That's got to get us a discount on a fortnight in Marbella. Are you sure it's not broken?" she said, mimicking regret. "I've always wanted a freebie to Bora Bora."

Millie laughed through the pain.

The buzzer went, indicating that there was a visitor downstairs at the front door. Laney picked up the bright pink phone – Millie had been responsible for the finishing touches – and answered with a bright, "Personal Proposals!" before following up with, "Yes, come on up. Second floor, I'll meet you at the lift."

She jumped off the desk, then smoothed down the navy crêpe pencil skirt that had been a self-indulgent treat from House of Fraser at the weekend. Laney treated every client with the utmost professionalism. That's what made them recommend their agency to friends, and with a fledgling concept like a proposal agency, word of mouth was invaluable. The agency was already breaking even, covering the bills and allowing each partner to take a basic wage, but Laney was determined to grow and turn this in to a flourishing success. To do that, they needed to secure every single prospective client that came through the door.

"Ready?" she asked, heading to the door.

"Yep. I'll put Rocky back on ice later," Tash said removing the cold leopard-print pack from Millie's swollen face.

"I'll quickly shove some thick make up on," Millie said. "Will that cover the damage?"

Tash's reply was an instant, "Only if it's under a paper bag."

As Laney waited for the lift doors to open, she took a deep breath and refreshed her memory of the initial call from this client.

It was a woman, which was unusual in itself. Ninety-nine per cent of their clients were men, with the only variation being on the last leap year when they'd had a female who wanted to propose while skydiving from a plane. Her partner said, "Yeeeeeeeeeeeeeees," before plummeting to earth and landing in cow dung in a large field.

There had also been one lesbian couple, now enjoying happy memories of a romantic proposal on a moonlit roof terrace surrounded by white blossom trees and lanterns. It had been utterly beautiful – one of

Laney's favourite matches ever.

But this one had definitely said she wanted to propose to her boyfriend. Usually Laney would have more background and details before the initial meeting, but the client hadn't had time to return the information form that had been emailed to her. Laney had assured her that bringing it along this morning would be fine, even it meant she was a little less prepared than she would have liked.

It was a very streamlined process. The clients got in touch and were invited to the office or – especially in the case of overseas clients – set up with an appointment for a conference call. In the meantime they were emailed a research questionnaire that aimed to establish their relationship history and their partner's personality traits, likes, dislikes, passions, loathes and loves.

At the meeting or conference call this was probed further, then the girls would meet to put together a couple of ideas that fell within their client's budget. Millie was the creative romantic, Laney the pragmatic bean counter and Tash the relentless organiser and official cheese monitor – if it got too over-the-top sentimental, she reined Millie in and reminded her that there was such a thing as too much slushy stuff.

The client chose from one of their ideas, signed on the dotted line, then celebrated with a glass of bubbly before going off to anticipate the big moment in relative calm, while the girls unleashed a flurry of activity and logistical planning. The client's job was to turn up on the day and savour every second, completely oblivious to the fact that the girls had been up until six a.m., making fake snow, coordinating a choir, or knitting heart-shaped parcels that would drop from the sky on little balloons, each containing declarations of love and devotion. That one had been a roaring success – if you didn't count the fact that three balloons had gone astray in the wind, one of them containing a message saying, "I want to live forever snuggled into my little BooBoo's secret places". They didn't ask.

Many of the proposals were on the low end of the budget scale, a few hundred pounds for beautiful, personal touches. Tash's favourite (and her conception) had been the girlfriend who was persuaded to go zorbing, rolling down a hill inside a huge, clear, plastic ball before crashing into five foot high inflatable letters that spelled out "Marry Me, Daisy!"

It was in the big extravaganzas that they really made their money. The *Braveheart* re-enactment. The heir to a Perthshire estate that had a flash mob take over a garden party and propose to his unsuspecting girlfriend, a Russian model with limited English who only realised what was going on when a Miley Cyrus look-a-like twerked over to her clutching a hundred grand sparkler. A helicopter to Skye where a sixty piece orchestra was waiting in the middle of a field at dusk, playing "Moonlight Sonata" while a very nervous seventy-year old man called Hugh proposed to Ella, the high school sweetheart he'd re-discovered six months before on Facebook. She said yes. Millie had cried all the way back to Glasgow after that one. "I'd have hated to see the state of you if she'd said no," Tash had remarked irritably after an hour of sniffing.

No one had ever said no. Every proposal had been greeted with ecstatic, shocked, overwhelmed or emotional reactions, but no blunt refusals. Tash always carried a bottle of medicinal Scotch just in case.

As Laney waited for the lift to arrive at their floor, her mind drifted again to her recollections of this client's original phone call. From her voice, she'd sounded like she was in her twenties, and fairly excited about the adventure in front of her.

No matter how often she did this, Laney knew that she would always get that little twinge of excitement right before every new client walked through the door. The unpredictability of it all thrilled her.

As did the challenge.

The client could ask them to do anything at all, and they'd metaphorically move mountains to accommodate. Then, forever more, they'd be part of that couple's history.

That was a special kind of job. And so far, every one of the people who had come out of those elevator doors had been ecstatic with the result.

When it was good, it was fabulous.

As she took a deep breath and greeted the latest chapter in the agency's history, she had no idea that she was about to discover that when it was bad, it was as horrific as it could possibly be.

6

On Laney's introduction, Tash leaned over to shake the new arrival's hand, her warm smile masking the cynical top to toe appraisal being carried out in her head.

OK, so she had long blonde hair, straight, glossy, probably a Brazilian blow dry and those came in at a hundred quid every few weeks, so money was clearly no object. Skinny Armani jeans, black vest designed to show off the pert, Fake Baked boobs and the Dolce and Gabbana jacket that had been in the window of Cruise, the upmarket designer store further along Ingram Street, for the last week. The black suede stiletto ankle boots looked expensive too. The bag was Stella McCartney, a steel grey Falabella tote edged with silver chains. Make-up flawless, smile wide, the whole package being one of perfection.

Tash hated her on sight.

Laney loved her on sight.

And Millie was having to squint through the swelling so she hadn't quite made up her mind yet.

"Cara Deacon," she announced to Tash, in a voice that oozed confidence, before turning to see Millie for the first time. "Nose job or eye bag removal?" she asked, in a tone that was completely matter of fact. Clearly these procedures were common occurrences in her circle.

"Car crash," Millie replied.

"Oh," Cara retorted casually. "Well, it'll heal."

For a moment, Tash wondered if she'd just met her evil twin. One with better shoes. She tucked her River Island heels under the sofa and cursed herself for not wearing her alarm-crushing Jimmy Choos.

"Please, have a seat," Laney interjected, smoothly taking things under her control. "Can I get you coffee, tea, a glass of wine?"

The champagne was reserved for after the client had been signed up. Cava came before.

"Coffee. Thanks. Do you have a skinny latte?"

"Of course," Laney replied, grateful for their Dolce Gusto coffee machine that came with pods in several different flavours.

"I'll get it," Tash offered, sweeping her inferior shoes out of the room.

They made small talk about the weather until she returned, delivering large steaming mugs to each of them.

Hospitality complete, she sat along from Laney on one soft grey velvet sofa, facing Cara and Millie on the other.

Laney took her silver Cross pen – a gift from her dad

when she'd started the agency – and placed it, ready for action, on the empty clipboard on her lap.

"So Cara," she started brightly, "did you bring along the questionnaire we sent out to you?"

Cara slid her hand into her over-sized handbag and produced a plastic A4 folder with the document inside.

"Great, thanks. We'll go over it in a minute. But perhaps you could start by telling us a bit about your relationship and what brought you here to us."

Cara smiled, revealing perfect, glistening white veneers, and nodded.

"Absolutely. So like, the thing is, I just don't have time to organise something spectacular and it has to be totally, like, amazing. Cameron has been promising to propose for ages, but I know exactly what I want, so I just decided to make it perfect. After all, it's about me, really, isn't it? It's not about the guy. They don't really care how it plays out as long as they get us in the end. Anyway, so I've dreamt of how I'll be proposed to for, like, ever. So instead of dropping hints and hoping he'll get it right, I just decided to make it happen."

For the first time, Tash felt a stirring of grudging respect for her proactivity. It took a lot of balls to achieve that level of high maintenance entitlement and arrogance.

Millie was passively horrified. Where was the romance? The adoration? This girl was all about herself and the show. She was grateful that the injury gave her the perfect excuse to remain unusually quiet on this one.

Laney, meanwhile, was just dealing in facts. If someone knew exactly what they wanted it made their job easier in the planning stages, although it did carry the risk that if a single thing was not as the client envisaged, it could blow the whole event. This one was going to ride or fall on the detail.

"I travel a lot with work. I'm a fashion stylist – photo-shoots and music videos, that kind of stuff – and my honey travels constantly too, so I need someone to work for me on this."

"So how do you see the proposal playing out? Can you paint a picture of it for us?" Tash asked, dying to know and ignoring an irritated look from Laney, who preferred to get all the background information first.

"OK, so …" Cara's words were accompanied by elaborate gestures with perfectly manicured hands, "it's like, totally *Sex And The City*. We fly first class to New York, and a limo collects us from the airport. Not one of the tacky, hen weekend ones. I'm talking black, sleek, pure class. It takes us to The Carlyle. I read somewhere that Jennifer Lopez stays there when she's in New York, so it's like, the only place to go. We go up to the room and there are rose petals everywhere. That evening, the limo collects us, I'm in a red Marchesa dress, Manolo heels, red Judith Leiber clutch …"

Millie uttered a soft sigh of wonder, her resistance to this woman now completely blown away by the romance and beauty of the scene she was describing. Tash focused on trying to prevent her eyes rolling at the overblown drama of it all – she thought about her coffee, she thought about biting the nipples of her neighbour's naked torso, she thought about getting a job that was more suited to her personality. Say, working for the police in kill-scene clean up.

Cara was in full flow now, her face animated with

excitement. "So like, Carrie Bradshaw, totally bite my ass. We drink champagne as we drive to the Museum of Modern Art. On the steps in front of it there is music."

"I think you mean the Metropolitan Museum of Art? That's the old grand one with the steps at the front," Millie suggested gently. Laney could see she didn't want to contradict, but just wanted to formulate the correct image in her mind.

Cara thought for a moment. "Yep, you're right! Always get those museums mixed up. I mean, who actually goes into them anyway?" She paused to reflect on her chain of events.

"Oh yes," she was off again, "so music on the steps. You know, like strings and violins. And a harp. A harp would look totally classy."

Laney's anxiety was increasing with every line. How the hell would they get a harp on to the steps of one of New York's most prestigious landmarks? And how many bylaws would that break?

"And the steps are covered in petals. White ones this time."

Laney added littering to their charge sheet.

"Then someone walks by … I'm thinking someone famous. Or like, a butler. They give my honey the ring and he just goes straight down on one knee and asks me, begs me, to marry him."

Cara paused to fan her welling eyes with her hands.

"Then there are fireworks. And he picks me up and carries me down the steps …"

Laney's practical mind was working overdrive. A major fireworks display would require official permissions. Running down the steps of the Met

37

carrying a grown woman in a long dress might require a paramedic.

"Then he whisks me off to the bar at the Mandarin Oriental, where champagne is waiting, and we have dinner and cocktails in Asiate – that's the restaurant overlooking the park – then we go back to The Carlyle …"

Without realising it, the others had all leaned slightly forward, hanging on every word.

"And I shag him senseless. Sorry. That might be TMI, but that's how it happens in my head."

"TMI?" Millie asked, wincing at the pain caused by a furrowed brow.

"Too much information," Tash replied, the edges of her mouth attempting to defy her orders not to laugh. "And no, I think that's a perfectly legitimate element of the plan. Although, not one that we would get involved in, per se."

Laney jumped right in, fearing what would come out of Tash's gob next.

"I think it sounds incredible," she assured Cara, "and definitely something that we can set up and take care of. We might have to tweak a couple of small details here and there depending on New York laws and official restrictions …"

Cara's expression immediately switched from "picture of wistfulness" to "threatening a strop". Laney spotted it and headed it off. "But we'll do everything we can to make sure it's exactly as you imagined it." There was no way she was losing this one. This was going to be a big budget affair and their commission would be significant – not to mention their expenses for the job and the fact that it would look incredible on their website and YouTube channel. Even without asking, she knew Cara would absolutely be up for allowing them to use the footage.

This was why she loved her job. This was why it had been worth giving up a lucrative career in pharmaceutical sales and persuading her lifelong best friends to join her.

"So Cara, when were you planning to do this?"

"Last weekend of the month," she said confidently, oblivious to the reactions of surprise on the faces of the other three. Tash did a quick calculation. That was three weeks away. In that time frame, they had two big proposals – one in Inverness – and then on the first day of the next month, one at Glasgow's Queen Street train station, so they'd need to speed back for that one. There were also a couple of smaller bookings that only required another day or so of prep. It would be tight, but they should be just about able to do it. "I'm sure you realise that we'll have to have a budget to work with and that some of the elements will be quite costly."

Cara shrugged insouciantly. "That's not a problem. He gave me a credit card and told me to use it for whatever I want. He'll love the fact that I spent it on something so wonderful for both of us."

"Great," Laney told her, mentally punching the air. An unlimited credit card was a seriously helpful aspect of any proposal. "So let's just go through all the details on your form and get the paperwork tied up, then we can start working on making this spectacular for you."

"Oh, and tell me, how did you hear about us?" she asked, as she pulled the information form out of the wallet and scanned the page.

Name: Cara Deacon.

Proposee's name: Cameron …

Laney stopped reading, her eyes locked on that name.

"Well, it's the strangest thing." Cara's voice was a sidetrack to her focus on the page.

"I found your business card in my honey's wallet."

"Oh. So do you think he's perhaps planning to propose to you already?" Millie asked excitedly. "Actually, we'd better check that he's not already contacted us to set something up. Wouldn't that be bizarre!"

"Oh my God, it like, totally, would," Cara agreed.

"Cara, what does your boyfriend do? You said he travelled." Both Tash and Millie caught the tremor in Laney's voice and looked at her quizzically.

"He's a corporate trainer. You know, one of those guys that big companies bring in to sort out their workforce. That's what attracted me to him in the first place. He's super-smart and just has a way of dealing with people."

"Oh, I'm sure he does," Laney said, questions exploding in her head as she stared again on the proposee's name on the application form. Cameron Cochrane. The same name as the man whom she'd left in bed that morning.

Were there two Cameron Cochranes?

What were the chances of the second Cameron Cochrane also being a corporate trainer?

And if the answers to both these questions were no and none, then why the fuck was this girl sitting in front of them, discussing how she wanted to propose to Laney's husband?

7

"Who does he work for?" Laney asked, the chill that had descended over her making her hands tremble as she fought to retain her composure.

"MindSoar. They're like the top company in the field."

"But …" Tash started to speak, obviously spotting the coincidence.

Laney could only hear white noise. And thunder. And a roar that seemed to be mushrooming from somewhere deep inside her gut.

A visceral reaction threatened to consume her, but just as quickly something else took over. A chill that made her insides plummet from hysteria to inner calm in a split second. She stood up, cutting off Tash's interjection, ignoring the confusion on Millie's bruised face, focusing only on the next thirty seconds, her fight or flight reflex screaming at her to escape the situation immediately. Get rid of it. Do anything to buy time to think and consider the next move.

"OK, lovely. Well, we'll get right on that. The credit card details are on the form here, so we'll charge our standard fee of engagement and then be back to you within a couple of days with preliminary costs."

"Laney…" Tash attempted to intercede again, but she was pointedly and firmly rebuked.

"But please don't worry about a thing. Between the info form and what you've told us today, I think we've got a perfectly clear vision for how this will play out. Leave it to us."

Cara smiled widely as she elegantly rose up on her skyscraper ankle boots, then leaned over and gave Laney a hug.

"Thank you so much. I was, like, totally unsure about doing this but now that I've met you all I know it'll be brilliant. I thought you'd all be like, totally stuffy, but you're not at all. I'm so glad I found that card in his wallet. I think this is going to be amazeballs."

"Amazeballs," Laney agreed, taking Cara's arm and walking her to the door. There would be no opening of the bubbly on this one.

"I'm going to meet him now and it'll be, like, impossible not to tell him. But I won't. I want this to be a total surprise. He's going to get the shock of his life." Cara giggled.

Laney opened the door, put her hand out to shake Cara's. "Oh yes, indeed he is."

As the lift doors closed, she felt her legs give way and numbness spread out from her heart to shut down every nerve ending in her body.

Did the last half an hour really happen?

Cara Deacon wanted to propose to Cameron Cochrane.

The man who had made love to Laney that morning and then told her he adored her as she waved him goodbye.

Laney somehow found the strength to stagger back into the office, where Tash and Millie were on their feet, regarding her with expressions of utter bewilderment.

As soon as the door closed behind her, Tash reacted with her usual calm, measured maturity, blurting, "What the hell was that about? Are you nuts?"

Millie was a little less forthcoming, preferring to fact check before escalating straight to explosive.

"Am I concussed or did she just ask us to set up a proposal to Cameron. *Your* Cameron?"

It took a few moments before Laney could reply. Robotically, she slowly walked back to the sofa, sat down, and exhaled.

"I have absolutely no idea what's going on," she whispered incredulously. "Is this a wind up? Some crazy joke Cameron is pulling? I don't get it. I don't understand."

Behind her, there was a rustle as Tash checked the large green artificial ferns for hidden cameras. This had to be a joke. Some kind of elaborate stunt. Only, wasn't setting up covert stuff supposed to be *their* job?

Millie's injuries forgotten, she was on her feet now. "But why didn't you say something to her? Ask her for more details? Reveal the not insignificant fact that the bloke she intends to propose to is already married. To you."

Laney didn't speak for a long time. "I don't know. I think I just wanted to … I don't know. I couldn't. I just wanted her out of here."

Laney did calm organisation. She did planning. Future

strategies. Covering bases. She did not do great bloody big catastrophes drop-kicked into the middle of her life.

"I just needed to think."

"About what?" Tash was pacing back and forth across the cream rug. Millie was now sitting next to Laney, her hand on hers, giving the only support she could.

"About what's going on. She seemed genuine, didn't she? But it has to be a joke. A crazy, messed up joke."

Tash grabbed her jacket and bag. "I'll find out. Stay here. I'll be right back."

She was out the door, and Laney was desperate to follow her, but her legs wouldn't move.

Yoga had taught her to focus on her breathing and she did that now, blocking out all other thoughts until she got her heart rate back down to something approaching normal.

But what was normal any more? Normal was making love to Cam this morning and then waving him off. Normal was having a husband who was away more than he was home, but who made up for it by being an incredible lover and her best friend. Normal was planning their family and ovulation kits and sex in the afternoon.

That was normal.

Think. This has to be a mistake. Or there has to be an explanation that is totally innocent.

"OK, so there's one of a couple of things going on here," she said, thinking out loud more than actually speaking to Millie, who had retreated to the kitchen and was now on the way back, multitasking by pouring cava into a glass as she crossed the room.

Laney took it without even looking up.

"Either this is a practical joke, and Cam is behind it and thinks it's funny, in which case, I'll be forced to kill him because it so isn't.

"Or else there are two Cameron Cochranes who work at MindSoar. It's a big company. But it's odd that he's never mentioned that before."

"But not impossible," Millie countered optimistically; her inherent need to look on the positive rising to the top as always.

"Nope, not impossible. But incredibly unlikely," Laney said. "But maybe this is one of those prank TV show stints and some MTV bloke is going to burst through the door at any moment."

"Maybe!" said Millie, looking anxiously at a door that was remaining resolutely shut.

"Or identity theft." Her face brightened. "That's it! Someone's stolen Cam's identity and they're pretending to be him. They've adopted his complete persona and they're living a huge big messed up lie. I saw a thing about it on TV the other night. It's rife and the criminals who do it are totally sophisticated. Yep, it's got to be that."

She visibly buoyed for a few moments then just as quickly deflated.

"Or maybe ... maybe ... Is he having an affair, Millie?"

For the first time, Laney's eyes welled up and Millie was faced with a scene she'd never experienced before: her cool, calm, super-together friend looking to her for reassurance.

"No, he can't be. He can't, Laney, honestly. He'd never do that to you. Cam loves you. He really does."

45

Until half an hour ago, Laney had thought the same. Now she was consumed with fear that she was about to discover that wasn't the case.

8

Tash watched the LED display at the top of the lift hit zero and decided not to wait for it to come back up. Pulling her shoes off, she dived to the stairway door, burst through it and ran all the way down to the ground floor, lungs exploding after fifty steps.

Christ, she needed a cig.

The lobby was deserted when she got there so, hopping across the mosaic tile floor, she pulled her heels back on before she reached the door and lurched into the daylight. Ingram Street was mobbed with the lunchtime shopping crowd.

Frantically looking left and right, she saw no sign of the blonde mane that belonged to the woman who had been in her office just a few minutes before.

Sod it. Shoes off again, she jumped up on to the large pot that stood at the entrance to their building and contained a green swirly tree of a plastic nature.

Desperately trying to keep her balance as it wobbled, she got enough height to see right down the street to her right. Nothing.

Bugger. Cara was probably in a cab and a mile away by now. She swirled her head to the left and … there! Tottering on her heels, she could see the unmistakable Dolce and Gabbana jacket about a hundred and fifty metres away, heading in the direction of Royal Exchange Square. OK, there was no way Cara was going to walk any distance in those shoes, so chances were she was either going to turn left and go down Buchanan Street, or head into one of the restaurants in the square. Tash jumped down and began to speed walk, figuring that running in heels at this time of the day would make her look like a shoplifter fleeing a scene with two pairs of tights up her shirt.

Sweat buds were popping on her forehead by the time she reached the end of the street. *Think. Come on, where would she go?* Princess Square was the obvious choice – an upmarket shopping mall with loads of trendy bars and restaurants. But parking was an arse-ache and she couldn't see Cam using public transport into the city centre.

The Hyperion Club! Laney had mentioned that he used the swanky private members club regularly for work lunches. It had valet parking and was only a couple of hundred metres away. Yes, that's exactly the type of place a cheating bastard who enjoyed acting like a big shot would arrange to meet his bit on the side.

Tash had no idea why she'd never liked Cam. Something about him put her hackles up. He was just always too smug, too smarmy, too irritatingly smart. As opposed to Millie's Leo, who was just a self-obsessed git who didn't – in Tash's opinion – treat her friend well enough.

But let's not get ahead of this. Maybe she was wrong. Perhaps there was a perfectly understandable explanation for this and they'd all laugh about it later.

For Laney's sake, she hoped that was exactly what was going to happen. Much as she thought Cam was a dickhead, the worst-case scenario here would break her friend's heart.

They had to be wrong. It had to be a big misunderstanding.

She swanned past the doorman with a wink and an air of confidence but she could see the receptionist wasn't going to be quite so easy to get past. This place was exclusive and strictly members only. If Tash got stuck at reception, then the last ten minutes of sweat and exertion would be for nothing. More importantly, there was no way she was going back to Laney without an answer.

The thirty something, impeccably shiny Gwyneth Paltrow look-a-like gatekeeper looked up from the desk and eyed her with the deadly gaze of someone who was under no illusion that she had the upper hand.

"Can I help you?"

Tash smiled. "Yes, I just need to pop up to the restaurant and deliver a message to my boss. Won't be two minutes. You'll never even know I was here."

"I'm sorry …" Gwyneth started, her imperious nasal whine making it perfectly clear that she wasn't, "… but you have to be a member to go through. If you'd like to let me know who exactly you're trying to contact, I'll have a message passed to him."

Petty. Snide. Sharp. The kind of woman, Tash decided, who never took her bra off or went to bed without a fifty-minute regime of cleansing, toning, moisturising and affirmations of superiority.

Not to mention sexist. Tash hadn't mentioned that her boss was male yet this aloof boot assumed he was.

Unfortunately, this was not the time for castigation and a stroppy lecture on the disgrace of sexist assumptions.

The ding of the elevator ten metres in front of her gave Tash her opportunity. "Thanks, you're a sweetheart. I bet everyone tells you how warm and fluffy you are. But I'd prefer to deliver it myself."

Gwyneth's face contorted with outrage as Tash streaked across the deep red plush carpet of the foyer, dodging the two suited gentlemen who had just alighted from the lift, and disappeared as the heavy brass inlaid doors closed behind her.

Inside the lift there was only one button so Tash pressed it and was transported to the first floor. The doors opened to an expansive dining area, the ceiling a jigsaw of chandeliers and elaborate cornicing, lined along one wall with fifteen foot high Georgian windows that looked down on the little people on the street below. Tash hated this kind of place. Elitist. Pompous. Delusions of importance. All back-slapping smugdom and vacant women with hundred grand rings sitting with men twice their age. Not a sexist assumption, just a depressing observation.

To her right, she saw the maître d' pick up a phone from his mahogany podium, listen and then fix his gaze directly on her. Busted. Gwyneth had obviously raised the alarm.

Tash realised she had seconds before an undignified ejection. Thankfully, it was still early for lunch, so there were only a few occupied tables to scan and …

There. There she was. Cara Deacon, flicking her hair while giggling as she relayed some obviously hilarious story to the man sitting across from her. The man who looked distinctly like an older version of the bloke from *Top Gun*. Bastard Cam Cochrane.

He was laughing too, the pair of them a shoo-in for a job in marketing as one of those perfect couples in hotel brochures. Here are Mr and Mrs Perfect Couple in the Jacuzzi. Look how they appear so carefree while sitting naked in hot water. Oh, here they are now in the bedroom, still smiling, showing no signs of the fact that Mr Perfect just farted in the bathroom. And here they are again, in the restaurant, congratulating each other on being utterly beautiful and having great taste in partner selection. Yes, the Dick family is utterly perfect.

Tash recoiled, stepped back into the shadows of the elevator bank, hands up in the surrender position to reassure the descending maître d' that she was on the retreat.

"It's OK, stand down. I just realised I forgot my balaclava and water pistol, so I'll storm the room another time," she told him as the lift doors pinged open and she stepped backwards through them.

Gwyneth was waiting for her at the entrance, but Tash just put her hand up to block the onslaught and strutted past. "Right, dear, don't get your thong in a twist, I'm just leaving."

Out in the late morning sunshine, she took a deep breath and clenched her fists as she processed what she'd just seen.

She needed to work out a plan for dealing with this. She needed to work out her next move. And she needed to get away from this building before she was arrested for going straight back up to that restaurant and kicking Cameron Cochrane's arse from one wood-panelled wall to another.

9

Laney didn't even need to ask. As soon as she saw the tight clench of Tash's jaw and the fury in her eyes, she knew.

But she asked anyway.

"Was it him?"

Tash nodded. "They're at the Hyperion Club."

"Did you kill him?" Millie asked in all seriousness.

Tash shook her head. "Wanted to, but no. He didn't see me. I wasn't sure what you wanted me to do, Lane, but I'm so up for heading back there right now …"

An involuntary gasp came from somewhere deep inside Laney's gut, and she instinctively closed her eyes to blank out the world. No tears. Like the rest of her, it was as if all her emotion receptors had been stunned into numbness.

"No. Don't go back. Just …"

Her head hurt. Really, really, hurt. Like a vice had her

temples in its jaws and was squeezing them together until her head exploded and splattered blood and grey matter across the walls. But that didn't even come close to the pain in her chest.

Cameron. Her Cameron.

This had to be some kind of sick joke but she wasn't laughing.

"Laney, I ..." Millie started to speak but Laney shushed her.

"Give me a minute. Just let me think," she said gently, trying to put some kind of order, some kind of system into this.

What was Cameron even doing here? He was supposed to have left the house and headed straight to the airport for his flight to Birmingham. Why was he still in Glasgow, not to mention sitting in some fancy bloody club with a walking Barbie?

This had to be a messed up dream. It couldn't be real. Any minute now she'd wake up and it would be the start of a brand new day where the sun was shining, Millie didn't have two rapidly forming black eyes, Tash wasn't pacing the room attempting to suppress a murderous rage and her husband was still monogamous. Was that really too much to ask?

Another glass of wine appeared in front of her courtesy of Millie, but she couldn't stomach it. Even the smell made her feel nauseous. Had she and Cam just shared a bottle of Rioja last night, before climbing into bed and ...?

Oh God, she was actually going to be sick. She took three deep breaths and fought the urge.

Unsurprisingly, it was Tash who broke first. "Ok, I'm

trying to do the supportive-friend, silent thing, but fuck that." Her shoes were off now, her black hair falling in messy straggles after her impromptu jog, her bright red lipstick dulled by too many cups of coffee.

"Laney, let's go down there right now and face him and little Miss Gucci. Maybe there's some explanation for this and it's all totally innocent. Maybe he's a cheating dick who deserves to have his bollocks severed. But if we go there now, at least we'll know."

Millie shook her head. "Come on, Tash, I don't think making a huge scene is the smartest thing to do. I mean, charging in there is only going to cause a drama ..."

"It's already a bloody drama!' Tash shouted, hands on hips now, battle stance.

"Yes, but there must be a less confrontational way to find out what's going on. The last thing Laney needs right now is to walk in there. They need to talk, but on their own, not in public."

"Why? Why does that matter? The faithless prick deserves every bit of public humiliation he gets. We should make him a fucking poster for around his neck that says 'I'm a lying bastard'. I'll make it. But we should go now, confront him and get this sorted," Tash said, painfully aware, even as the words came out of her mouth, that there was no sorting this.

"No." Laney spoke for the first time, in a voice that didn't even sound like hers.

Taking her mobile phone from the glass coffee table in front of her, she dialled a number. If she heard his voice, she'd know. Her internal lie detector would kick in and she'd just know.

He answered on the second ring, with a cheery, "Hey,

can you hang on one second?"

Oh God. How many times had their calls started that way and why hadn't she ever wondered if there was any kind of significance to it? He'd always explained it away with some absolutely feasible excuse. "Sorry, I was in front of a client." "I was in the gents." "I was screwing my girlfriend and by the way, I've even given her a credit card to buy anything she wants." OK, so he'd never actually used that excuse, but what if it was true? In her mind's eye she suddenly had a vision of him getting up and excusing himself from the table where he was sitting with Cara, telling her all the things Laney had always thought were reserved just for her.

No.

It couldn't be.

This was her husband. Her love. He wasn't going to lie to her or spin her a line. There was going to be some kind of simple explanation for all this. He was planning something. A surprise for her, perhaps? Yeah, that was it. Cam was always the spontaneous type. This was all a big ruse and there would be some hilarious reason for it all.

There was a clearing of the throat at the other end of the line.

"Sorry about that, babe, I was at the ticket desk and you know how some of those check in agents can be. Honestly, how many ways are there to ask if someone else tampered with my luggage? No, they didn't. And if I'm some crazed terrorist, I'm hardly going to tell you if they did." His laughter indicated that this seemed to amuse him greatly.

Oh dear Lord, her world was falling apart and he was

laughing.

Her hand tightened around the phone. "So you're already at the airport?"

More laughter. "Of course I am. Flight's leaving in an hour or so. I'm just going to grab a quick beer at the departure gate and wait to be called through." He paused. "Oh. Sorry darling, there's a huge bloke at security giving me the evil eye because I'm on the phone. I'll go for now and call you as soon as we land." Then, almost as an afterthought, "Is everything OK with you?"

Now was the time to call him out, to tell him she knew he was lying and force him to tell her the truth.

"OK?" she repeated. Now. Right now. Confront him with the evidence. "Everything is fine. Absolutely fine."

"Great, speak to you later, gorgeous." The click told her he was gone. He'd lied to her, treacherous, twisted, killer lies. And like a fool, she'd believed every word that had ever come out of his mouth.

All those other times that he'd been travelling ... Hang on, had he ever even been away? She'd never called hotels, always his mobile. Checking up on him had never crossed her mind and why should it have?

Never once had she ever suspected that he could have been deceiving her. Sometimes there would be just one quick call in a day, but she'd always been absolutely fine with that because he was working hard, training clients all day, then entertaining them at night. Those intensive courses required focus and he couldn't be sneaking out to phone home every five minutes. She knew that and it suited her fine. Over the last year or so she'd been working flat out, too, building this business, bringing in clients, working on the proposals. Neither of them kept regular hours and sometimes, yes, that got in the way of the relationship, but they were both OK with that because they were building for the future. Their future. The one that they were now apparently sharing with a stylist called Cara.

Ever practical, Laney tossed the phone on the couch. Tash would have launched it at the wall, but all that would accomplish was a five hundred quid bill for a new iPhone 5.

Something else flashed through her mind. Facetime. All those occasions where she'd asked him to use Facetime when they were chatting and on at least half of them, he'd come up with some excuse. His Facetime was playing up. The signal wasn't strong enough. He didn't have time because it was just a quick call.

Had he been playing her on every brutal, lying occasion?

The constriction of her lungs forced her breaths to come in short sharp bursts. For a moment she wondered if this was what a heart attack felt like, but no. This was the more traitorous version – chronic heartbreak.

"Fine?" Tash asked, arms folded, eyeing her with incomprehension. "Like, fire and petulance are *'fine'*? The situation in the Middle East is *'fine'*? Global fucking warming that will lead to our bodies heating up until we spontaneously combust is *'fine'*?"

Laney ignored her, instead tuning in to Millie, who was again sitting next to her, poised and ready to hug her as she asked the toughest question. "So what are we going to do, Laney?"

We. Not I. Somehow that gave Laney a tiny shred of

comfort. Since they were kids in the playground it had always been that way. The three of them. So different. So close. Always ready to take the blame for each other and back each other up against predatory forces. The times that Laney had done the others' homework. Those many mornings that the entirely trustworthy Millie, with her big innocent eyes, had manufactured lies to the teachers to cover up for the fact that Tash was absent because she was in Matalan, looking for something to wear to the school disco. The time that Tash had punched Danny Miller in the face because he'd two-timed Laney with a sixth year that gave blow jobs to anyone she fancied. Somehow, this one required a better plan than letting Tash punch him in the face.

Laney fought to organise the thoughts ricocheting round her brain.

She wanted to go now to the Hyperion Club and confront him, but would he even still be there? She wanted to phone him back, tell him she knew and order him home to thrash this out and get to the truth. She wanted to take the silver dagger on her desk, the one that was used for opening mail and occasionally peeling a stubborn orange, and plunge it into his chest.

However, there was a chance that none of those actions would truly sort this out. If he was guilty, then they'd already established with that last phone call that he could lie through his teeth. He'd squirm out of it. Oh dear Lord, had she just had a thought about the love of her life "squirming" out of a lie? Before this morning, she'd have trusted him with her life and sworn with her last breath that he was the most honest, stand up, decent man you could ever meet. This was all just so surreal.

However, if there was even a grain of truth in it, any at all, then she wanted to know the extent of every single detail and to do that she had to see it for herself.

"There's only one thing we can do," she finally spoke. "If this is real, I want proof. I want to know everything and there's only one way that can happen. We're going to plan my husband's proposal."

10

What a bloody day.

Tash tossed her handbag into the corner of the room and swayed a little tipsily as she padded across her living room. That's what happened after a full afternoon of alternating between drinking wine, trying to console a friend and making offers to murder her husband as he slept. Assuming they could actually find out where he slept these days.

On first contemplation, Tash found Laney's decision difficult to understand. If it had been her, she'd have stormed the Hyperion Club that afternoon and the rest of the city would be reading about it the next morning under the heading "Woman Catches Cheating Husband, Sets Fire To His Bollocks With A Crème Brûlée Torch".

In hindsight, though, Laney's plan did have some advantages over the third degree burns route – the most obvious one being the lack of requirement for a lawyer or the stamina to do five to ten years as someone called

Big Janie's bitch.

After an all-day analysis fuelled by cava, then two bottles of Moët (taken from the store and already added to Cara's account), she could see the logic in it. It was like ripping the plaster off a deep wound. Or the families of the victims on CSI that insisted on seeing their loved one after he'd been assassinated by a drug cartel in a seedy yet accessible warehouse.

Sometimes you had to actually face the horror and completely understand the magnitude of the situation in order to accept it.

After several large glasses of alcohol logic it actually made sense.

Tash unzipped her black crepe skirt and let it fall, stepping out of it before moving across to the couch, where she pulled off her red jersey T-shirt and tossed it across the room. It landed in a heap on the breakfast bar. The open plan layout of this room had made her fall in love with it on sight. The show house of the one bedroom apartments, it had already been decorated with stunning dark cream jacquard wallpaper on the main wall, a contrasting silk sheen on the others. Unlike the bedroom, where the over-patterned curtains had been removed on day one for fear of exacerbating a hangover, in the lounge the show house curtains remained, classic taffeta creations in muted gold and edged with thick cream brocade. They resembled something out of a home-style magazine. The rest of the apartment looked like it had been furnished by a top class designer – one who had absolutely no imagination and his eyes shut.

There was a huge plasma on the wall, all the better to watch sport on. Across from it, spanning at least ten feet, was a cream leather couch. In front of it, a glass coffee table that proudly held a year's worth of Vogues, two cans of Red Bull and last night's ashtray.

That was it.

Nothing else. Not a single picture or candle or ornament. Tash had absolutely no idea why anyone needed a vanilla candle and a large bowl of pot-pourri to make their life complete. All of that stuff seemed so surplus to requirements.

Now in her bra and knickers, she wandered behind the breakfast bar into the kitchen area, all cream units with dark walnut tops, only a steel kettle and toaster providing any hint that the kitchen had actually been inhabited since installation, and pulled a bottle of beer from the fridge. The top screwed off and landed with a clank when it was tossed in the sink.

Plumping down on the couch, she rested her head against the back cushion and took a large slug of beer. What. A. Day. Emotional. Painful. Infuriating.

At the end of it, she'd begged Laney to come home with her, to stay here for the night or let Tash and Millie crash at her place, but Laney was having none of it. She wanted to think, she said yet again. How much thinking could one person do? In the end, Tash had given up trying and hugged Laney instead. "You know that if he turns up dead in the morning, we'll totally give you an alibi, right?"

Laney had nodded gratefully; like it was the kind of offer she heard every day.

Tash meant it.

Even thinking about that vile arse made her blood pressure rise, so she resolved not to.

Instead she grabbed the remote control for the TV and searched. She knew exactly what she needed right now. Big, muscular men. Biceps rippling. Sweat pouring from them as they gave the ultimate in energetic performance. The sports channels flicked in front of her. There must be rugby or basketball on somewhere.

Bingo! The camera zoomed in on the scoreboard and reported that The Brooklyn Nets were up four points on Miami Heat at the start of the second quarter. That was the next couple of hours taken care of, then. There was a ready-made Caesar salad in the fridge that she mentally slotted in for half time and she was set.

Peace. Quiet. Bliss.

At first she thought the buzzer was on the TV and it took four or five rings before she realised it was the front door.

Why would anyone be ringing her bell at this time of night? And how did they get into the building in the first place? It had to be Gladys from across the hallway. Not the most conventional of seventy-year-olds, she swore she was a Playboy bunny in the London club back in the day and had once shagged Hugh Hefner until he begged for mercy. Tash had no idea if it was true but she hoped it was. Occasionally Gladys would join her for a box set binge or a late night pizza, but she was pretty sure they didn't have plans for tonight.

Checking the peephole, she realised she'd been right on the neighbour aspect, but wrong on the actual identity of the neighbour.

Bugger. She'd completely forgotten. What time had she said she'd go there? Eight? It was well past that now, which might explain why Mr Next-Door-Sexy-Porsche-dating-Giselle was leaning against the doorway, bottle of wine held lazily at his side when she opened the door. His grin told her that the fact she'd stood him up hadn't left scar tissue on his heart.

"Do you answer the door to everyone like that?" Sy asked her, gesturing to the near-nakedness of her black lace thong and non-matching red balconette bra. Underwear co-ordination was only for the supremely organised, porn stars, first dates and special occasions.

"Only to Gladys. We've got an … *arrangement*," she said, one eyebrow raised, grin set to cheeky.

His laughter was low and throaty. She liked that about him. He had a great laugh and an incredibly sexy twinkle in his eye. And as he stood there in beautifully cut trousers, his white shirt casually opened at the top two buttons, smelling like the most expensive cologne money could buy, she experienced a rush of blood to the nipples.

"My place? Or yours?" he asked, spotting the addition of erect erogenous zones to the party.

She opened the door wide and let him in, trying desperately to remember what kind of state she'd left the bedroom in that morning. Not that she supposed he would pause to check if she'd dusted under the bed before he ravished her.

This was how it was with them. Great sex, when both of them were up for it. No strings. No ties. No promises. The perfect relationship. It wasn't until their third encounter that she'd actually learned his name.

She'd expected something unusual to go with his maverick attitude and cavalier career. Something highbrow to match his wealth and expensive tastes.

65

Perhaps even exotic, to complement the sallow skin and dark hair, now flecked with grey in a total Richard Gere *Pretty Woman* phase.

She thought Conrad. Or Colton. Perhaps even Addison or Zac.

But no. Simon. Bloody Simon. Which just made her think of Simon Cowell and that totally turned her off. She'd never considered there to be much attraction in a bloke who wore badly fitting jeans and whose hair suggested he'd just stepped off an open top bus. It took her a few moments to get that mental image out of her head before she could revert to viewing him as a suitable sexual companion.

So she had a fuck-buddy called Simon. Which was why she preferred to call him Sy, and think of him as Mr Next-Door-Sexy-Porsche-dating-Giselle. And sexy he was. He had that walk of supreme confidence. Not quite a swagger, but one that oozed sex and supreme confidence with every step. Forget Lord Cowell of the High Waist Jeans, he was the decidedly libido-enhancing Harvey Specter in *Suits*.

"Good day?" he asked, heading to the kitchen, depositing the wine bottle in the fridge and swapping it for a beer instead.

Tash shook her head, the edges of her jet black bob swishing against her neck. "Don't re-open the wound. Bad day. Really bad. The male species really has to get a grip on some of your members."

Was she imagining it, or was that a flicker of concern? "What happened?"

Tash sat back down on the couch, automatically pulling her legs up and crossing them in front of her, mentally chiding her extremities to behave themselves. Civilised people had at least some conversation before sex, no?

"My friend. Laney?"

After a second of deliberation he nodded. "The one I met the day you moved in?"

Tash nodded. Laney and Cam, Millie and Leo had pitched in with her brothers, Jordan and John to move what little belongings she had into this apartment. Jordan and John had carried the sofa up like it was no heavier than a bean bag. If rugby didn't work out, they had a career in removals. Laney had bumped into Mr Next-Door-Sexy-Porsche-dating-Giselle while she lumbered a large steel bin out of the lift. It hadn't been her finest moment.

"Yeah, well the guy who was with her was her husband."

"Don't think I met him."

"Well, if you ever do, feel free to point out that he's a dickhead. We had a new client today, turns out that she's seeing Laney's husband. Wants to propose to him. God, I can't believe I'm even saying that. What a mess. Anyway, let's stop talking about it in case it puts me off men for life and I'll have to reject all future advances from my persistent neighbour."

He was sitting on the edge of the glass coffee table now, directly across from her, unable to hide his amusement as he struggled to swallow his drink while laughing. "You're not one for small talk are you? If you carry on like this I'm going to feel like I'm being used and exploited."

Tash unfurled her legs, wrapped one of them around

each side of his hips and pulled him towards her, tasting the cold beer as their lips met, feeling the hardness of his instant erection against her stomach.

He kissed her again, harder this time as her hand cupped his neck, feeling the familiar little pulse that told her his heart was beating faster than normal. With a few flicks of the other hand, she had his shirt off, then worked south, flipping open his button and then teasing down his zip. His erection immediately sprang free. Gotta love a man who has the confidence to go commando.

Her bra was soon gone, and he moved downwards from her mouth to her neck, leaving a trail of kisses on the way.

When this kind of arrangement was available, why would anyone want to spoil a great time with something so unfailingly risky and disappointing as marriage?

11

In the taxi on the way home, Millie couldn't shift the knot in her stomach. Of all the ways she thought today would play out, this wasn't even up for consideration. A car crash. A burst face. Two black eyes. Her best friend's heart split in two. Poor Laney. There had to be some mistake, some logical reason for this but no matter how many ways she'd analysed it, nothing had sprung to mind. Cam had always seemed like such a nice guy, but then she thought that about most people. Sure, he was a workaholic, but that didn't make him a bad person. However, having a secret girlfriend who wanted to shag him senseless in New York most definitely did.

Like Tash, she'd asked Laney to come home with her and been met with a firm refusal. Understandable. This was going to take some amount of processing, even for someone as switched on and together as Laney.

At home, she paid the driver and wandered up the path, spotting a light on in the kitchen. Great. Leo was home. In between all the drama today, she'd managed to text him to say good luck in the audition, and then afterwards, texted him again to ask how it went. There had been no reply to either. His phone was probably out of credit again. They could manage the bills and necessities on her salary and his basic wage from the bar, but when it came close to the end of the month phones started running out of credit and they cut right back on luxuries.

If he got this part, that would all change, especially if it led to more work and perhaps even something regular. It didn't bother her at all that they were permanently skint, but for his sake, she hoped it didn't last much longer. He was so talented that he deserved to be working and be earning decent money. If both of those things happened – sorry, *when* both those things happened – it could change so much for them. They could start to enjoy going out more, maybe a holiday or two and, of course, they could finally get engaged, married and perhaps even start thinking about a family.

One day.

Right now, all she wanted to do was to go in, hear his audition had gone well, and then snuggle up on the sofa with a good movie.

"Hello?" she shouted, her sing-song voice concealing a bugger of a day. There was no point in letting today's crapness overtake the night too.

"In here," he yelled from the kitchen. Brilliant. With any luck he'd have started dinner and they could move straight to sofa/food/cuddles.

The kitchen door was already half open. "Hi babe!" she said as she spotted him, fixing his hair in the mirror next to the fridge freezer on the far wall.

He caught her reflection. "Hi babe, I'm just … Bloody hell, what happened?"

It took her a moment to catch up and when she did, a hand automatically went to her face. "Oh, nothing. Well, something I suppose. A car hit me this morning and I smacked my face against the steering wheel. I'm fine, though, honestly. It's not even particularly sore now, but that might have something to do with half a dozen painkillers and a bottle of wine. I got a taxi home," she conceded, ignoring the look of horror on his face and the slight recoil as she stretched up to kiss him. His reaction caused her to miss his mouth and she managed brief contact with his cheek. She didn't blame him – unless there had been a miraculous healing in the last couple of hours, she knew she looked like she'd been smacked by a shovel. And it probably appeared even worse now that her make-up had probably worn off and her unruly mane was pulled back and twisted into a plait that fell down across one shoulder. No camouflage, no subtle hair coverage.

His horror was written all over his appalled face.

"Did they X-ray it at hospital?"

Millie swatted away the question. "I didn't bother going. I'm fine. Really. It's nothing. Anyway, tell me about the audition. How did it go?"

He shrugged, and ran his finger through his dark shoulder length, hair. On other guys it would look a bit "eighties grunge rock". Or "seventies Italian Football Squad". Or worse, "young Bruce Jenner". But on Leo it came off as "cool surfer dude crossed with rock god". Millie was so distracted by the way that his shoulders

71

moved when he put his arms above his head that she almost lost focus on what he was saying, just zoning back in when he finished with, "… they'll call me in the next couple of days."

"That's brilliant. I have such a good feeling about it. And wait until I tell you what happened today."

"You mean, other than you going stunt-mania with your car?" he asked, hands clasped behind his neck now as he did side bends. Every moment was an opportunity for exercise in his world.

Millie pulled a loaf of bread out of the cupboard, followed by butter and jam from the fridge. Sod exercise. Today called for comfort snacks.

"Yeah, but this is much more devastating. So we got a new client this morning, a gorgeous blonde and she …"

The ringing of the phone interrupted her mid-flow.

Millie was happy to leave it. It wouldn't be important. Calls to the house were mainly sales pitches and automated recordings promising her PPI rebates. Anyone who mattered had her mobile number.

"It's for you," Leo told her, handing over the receiver to a puzzled reception. Those blooming sales calls were getting beyond a joke, asking for her in person.

"Hi, Millie? It's Guy Dixon. From Ocean Sky Travel. I just wanted to apologise again for this morning and check how you were doing."

Either this bloke was the nicest guy in the world or he was terrified of getting sued.

"I'm fine, thanks," she said, for what seemed like the twentieth time that day. "Nothing a bit of make-up won't cover."

Leo rolled his eyes, and then patted down his jeans

pocket to locate the source of a distinct buzzing sound.

When he found it, he headed out into the hallway to take the call, leaving Guy to explain to Millie that he'd assured his insurers that he was at fault and told them to expect a call from her insurance company. "Thanks, I appreciate that. I'm sure it will all work out fine," Millie told him, taking a large bite of jam-covered bread at the end of the sentence.

This was the first thing she'd had to eat since breakfast and she couldn't wait any longer. No doubt he'd wonder why her goodbye sounded like she was speaking while chewing a packet of marshmallows.

She'd just pressed the red button to disconnect the call when Leo returned, his complexion deathly white, his walk slow and dazed. If he was auditioning for a part as a spaced out zombie, he just got the job.

Millie jumped to the obvious conclusion. "Oh honey, I'm so sorry. And I know it's a cliché but it's absolutely their loss. It'll happen, Leo, I promise it will."

He nodded slowly. "It has," he whispered.

Millie's jaw froze mid-bite. "It has?" she asked, confused.

He nodded like one of the less animated characters in the "Thriller" video.

"I got it. Three months initially, but if it goes well, they're already talking about a sequel. They want me to sign an option for that, too. Thirty grand for this stint, sixty for the next one. Starting next week."

The jam sandwich was tossed in the air as she shrieked and flew to hug him.

"Yesssss! That's amazing, babe. Oh my God, you deserve this so much. I'm so bloody proud of you."

He picked her up and swung her around, knocking over two chairs and a vegetable rack. Neither of them cared.

"I can't believe it," he roared, then stopped, held her tight and looked into her eyes. "Baby, you know what this means?"

Millie could feel the tears of joy pour down her cheeks. Yes, she did. It meant celebrations, and an end to struggling. It meant she wouldn't have to support them any more. It meant engagement and marriage. It meant a family. It meant everything they'd ever dreamt of.

"I do," she said, the irony of those two words not escaping her.

He nodded, before placing his forehead against hers, their eye contact broken.

"It means …" he began, making Millie freeze so that she didn't miss a single second of what was about to come. She spent her whole life planning the most romantic, emotional moments for other people and now she was about to have hers. And the strange thing was, she didn't need flowers or gestures or bloody harps on stone steps. She just needed him and the future they had ahead of them.

There was a pause as he choked on the words. Understandable. It was the most important thing that he was ever going to utter. Millie primed herself, ready to say yes, ready to salvage something utterly incredible from a devastating day.

"It means …" he repeated slowly, voice oozing emotion. "… that I'm going to be a star."

12

Laney stared at the ceiling, eyes locked on the same spot they'd been focused on for the last two hours. This was absurd. Just completely surreal. When Cam was away she usually filled her time by bringing work home, doing a bit of marketing or updating their website and social networking sites, or perhaps a quick look over the accounts. Afterwards, she'd maybe go down to the gym or pour a glass of wine and snuggle under the duvet to binge watch some American cop show, or head out with Laney or Tash, or over to her dad's house for dinner and chat.

Her life was fantastic. The perfect mix of busy and calm.

Right now, she couldn't imagine ever feeling calm again.

The clothes that she wore to work were already gone, her skirt in the trouser press having its creases removed, her pale blue silk shirt already in the washing basket.

A black velour onesie and thick furry socks had replaced them, but despite being well insulated and only a few feet from a huge, high-tech glass radiator, she felt like her bones were turning to ice. The shivering just wouldn't stop.

Perhaps she should have taken one of the girls up on the offer of company. At the time she'd been so sure she needed to be on her own, to rage and cry and kick the crap out of his ultra-swanky, thousand quid speaker system, but now she just felt empty.

The worst thing was, the one person she wanted to phone and talk to about it was the person who'd caused it.

Since the day they'd met, she'd told him everything, looked forward to seeing him or speaking to him every night to share the good and the bad.

This was as bad as it had ever been. And she couldn't tell him. Wouldn't tell him.

As if some kind of paranormal communication system had just passed the message on, the phone rang. Cam's face flashed on the screen, the picture taken last summer as they wandered down Grafton Street in Dublin on a weekend break. Their favourite place, Dublin. The beer and the music and the craic.

The explosion of pain came from nowhere, sharp, crippling and so physical she lurched forward, arms around her torso, struggling to breathe. Her glass fell, spilling wine across the rug, but she didn't care. It would clean, reverse the damage, be back to perfect in no time.

Unlike her marriage. Or her life.

With a trembling finger, she rejected the call.

There was no way she could speak to him right now. Her dad always told her that she had the answer to everything; she just had to work it out.

There was never going to be any working out of this one.

Why? How?

The where and when were easier to work out. Cam was only ever home a couple of days a week at the very most and she'd always taken his trips at face value. Where was he right now, though?

He was supposed to be in Birmingham, but was he actually still in Glasgow? Maybe just a few miles away? And was he lying next to Cara Deacon? Was he shagging her right now?

If the neighbours didn't have their TV on they'd hear her roar, but she didn't care and was barely aware that she was doing it.

On her feet now, she was pacing, careful not to stand on the dropped glass but almost hoping she would so that the ripping flesh could distract her from the excruciating pain inside.

This was unbearable. She had to know. Picking up the phone she steeled herself to do the unthinkable – act like there was nothing wrong. It was a skill she'd developed when her parents had split up when she was fifteen. Smile on, chirpy voice, act like everything was a breeze. It was the least she could do to help her dad, devastated over the departure of his wife of twenty years with the fellow cop he'd thought was his best friend. It had been painful, hard, and on the occasions her mum returned for a flying visit from her home on Arran, an island off the west coast, it was tempting to remonstrate and point out what a heartless cow she'd been.

But what would that achieve?

Many times, she and her dad had talked long into the night and agreed that the best thing was to keep it all pleasant. Superficially civil. Lock away the true feelings and pretend you're happy, act like all is fine.

In the meantime, the experience gave her a core of … well, perhaps not steel, but definitely strength.

And she'd never needed it more than now.

Picking up the phone, she dialled his number.

"Hey, sorry I missed your call. I was in the shower."

"No worries, babe. How was your day?" he asked, as breezy and warm as ever.

Oh, for fuck's sake. He sounded exactly the same as he always did. Not even the slightest change in the timbre of his voice. Yet she didn't even recognise the man she'd thought he was before today.

"Erm …" Don't crack. Do not ask him. Do not. "Oh, you know, same as always. Landed that new client, should be a pretty big deal."

"Brilliant. Well done, honey. Let's celebrate when I get home. I'm sure I can think of a way or two to congratulate you."

The urge to throw up was only quelled by closing her eyes and inhaling deeply.

"That sounds like a plan," she replied, trying desperately to sound like it was the best idea she'd ever heard. "But right now I have to get some work done. This new job is going to take a load of organising. How's Birmingham?"

"Oh, you know – another chain hotel, another preparation session for tomorrow."

He sounded so sincere that she doubted a jury would find him guilty.

"What hotel are you in?" she asked casually.

There it was. If she hadn't been looking for it, she'd never have even noticed. The slight hesitation, then the almost indecipherable change in his tone that convinced her that whatever came out of his mouth next would be a lie.

"The Holiday Inn. And I almost went to the wrong one. Luckily I checked right at the last minute and saw an email from travel with the right address. Taxi driver must have thought I was witless, changing the destination. He was a nice guy though. Been up in Glasgow for the rugby a few times."

He was rambling now and she knew she shouldn't push it. Didn't want to make him suspicious. But didn't those documentaries about psychopaths always say that when someone was lying they gave loads of unnecessary details?

The travel department? Taxi drivers? Rugby? What the hell was he on about? Hello, my name is Cam Cochrane and I lie like a serial killer.

"Glad you got there OK in the end …"

Another pause. She could almost hear his brain whirring. Making him suspicious wouldn't achieve anything. If he was betraying her, she didn't want to give him so much warning that he stopped before she found out for sure. Then she'd never know and that would eat away at her. That's why she put on her brightest voice and added, "… and I'll give you a call tomorrow morning. Love you."

"Love you too, baby. Miss you."

"You too," she said, repeating the same close as hundreds of similar conversations they'd had over the years.

Within ten minutes of hanging up, she'd Googled every Holiday Inn within a ten mile radius of Birmingham and called them up, asking to be put through to a guest called Cameron Cochrane. No such guest? Perhaps it's booked under MindSoar? No? OK, thanks so much for ripping my heart out of my chest.

There was no avoiding the reality. He'd lied. He wasn't there.

She should go to her bed now, stare at the bedroom ceiling instead.

Yet … she couldn't. How could she sleep? Lying next to the scent of his pillow would kill her.

She had to know more and it had to be now.

Cursing the fact that the wine had put her over the driving limit, she called a cab and scanned the form that she'd read so many times today, she knew it off by heart.

According to the details, Cara lived in Finnieston, not far from the city centre, but just far enough that the prices for a Georgian flat dropped by about a hundred grand.

Although it was ten p.m., the traffic still buzzed with revellers on nights out in the busy Dumbarton Road area. When they reached the destination, a terrace of sandstone tenements, she gazed up and calculated which one was Cara's. Two up, three across – darkness.

"Look love, I'll sit here all night if you want but it's going to cost a fortune," the taxi driver told her with a touch of sympathy that made her eyes fill up. The last thing Laney needed right now was someone being nice to her. First sign of affection and she knew she'd crumble.

"You're right, I'm sorry, I'll …" What? The most sensible idea was to go home, but she'd only lie awake all night wondering. To her left her eye caught a blue neon sign – all night café. Scrambling in her bag, she found her purse, paid the driver off and crossed the road, the smell of coffee and toast beckoning her in, yet turning her stomach at the same time.

Only a few of the ten or so red Formica tables were taken. A bearded young guy lay semi-slouched over the condiments in the corner, clearly no stranger to a drink or twelve. A couple of tables along, a twenty something couple, the girl sporting false eyelashes that came from the tarantula family and emanating irritation at her boyfriend as he studied his phone. With a roll of the eyes and a sigh, she applied lip gloss to a mouth that was already adorned with Sheen De Oil Slick.

In the centre of the room, at the biggest table, was a group in black T-shirts and trousers that Laney guessed were bar staff just clocked off for the night. For a second she had a pang of nostalgia. A dozen years ago that would have been her, out for a drink after finishing work, glad she had another forty quid to go towards the rent of her student flat that week.

Head down, she slipped into a window table that gave a clear view of Cara Deacon's flat across the road. Almost immediately, a plump, smiling waitress breezed over.

"Hello love, how are you tonight?" she chirped.

Heartbroken. Devastated. Crushed. Broken.

"Good, thanks," Laney managed. "Just a cup of tea,

please."

"Nothing to eat?"

"No, thank you. Maybe later."

The waitress headed back behind the counter and got to work on the tea.

Laney laid her phone on the table in front of her, desperate to call Tash or Millie and ask them to come join her in her new role as deranged stalker. The company would make her feel better, but she didn't dial. It was bad enough that one of them was going to be an exhausted mess tomorrow, never mind dragging the whole team out. And besides, if she lost the plot, stormed the building and battered Cam with his two grand, top of the range laptop – the one she'd bought him for Christmas and hadn't even finished bloody paying for – she wanted them to have plausible deniability as to her actions.

Instead, she turned to face enemy territory, locked eyes on target, jaw set to utter fury.

There may be no activity there now, but that was fine. Laney was known for her solid, patient nature. And if she had to sit there all night for a sign of that faithless prick, that was exactly what she would do.

13

Tash took a deep breath. "Millie, I love you, but you need help. We are going to die. We are. We're going to plummet to earth and some smart arse at a newspaper is going to come up with a headline that will not even begin to capture how fucking ridiculous this is. It'll read, 'I've fallen for you … Splat'."

Millie's cheeks flushed pink as she laughed, a sharp contrast to the blue/black bruised eyes that no amount of concealer could completely disguise. "Where's your sense of adventure? This is a brilliant idea! Best one I've come up with yet."

Tash responded with a glare that sat between violent and murderous on the evil scale.

Millie ignored it, too busy double checking all the details for her latest episode of romantic creativity – a CD player with PA system that would amplify sound enough to be heard through the thick glass exterior wall of a building, a huge banner, a video camera to record reactions and a window cleaner's gondola, currently attached to a Glasgow high rise office block at roof level, with Tash and Millie standing in it as it shuddered in the breeze.

Tash looked pleadingly at Laney, standing on the roof a few feet away. They'd decided who would go in the gondola in a professional and arbitrary manner – rock, paper, scissors – and Laney had won, allowing her to stay on the roof while the others took part in the stunt, descending from the fortieth floor to the twenty-ninth, where they would stop and stage the proposal. At the time, Tash had thought it churlish to object on account of the fact Laney's life had gone to crap and the last thing she needed was to be dangling in the air above the streets of Glasgow, but now civility and compassion had been unceremoniously gazumped by fear of imminent death.

"Look, I know you're suffering from acute heartbreak, but if you take my place I'll do anything for you. Anything. I'll clean your house. Give you a kidney. Kill Cam. Or all three."

While the sentiment behind it was genuine, Tash's main motivation – other than the wish not to die from falling forty storeys to the ground – was to try to make Laney smile. God, she looked awful. Grey. Bloodshot eyes surrounded by dark circles. Posture that just oozed misery. Tash felt her teeth clench in anger yet again. What a bastard he was for doing this. It didn't even give her an iota of satisfaction that she'd been right about him all along. From the very start, there had been something about him that rubbed her up the wrong way. Now she had an inkling of what it was – he was a lying, cheating prick. That would do it.

"Right, behave, here comes Dave," Laney announced, the warning clear in her raised eyebrows.

The door that led from the inside of the building slammed as the bold Dave headed towards them, dressed identically to Millie and Tash in a bright orange boiler suit and hardhat.

"Oh bugger, we're going to die looking like Teletubbies at an easyJet interview," Tash hissed, receiving a sharp dig in the ribs from Millie in return.

Laney shook his hand, going immediately into professional mode. "Ready?" He nodded tentatively, his face paling as the health and safety officer they'd recruited helped him with the final preparations.

Tash leaned in to whisper to Millie, "Yep, this all sounded great when it was on the drawing board, but it's a bit different when the wind is whistling around his arse and he's being strapped into a harness that could result in amputation of the bollocks." As he came within earshot, her demeanour immediately changed and she greeted him with a wide, cheery smile.

"Dave, come on board! Are you ready for this?"

He nodded and said something, but Tash couldn't hear thanks to the wind and the noise of the gondola creaking to life. At least if she died today, she'd go knowing that she'd had great sex last night. Sy had stayed until she'd kicked him out and sent him back to his own apartment at two a.m. That man knew what buttons to press and he did it exquisitely well, but she had no desire to wake up next to him or anyone else in the morning. That was her time. The early morning coffee while still under the duvet. Padding about in peace and not caring a jot that some bloke may be transfixed by your cellulite as you head for the loo. Not that she had much of it, but that wasn't the point. It was her time.

"You seriously want me to go?" He'd asked as they shared a cigarette, the ashtray balanced on his naked torso. Waxed. Buff. His six pack so defined she could use it as a toast rack.

"Indeed I do. Look, I'm doing you a favour. Giselle might swing past in the morning and you'll have time for a quickie before work."

It was said with absolutely no bitterness or jealousy. She really didn't care. As long as condoms were involved all round, he was free to have as many partners as he wanted and – the best part – so was she. That had always been the deal.

"Let me take you to dinner tomorrow night," he'd said as he pulled on his trousers, his magnificent delts rippling with every movement.

Tash had shrugged. "Can't, sorry. Need to be around in case Laney needs me."

"See, somewhere in there is a heart," he'd joked, with a smile that made his piercing blue eyes crinkle at the sides, before leaning over and tracing a circle around one of her nipples with his finger, then kissing her, the salty taste of his lips turning her on so much that the trousers were swiftly discarded in favour of another blissful encounter before he left.

That was romance. That was attraction. That was worth dangling a hundred feet in the air for. Helping a bloke called Dave propose to his girlfriend Mia?

Hardly a glorious end.

She tried not to grimace as the health and safety guy checked her harness for the third time, then gave them the thumbs up. Bert, the lovely window cleaner for this building who was happy, if a little bemused, to lend his services to the event, pressed a button on his control pad and, with a vibration that sent shock waves through their bodies, the descent began. Thirty-ninth floor. Thirty-eight. Thirty-seven. As each level passed, Tash willed herself not to look down and made another bargain with God.

Thirty-six. "I will buy a magazine from every Big Issue seller I ever encounter if you let us live."

Thirty-five. "I will donate ten per cent of my salary to charity."

Thirty-four. "I will devote my life to standing at traffic lights and helping old ladies cross roads."

Thirty-three. "I will stop being recklessly judgemental and critical of others."

Suddenly the wind sounded decidedly like God laughing.

When they reached the twenty-ninth floor, the gondola stopped with a screeching jolt that made Tash and Millie yelp in unison. Her friend's momentary reaction of fear gave Tash a small sense of satisfaction.

Inside the office in front of them, no one even acknowledged their existence, which made Tash want to do something ridiculous, like dance the Locomotion or moon them. She refrained. Crashing to earth with her buttocks hanging out held no appeal.

Doing a quick scan of the open plan office in front of her, she reckoned there were about sixty people there, all going about their day, completely unaware what the next couple of minutes would hold. Dave had told them that his dearly intended worked in the cubicle that would be directly in front of them as they stopped. Tash quickly locked on the typist sitting at the computer only feet away.

Holy shit, she hadn't realised Davie was into vintage. And by that she didn't mean the natty twinset with a forties flavour, but the lady inside it. The woman –and yes, it was a woman, not a girl – was at least sixty, with a sour expression and bright white bouffant that looked like a motorcycle helmet. Well, everyone to their own. Maybe he liked the smell of hairspray and running his fingers through a solid mass that could save her from concussion should she hit an obstacle while moving at speed.

Millie nudged Tash's shoulder and then gave her the thumbs up. OK, time to execute the plan. Ear defenders on. Bang on window. Press play. Then watch as an office full of incredulous people turned, their astonishment giving way almost immediately to smiles. Bert, the gondola operator, commenced his duties – holding up a large flip chart that had the words of the song that was now blasting from the PA – "Marry You", by Bruno Mars.

Millie, Tash and Dave went into a well-rehearsed dance routine, performing the actions to the song, making the gondola sway so perilously it was difficult to keep the mandatory huge grins on their faces.

Before they were even halfway through the first verse, Tash could see it was all going wrong. The eyes of the entire staff of the office were fixed on them now and there were grins, giggles and hands clasped over mouths in puzzlement.

All, that is, except the target of the proposal, who was still sitting in her chair, face a mask of fury.

Tash felt her blood pressure rise even further. There was no bloody way she was risking life and limb for someone so unappreciative. This wasn't going to be the first "no". Absolutely no bloody way.

Tash put even more energy into her moves, her gaze now locked with Miss Frosty Knickers, willing her to play along, to realise how incredible this was, to lighten up and go along with it.

But no. What a cow. What a miserable ...

Millie nudged her again as the song came to a close and Tash reluctantly went into the finale. What was the point? This wasn't going to go well. And they were in mid-air. How were they going to console poor Dave when they were dangling from a great height? He'd better not demand a refund. She'd need the fee from this job for the therapy bill to get over her new phobia of dropping to earth with a loud thud.

Regardless, he wasn't going to be able to claim she didn't do her job.

From the front of her boiler suit she removed a roll of paper about fifty centimetres high; she held on to the edge of it and passed the roll to Millie, allowing it to unravel foot by foot until it reached Dave and spelled out his message.

"Mia, will you marry me?"

On the other side of the window, Mia's face went to a place that was even more furious than before.

Tash's anxiety flipped up a notch. Oh no. No. No. No. This couldn't happen. This wasn't ...

Hang on. Every other person in the room was now cheering, a strange reaction to the lack of enthusiasm from Mia. Tash quickly glanced at Millie and Dave, realised their gazes were off to the extreme left and followed them to see a pretty young woman in a tartan dress and Doc Marten boots, holding a tray of coffees and snacks, frozen to the spot, motionless except for her head, which was now nodding furiously, making the tears that were running down her cheeks splash onto a plate of custard creams.

Tash let off a roar of laughter and gave her the thumbs up. She'd been staring at the wrong woman, while The Gods of Sentimental Tosh had triumphed once again and another one was in the engagement bag. Mistaken identity just turned into mission accomplished.

Dave signalled to Mia to head upwards to the roof, and she dropped the tray on to a photocopier and ran from the room. Meanwhile, Bert the Gondola Operator placed his flip chart in the open bucket in front of him, pressed the up button on the control panel and held on as they began to head for the safety of solid ground. Or solid rooftop.

They arrived at the same time as Mia burst through the door, and Dave unharnessed, climbed out of the moving platform and ran towards her. Just feet away from his dearly beloved, he stopped in his tracks, dropped down on one knee and held out the ring that had been in his boiler suit pocket. A solitaire. Diamond. White gold. Simple and beautiful. Mia screamed with delight as he slipped it on her finger, then laughed as he swung her round on the spot.

Out of the corner of her eye, Tash could see that Millie

was crying. As usual. But it was Laney's reaction that concerned her more.

As she stared at the happy couple, Laney, their pragmatic, even, non-gushy chum, was crying too. And they weren't tears of joy.

Suddenly Tash spotted another arrival to the happy scene. "Code red, code red, possible enemy combatant approaching," she hissed to Millie.

The white bouffant had come through the door and was headed straight for the happy couple, her helmet of hair not even budging despite the gusting wind.

"Who's she?" Millie asked. "Oh God, she doesn't look happy."

Helmet head was just a few metres from the couple now, expression still murderous. "I reckon I could take her down. Do I go? Do I?" Tash asked frantically.

Millie put an arm out to stop her. "Tash, don't. Whatever's going on it's nothing to do with us."

The woman reached Dave and Mia, and, with super-fast reflexes, reached out and flicked the back of Dave's head. He jerked back, before spinning around, breaking into a wide smile, lifting the woman up and spinning her around.

Tash and Millie reached them just as he deposited her back on the ground. "This is Mia's mother," he explained. "She's just congratulating us."

Dave's future mother-in-law was clearly trying to re-arrange her face into a smile, but not quite succeeding. Dave, completely oblivious, was waiting for a reaction to his introduction.

"Pleased to meet you," Millie gushed. "I bet this is a thrilling moment for you, too."

Her answer was lost in another gust of wind which, going by the grimace that didn't exactly light up the future mother-in-law's face, maybe wasn't a bad thing. Dave and Mia were too busy staring lovingly at each other to notice.

Only when they were back in the safety of the building did Tash feel free to comment.

"Man, I would not want to get on the wrong side of the mother-in-law. Scary woman."

Millie giggled as she shook her head. "But Dave seems totally oblivious. Somehow, I'm not sure that one will make it to the altar. Especially if Mia's mum has anything to do with it."

"It's probably better that they don't. Mia seems like a lovely girl, but you know what they say – if you want to know what a woman will be like when she's older, just look at her mother. Given that my mother is currently ensconced on a Majorcan sun lounger, clearly I'm going to be a middle-aged expat, with a tan the colour of teak, who spends her days having cocktails delivered by a bloke called Miguel."

"Does the same theory apply to men?" Laney's voice made the two of them jump. They'd left her on the roof tying up all the loose ends – paying the health and safety guy and Bert the window cleaner – and hadn't realised she'd caught up with them. Tash, her sleek black bob a windswept bush, pressed the elevator button then jumped from foot to foot to try to get some heat back into her bones.

"Dunno, why?"

Laney sighed as she leaned against the wall. "Because Cam's dad has been married three times – cheated on every one of them."

There was a pause as everyone let that little nugget of information settle. No one registered the ping of the lift as the doors flew open. Inside, a suited businessman stared at them, his confusion obvious as they completely ignored him and let the doors close again.

"Have you decided what you're going to do, luvly?" Millie asked her gently.

Laney nodded. "Let's talk about it back at the office. If I'm going to ruin my life I want to have a glass of wine in my hand when I do it."

14

The rain was battering against the windows by the time they got back to the Proposal Planners office, a dramatic soundtrack for the gloom inside. Millie broke into the alcohol supplies yet again. Two days in row had required alcoholic fortification. This wasn't a great sign.

Sitting on the sofa, Laney kicked off her suede boots and pulled her legs up on the couch beside her, just in time to take the glass from Millie's hand, doing it slowly, so as not to cause Millie to drop the other two she was expertly balancing in a triangle formation.

They were all back in civvy clothes now – Millie in a floor length psychedelic maxi, Tash in tight dark navy jeans and a white chiffon top, and Laney in the first thing she pulled out of the wardrobe – a deep red body-hugging dress that she'd bought for a "Women In Business" lunch the month before. A tad over dressed for a normal day at the office, but at least she'd get some wear out of it.

The others got comfortable. Millie took the space next to her, with Tash lying on the opposite sofa, one head raised against the arm, her feet dangling over the other arm.

Tash kicked off the discussion with, "Am I going to need aspirin for this conversation? Only the combination of yesterday's booze, a late night last night and risking my life for a bloke called Dave this morning is making my head hurt. I just need to know if it's about to take a turn for the worse. Not that I'm trying to steal your thunder with the whole internal pain thing."

Laney couldn't help but smile. "Then aspirin might be wise," she said, before taking a large sip of Prosecco, taken from one of four bottles that she'd dropped off at the office on the way to the proposal that morning. There was no way she was wasting more champagne, especially when it did absolutely nothing to soothe the pain.

"So where are we at?" Millie asked gently, her eyes filled with concern. It was weird, Laney knew, but she'd rather deal with Tash's brutal approach than Millie's sympathy and worry. Somehow that just made her feel more vulnerable.

"I called him last night."

Tash lifted her head at that announcement. "And?"

"Said he was in Birmingham. Acted completely normally. Completely."

"Well, maybe that means this is all just some simple misunderstanding," Millie said, hopefully.

"It's not. He was lying."

"How do you know?"

"I just know. There was something in his voice that wasn't there before. I don't know – a hesitation. A pause. Like he was trying to be careful what he said. And then he gave me loads of details. Cam never does that. Unless he's talking about some new gadget, he's a big picture, minimise the chat kinda guy."

"Dickhead," Tash added, completely unhelpfully.

"Yep, that too."

Laney ran her fingers through what little hair she had left. This felt so strange. Like it was happening to someone else. How could this suddenly be her life?

For a moment, she thought about telling them she'd spent the whole night at the café last night but decided against it. That was probably best kept to herself, otherwise Tash would start doing drive-bys to check on her whereabouts. Also, she could see that sitting for six hours in an all-night greasy spoon probably didn't give a particularly positive view of her state of mind.

"So I think I want to stick with the plan to carry the proposal through. I need to know the truth. I need to see it. I need to know how bad this is and I need to know …"

The words caught in her throat like a toxic lump.

"I need to know what he'll say."

There was a sharp intake of breath from Millie's direction. "Laney, come on, that's … that's …" She struggled to find the words.

"Completely crazy and borderline masochistic," Tash offered.

"I know," Laney said with a sigh, a hint of inevitability in her voice now, "but I still think if I confront him first, he might lie his way out of it, cover his tracks. This way, there will be no doubt."

There was no satisfaction, only regret there. But for six hours, as she got giddy on the scent of sausages and the fumes from the Calor gas heater in the all-night café, she'd thought the situation through from every angle.

Staring at the ceiling, Tash exhaled loudly. "Laney are you sure? That's going to be brutal. Do you really want to do that to yourself?"

"I think I have to. Maybe I'll be pleasantly surprised. Maybe Cara is a mad stalker and this is all a figment of her imagination. Maybe she's a work contact and his lunch with her was completely innocent, but he just didn't tell me in case I read something into it."

"Yes!" Millie blurted, latching on to that idea with buoyant optimism. "That's exactly what could have happened. You could be right."

"But I'm not," Laney told her calmly, "and we all know it, really. So the only way is to go through with this. Starting now."

"What are you going to do?" Millie asked, but an answer wasn't necessary, as Laney had already picked up her phone and was dialling the number she'd saved in the contacts the day before.

She flicked to loudspeaker, letting the girls listen as Cara answered on the third ring.

"Hello?"

"Cara, it's Laney from Personal Proposals. How are you?"

The other two girls leaned forward to pick up her response, despite the loudspeaker on the phone relaying Cara's replies loud and clear.

"I'm great! Excited. Can't wait to get started."

Laney closed her eyes for a couple of seconds, before she mustered the strength to get back in the game.

"Great. So you still want to go ahead?"

"Absolutely."

OK. In that case I just wanted to let you know that I'm sending some paperwork over to you today – a more detailed itinerary, as well as our contract and terms and conditions. If we could have them signed and returned in the next day or two that would be great."

"No problem at all. OMG I can't, like, really believe this is going to happen. It's what I've always wanted."

Laney was struggling to keep it together now, but she had to go on. What was it Tash had called her? Masochistic. Yep, that just about covered the last five minutes – especially if you added in "devastated" and "horrified".

"Great. And Cara …"

"Yes?"

Millie and Tash were quite literally on the edge of their couch, watching her in the same way you'd stare at a slow motion car crash, knowing that it was going to be brutal and bloody, but painfully aware there was nothing you could do to stop it.

"Are you sure you'll be able to keep it a secret? I mean, it's an exciting thing and the natural instinct is to share it with the …" Laney broke off, coughing, desperately fighting the urge to vomit, until she made herself say the words, "with your partner."

"Oh, I'm sure. I'm, like, great at keeping secrets. I didn't tell him that I'd bought him the latest iPad for his birthday a few months ago and he was like, totally surprised. Took me to Paris to thank me."

Laney dropped the phone. There was only so much she could take. Fuck. Cameron had appeared with an iPad Air the day after he'd turned thirty-five and told her the company had issued them to all the consultants. She hadn't doubted it for a single moment. Not one. Nor had she batted an eyelid when he'd come home from a "working" trip to Paris the following weekend complaining that he was exhausted. Fuck. Laney closed her eyes again as she sat completely still, completely unable even move as the pain seared through her.

Tash swooped in and snatched up the phone from the steel grey rug.

"Sorry, Cara, this is Tash. Laney just got an unexpected visitor so she's handed you over to me. So, tell me, I bet you've been thinking about this since the moment you left our office yesterday."

Not particularly subtle, but Tash's pretence of girly warmth masked the slight oddness of the question.

"I *so* have. Oh my God. I met Cameron for lunch and it was all I could do not to blurt it out right then and there. But I, like, totally don't want to spoil the surprise. I was glad when he went off to work and I could breathe again."

"Oh. What is it Cameron does, again?" Tash asked innocently.

"He's a corporate trainer. That's what makes him so smart. He totally sees into people's minds and he can get them to do anything."

Laney's stomach lurched as she realised the truth of that – he'd certainly got her to believe every lying, cheating thing he'd ever said.

"Wow, that must mean loads of travelling. I bet he

SHARI LOW

racks up the air miles doing that job."

"Absolutely. He's so dedicated. Straight after lunch he had to jet off …"

The three of them looked at each other, eyes wide, all desperately hoping that this played into their earlier wild explanation of innocence.

"… to London."

The wide eyes changed to quizzical expressions. London? He'd said he was in Birmingham. So maybe their outlandish theory was true. Perhaps she really was some mad stalker / work colleague and he had a business meeting at lunch and then fed her false information about where he was going because he didn't want her tracking him down. Grasping. Straws. It sounded ridiculous. It *was* bloody ridiculous. Yet Laney hoped. Hoped so much that her nails dug into the palms of her hands and sent shooting pains up her arms. There was a glimmer of a chance that this was all some big mistake they'd laugh about later.

"Oh, that must be hard, him being away so much," Tash probed, making the other two wonder why MI6 had never discovered her brilliance.

"Not really. I mean, he calls me every night at midnight …"

Hope gone.

Completely.

It was always one of Cam's things – when he called Laney, he'd joke that midnight was his cut off point, so he always hung up just before. She'd thought it was due to dedication to his craft. An urge to get an early night to be ready for the next morning. Now she realised it was to call someone else. Cara's words were only vaguely registering now, but somehow the innuendo when she giggled, "Actually we Skype. It's great for long distance relationships. Very *intimate*, if you know what I mean," got through.

"Remind me never to borrow your phone," Tash replied, somehow managing to inject just enough levity into it to make it sound like a witty retort. "Anyway, glad we're organised and on track with a plan, and as Laney said, we'll get more details fired over to you in the next couple of days and then the countdown begins. Take care."

Cara was still trilling, "Byeeeeee," when Tash hung up and tossed the phone over the back of the couch. "I know it's not her fault, but I'm starting to really hate her."

"You're right with the first bit – it's not her fault. And she's not lying or making this up," Laney added. "He always cuts off our calls before midnight. Says it's so he can get enough sleep to get up for a workout in the morning before work."

"Think it's more down to his late night Skype workout," Tash observed dryly.

Laney wearily reached over and refilled her glass from the bottle on the coffee table. "Sounds like it. Christ, every time I think this is as bad as it gets, it takes a turn for the worse."

Millie was nodding thoughtfully. "I know, but what you were saying before, about Cara? About it not being her fault. Shouldn't we warn her? Don't we have an obligation to tell her the truth? Expose him now?"

"I've thought about that a lot," Laney countered, "and you're right – she should know. But I can't help thinking that it's better for her to know the extent he's willing to go to, too. If we tell the truth now, it gives him a chance to lie his way out of it, maybe to her, too. He could say we're separated. Or living separate lives. Or, I don't know, some other bullshit story. We've already established that he's pretty good at this. She says on her form that they've been going out together for two years. Two years of lies. How could I miss that? And how could she not notice that there were inconsistencies? I mean, where did she think he was on Christmas day? Or Hogmanay? He was with me, so he couldn't have been with her. How did he explain that to her? I agree she needs to know about this, but I just hope she understands why I had to do it this way and why I thought it was the best thing for her, too. And if she still wants him afterwards … well, that's up to her. She's welcome to him. There's no going back for us."

It was the first time she'd said it. It was definitely over. And yet, even knowing that, she couldn't walk away without confronting him in the act, because she had to be sure, without an iota of doubt, that she was doing the right thing. She'd do everything she could to minimise the shock and pain for Cara, but surely they would both benefit from finding out just how far his lies would go?

It didn't sit easy with her but in this new surreal existence, where nothing was as it seemed, she'd go with it for now. At least the costs were coming directly from Cam – that was still a tiny, if admittedly petty, consolation.

The buzzer of the office intercom made them all jump.

Tash was up first and padded over to the phone on Laney's desk.

She listened for a moment. "Of course, come on up."

As soon as she replaced the phone, her tone shifted to bewilderment.

"It's a delivery. Interflora. Any ideas?"

The response was negative all round.

When the delivery guy reached the open door, his face was barely visible behind a huge bouquet of lilies and white roses.

"Ah, white roses are my favourites," Millie breathed giddily, jumping to her feet.

Tash rolled her eyes. "Who would have thought it would be Leo who would contribute a redeeming act from the male species."

Hands on hips, Millie replied tartly, "My boyfriend is a lovely man. And he's got every right to spoil me."

"You deserve it, honey," Laney said, trying her best not to spoil Millie's moment. This wasn't all about her. Millie had had a really tough couple of years, supporting Leo while he tried to make it in acting, and it was about time Leo repaid the favour by making Millie feel as special as everyone knew she was.

Tipping the delivery guy a fiver, Millie relieved him of his blooms and rushed back over to the sofa, laying them down gently on the coffee table before opening the card.

Her expression immediately flicked from joy to incomprehension to disappointment.

"What's up?" Laney asked.

Millie answered the question by reaching over and giving the card to Tash.

Millie would have been thrilled if the flowers had been for her.

Laney would have been disgusted if they'd come to

her from Cam.

But Tash?

Tash was clearly just overcome with disdainful apathy as she read out the note: "Giselle chose them. Thanks for last night." She groaned, "Urgh, you know what this means, don't you?"

"That your fuck-buddy wants more than the job description?" Laney suggested.

"That he's falling in love with you?" Millie said, her inherent love of romance overcoming the disappointment that they weren't from Leo.

"Nope, it means …" Tash sighed, tossing the card on the table, "… that he's absolutely and totally chucked."

15

For a moment Millie thought the person sitting on the front step was Leo. It wouldn't be the first time he'd forgotten his keys. It was a creative, artistic thing, she'd decided. The parts of his brain that were the most developed were imagination and creativity, so logical things like bills, shopping and housework didn't factor in the priorities. Or keys, it would seem.

As she approached, she realised she'd got it wrong, when Guy from the travel agency jumped up, hands in the air.

"Sorry, I didn't mean to freak you out," he said, clearly mistaking her expression of bewilderment for horror. "I'm not actually sitting on your step like a deranged stalker. I mean, I was. Sitting on your step. But not being a stalker. Just being … I mean, just doing … writing a note for you. Oh God, your face looks so sore. Does it still hurt?"

It was impossible not to laugh at his flustered explanation. "No," Millie said, grinning. "Only when I laugh. Like now."

"Ah, sorry again. I'm like an ongoing jinx for you. I promise I don't do this to everyone I meet. Hit them with my car or stalk them, that is."

"I should hope not. It's an expensive way to expand your social circle."

There was an easy pause, before Guy realised he should be the one to fill in the blanks.

"Oh, OK. Sorry. Right. So it was just to say again that my insurance company will pay out because I told them it was my fault, but in the meantime my mate owns a garage over on Mount Vernon Road and he says he'd be happy to come and get the car tomorrow, fix it, and return it to you straight away, and that way you're not inconvenienced by having to wait for the insurance company to arrange the repair."

"Cool," Millie told him, fishing in her bag for her keys. "If you let me know the number I'll give him a call."

"That's what I was doing – writing down the number," he explained, gesturing with the pen and paper in his left hand. "In a totally non-stalking manner," he jested.

Millie felt herself warming to him even more. He was such a sweet guy. Good looking. A bit of the Gerard Butlers about him. There was no doubt that all the girls in his office would totally fancy him, especially if he was as nice and decent as he seemed to be. But then, her judgement wasn't exactly foolproof these days. Hadn't she thought Laney's Cam was a lovely guy?

Millie located her keys and pulled them from the

bottom of her bag. "If you absolutely promise that you're not a stalker, do you want to come in for a coffee? It doesn't look like my boyfriend's home yet so I don't have any urgent plans for the next half an hour. And it's the least I can do since you've come over her to help me out."

"Erm, sure, yeah. That would be great, actually."

Millie let him follow her into the kitchen, blissfully unaware that, as always, there were half a dozen pairs of pants lined along the radiator. She loved the clutter of her kitchen. Some might call it untidy or messy, completely disorganised, or – in the case of Tash – "the closest thing to a landfill site inside four walls," but Millie didn't care. She loved the mishmash of china cups and saucers, rescued from charity shops and car boot sales. She adored the pulley in the middle of the room, a hanging frame for pots, pans, dried flowers and – occasionally – wet tights.

The wallpaper, a faded white with tiny pink roses, had been there when she first moved in and she reckoned it dated back to the fifties. Everything came back into fashion if you waited around long enough. Cath Kidston was making a fortune off this retro style these days.

Guy pulled out a wooden chair, one of six non-matching seats positioned around a battered wooden table that Millie had found in a second-hand furniture shop and restored. Actually, that wasn't strictly true. Leo had started to restore it, given up halfway, and then Millie had splodged on a coat of varnish to protect the sanded top. The result was a half painted, half bare wood, well-worn piece of furniture that she loved because it was gloriously unique.

"Coffee or tea?" she asked, filling the kettle from the tap on the Belfast sink, another inheritance from the previous owners. If anyone else had bought the flat, they'd probably have ripped out the kitchen and replaced it with something sleek, glossy, white and trendy. Instead, Millie had painted the yellowing wooden units, some pale pink, some pale blue, and splashed out on a new white worktop. She loved how it looked. If a kitchen could sum up a person, this did the job – Bohemian, bright, quirky and a little dreamy.

"Tea, please. I love this room. It's really …"

"Chaotic?" Millie helped him out.

"Quaint and cosy," Guy replied, laughing.

Millie switched on the gas ring and placed the kettle on top, then busied herself getting cups and loading the teapot with teabags. Yes, she still liked her flowery teapot. It reminded her of sitting at the family table after school when she was a kid and her mum and her friends would chat and laugh while drinking cup after cup from a teapot in the middle of the table, that never seemed to run dry.

Gathering the tea accessories, she placed them in the middle of the table and then turned back to the fridge, taking out a lasagne she'd made last night when she was trying to keep her mind off Laney's devastation. Once again, Millie had offered to go home with her and been gently refused. That was just Laney's bolshy, independent way.

She slipped the pasta in the oven just in time for the kettle to whistle.

Guy smiled as she poured his cup first.

"Does it hurt when you eat or drink?" he asked.

"No. I promise, it's not nearly as bad as it looks. You really need to stop beating yourself up about it. That wasn't a pun, by the way. It's absolutely fine. Let it go," she told him, smiling as she offered him a Jaffa cake.

'OK, I promise I won't ask again."

Millie kicked off her sandals as she sat down, and then joined him in the partaking of an orange and spongy biscuit. "Ah, that's better. Bit of a rough day at work today."

"I never asked, what is it you do?"

"I'm a partner in a proposal agency."

"A what?" he asked, mimicking the reaction of everyone they'd ever told, in the history of the whole wide world.

"A proposal agency. We help people who want to ask their partners to marry them in an unusual way. Today we dropped down the outside of a forty storey building and danced to a Bruno Mars song while holding up a banner saying, 'Mia, Will You Marry Me?'"

Guy was laughing properly now, completely incredulous. "Honestly? That's brilliant. I hope she said yes."

"She did."

He thought for a moment. "You know, you should give me some cards for the office. Loads of our customers book romantic holidays or weekends away and that would be a fantastic service to suggest. Do you set things up abroad, too?"

Millie nodded, her enthusiasm bubbling over. "Absolutely. We're just about to start working on one in New York." The last word tailed off as reality kicked in and the horror of that particular job came back to the forefront. That one wasn't going to be their finest moment.

'That's excellent. Look, I know our only contact so far has been a pretty unfortunate incident …" He trailed off, distracted. "Can I have another Jaffa cake, please? Only I haven't had them since I was about eight and I'd forgotten how brilliant they are. Don't suppose you've got a packet of Wagon Wheels stashed anywhere?"

"Help yourself and sorry, no on the Wagon Wheels," she said, happily pushing the plate towards him.

He took one and then got back to his point. "What was I saying? Oh yes, so the whole bruising injury thing aside, I'm just thinking, perhaps we can look at some kind of mutual agreement on the work front? If you used our service for your bookings, I'd be happy to offer some kind of discount, and we can also promote your business in our branches."

Millie could see the absolute sense in his proposal. "I'll speak to Laney. That's one of the other partners. Laney handles the business side of things, and Tash handles logistics, planning and moving mountains."

"And what's your role?" he asked, genuinely interested.

Millie shrugged. "I guess I'm the – oh, God, this is going to sound really naff – but I'm the one that comes up with the fantasies. Not *those* kind of fantasies!"

"I didn't think for a minute that's what you meant. But I might need another Jaffa cake to get over that."

"*Romantic* fantasies," she stressed, watching as he took a bite of yet another biscuit. Where did he put it? This guy didn't have an extra ounce of fat on him and yet he was practically inhaling the biscuit plate.

"So that must be a lot of pressure for your boyfriend to live up to, then. Someone who deals in big gestures all day must have high expectations of romance." He was teasing her, but in such a nice way she was actually enjoying the banter.

"Absolutely. If I don't get a trail of rose petals in front of me at all times, I have a total diva strop."

He puffed out his cheeks. "Poor guy. That's serious stress. Anyway, listen, I'd better get off and let you get back to your night. Thanks for the tea. And do call that mechanic and he'll take care of everything for you."

"Thanks," Millie repeated. "And I'll say to Laney to get in touch about the New York trip. The flights and hotel haven't been arranged for that yet."

"No problem at all."

Millie saw him to the door and waved him off, feeling strangely happier and less weary than she had when she'd walked up the path an hour before.

She picked up the phone and speed-dialled Laney.

"Hey, just making sure you got home OK."

"I did, honey. Thanks."

"Want to come over here and we'll be totally clichéd and watch chick films and discuss Jennifer Aniston's unappreciated brilliance?"

Laney laughed. "Tempting, but I'm just going to hang here."

"Are you sure?"

"Positive."

"OK. But promise me if you feel rubbish later you'll come over or call me. I don't think we're doing anything tonight, so I'll be around. Promise?"

"I promise."

Taking her tea with her, Millie curled into the faded rose pink armchair in the corner and let the heat of the Aga warm her. She'd do anything to fix this for Laney, but it didn't look like there was going to be any way to stop the train of pain and heartache that was trundling towards them.

Picking up this month's copy of *Marie Claire* from the rickety oak side table to her right, she started flicking aimlessly through the pages, her thoughts stopping her from taking any more than a cursory interest in any of the features or photo shoots. It took her a few moments before she realised where her mind had wandered to.

Guy's statement about pressure replayed in her mind.

"So that must be a lot of pressure for your boyfriend to live up to, then. Someone who deals in big gestures all day must have high expectations of romance."

Was that why he'd never proposed or mentioned the wedding?

All this time, she'd put it down to money, but let's be honest, you could get married for the cost of a licence and that would be absolutely fine with her.

Wouldn't it?

There was no time to answer before Leo sauntered into the room, dropped down and kissed her on the lips. He tasted of coffee and him. His hair was pulled back in a ponytail and he was wearing battered jeans and her favourite grey T-shirt.

"Hey babe, good day?"

"Not really."

"How's Laney?"

Leo and Laney didn't know each other particularly well, but Millie was touched that he cared enough to ask.

"Not great. How were your meetings?"

He took a slug of milk from the carton, a couple of white drops landing on his T-shirt. He didn't notice.

"Yeah, great. We sorted out the paperwork and I start this week. My agent is stoked."

The chair Guy had just vacated half an hour before made a grating noise on the tile floor as he pulled it out, turned it around and straddled it, facing Millie. The macho pose made her smile as it was so unlike him. Leo was measured. Gentle. A bit theatrical. A Bohemian soul, like her. This new role was obviously making him channel his inner gangster. Millie hadn't even realised he possessed one of those.

"Babes, you know this gig is going to mean really long hours. Are you OK with that?"

"Of course! Leo, this is the break! It's your … your …" Not for the first time did she curse her lack of movie knowledge. "It's your *Pretty Woman*!" she finished triumphantly.

He thought for a moment. "Nope, no idea what that means."

"Sorry, bad example. But it was the only one I could think of that turned someone into a huge star. You know, the Julia Roberts thing."

He shook his head, smiling. "Brilliant. Now I'm a hooker with a thing for rich guys. You couldn't have gone for De Niro in *The Godfather*. Or Affleck and Damon in *Good Will Hunting*?"

She used her toe to poke his thigh. "You know what I mean. Sorry. I will spend every night you're working late brushing up my movie knowledge."

"Excellent. I'll be asking questions."

It was only later, their lasagne gone, a bottle of wine empty, both of them wrapped in each other on the sofa as they watched some Will Smith movie, that she remembered what Guy had said.

Propping up on one elbow, she rested her chin on his chest, her face only inches from his.

"Do you ever feel pressure because of my job?"

"Pressure how?" he asked, trying to look around her to see the TV screen.

"Pressure to be – oh, I don't know – romantic?" It made absolute sense. Why had she never sussed it out before? Of course it would be tough to come up with a romantic proposal, to make something uniquely theirs and personal, when she spent all day long, sometimes using vast sums of cash, to plan these extraordinary events for other people.

His gaze finally left the screen as he locked eyes on hers. "No," he said simply, before turning his head away and losing himself once more in Will Smith saving the world.

Millie put her head back down on his chest.

So if that wasn't the problem, then what exactly was?

16

Laney had been staring at it for twenty minutes, but dread had made her physically incapable of action. It should be easy. Open. Click. Start searching.

When she'd first sat down there was still a little daylight coming in the hallway window; now it was dark.

From her position on the floor of the hall, she stared a little longer. OK, come on. This could be done.

Placing her coffee mug on the cream carpet, she pushed herself up, and opened the door to his study. Her stomach lurched. The room smelled of him. Not a bad smell, or a scent of aftershave or sweat, just him. Just Cam. She could be led in here blindfolded and she'd still know where she was.

Fingers trembling, they traced a line as she walked around his desk, then sat in his leather chair. She could only remember sitting here a couple of times before.

Once when the chair arrived and she and Cam were trying it out, and one other time when her laptop was down and she'd used his computer to pay a couple of bills. He'd been in the room both times.

This felt weird. Intrusive. And no, the irony wasn't lost on her that she felt guilty despite the fact that he'd been intruding on someone else's knickers.

His desk was black gloss, sleek and shiny. When it was delivered she'd thought it a bit over the top for a study that no one ever saw except him, but then she figured he worked hard – why shouldn't he have a flash desk if it made him happy?

Where was the line? A nice car? Expensive holidays? Designer suits? A twenty-five-year-old stylist who over populated her sentences with the words "like" and "totally"?

That was, like, just totally where the line was.

Not that Laney was innocent in that direction. It seemed like recently her sentences had been over-populated with the words "prick" and "bastard".

Starting with the drawer to her left, she pulled them all open and searched them one by one. Stationery. An old mobile phone. His old iPad. Dozens of chargers and miscellaneous cables. A couple of notebooks. Nothing at all suspicious or incriminating.

The computer next. Flipping the on switch, she felt a couple of sweat beads pop on her brow as she waited for it to boot up.

Password.

Shit.

It was a numeric one – six digits. She tried all the obvious ones. Date of birth. Date they met. Date of their anniversary. Variations of the house and work phone number. Even his National Insurance number, which was conveniently located on a payslip in the third drawer down on the left.

She sat back, the cool of the leather soothing the headache that had started at the top of her neck and was now reaching around her temples and squeezing tight.

Her chest felt the same kind of constriction despite the fact that her bra had come off within minutes of arriving home and she was now wearing a white, oversized scoop-neck T-shirt above her grey yoga pants and chunky knit socks.

Every number she could think of was summoned to her brain, tried, then dismissed. Nope, nothing worked.

She was on the verge of giving up when something twigged. No, he wouldn't, would he? Pulling her phone from her pants pocket, she checked that number again, then typed in the last six digits.

The screen opened. Laney crashed.

He used Cara's phone number as his computer password. Somehow that seemed like even more of a violation than shagging her. Even in her blur of pain, she could see that thought was irrational, but it was almost like he'd brought her into their home.

Wait a minute. Had he actually brought her into their home?

Laney was occasionally away overnight. She worked long hours. Had he brought her here and screwed her in their house? In their bed? On the top of his shiny glossy desk?

The jolt as her reflexes made her jerk backwards was instinctive, like the reaction when a doctor tapped on a knee with a hammer.

It took a moment to steady, to decide to carry on when all she wanted to do was leave there right now and go anywhere. Anywhere at all. As long as it was far from Cam Cochrane and everything connected to him.

No. She'd come this far and if there was anything here that she should know about then she wanted to find it.

Her hand reached for the mouse and she methodically worked her way through his files. Photos? Nothing. Just dozens of selfies, scenery shots, and images from parties they'd had over the years.

She went through his emails. Nothing there, either. The electricity company. Correspondence with a couple of his university mates. But then, this was his private email and he used his work email for most correspondence. That was server based and accessed remotely, but she had no idea how to go about hacking it.

She shuddered as she realised how much she hated doing this. Snooping and checking up on someone just felt so invasive, so utterly wrong, and yet she couldn't stop. She had to know if there were any clues and she had to know right now.

Opening and closing every file on his desktop, she realised that there was absolutely nothing obvious there. But then, Cam was a smart guy. If he was doing this, he wasn't going to leave clues.

A wry smile reached her lips as she realised she'd just started that thought with "if". The evidence was stacking up like Jenga blocks and yet something deep inside her still wanted to give him the benefit of the doubt.

Shutting the computer down, head pounding with

unanswered questions, she picked up the phone and called her dad's number.

"Hey, Dad, it's me." Before he even spoke, she could picture him sitting at the kitchen table, specs halfway down his nose, reading one of the four newspapers he perused every day. Since he'd retired from the police six months ago at sixty, Fred had been methodical about keeping his mind as active as his half-hour daily run kept his body. Tall and fit, he was still a catch, but a lifetime of long hours and shift work had left him at a loss as to how else to fill his time. He'd been asked to return as a consultant to the new, unified Police Scotland force but he'd refused, saying he needed time to de-pressurise. Instead he helped them out with the occasional proposal or case, and spent the rest of the time doing all the things he had missed when he was working fourteen-hour days putting away bad guys.

"Laney, love. How's things? How did the abseiling down the building thing go this morning?"

"Great. Only it wasn't abseiling, they were on a window cleaner's gondola. I took some pictures. I'll bring them over at the weekend."

"Great, love. Sounds like a good one. I take it she said yes?"

"She did."

"Och, fools, eh?" he joked.

"Absolutely," she answered with more vehemence than she'd intended.

"You OK, Lanes?" he asked, spotting the tone.

"Yeah, I'm fab, Dad. Just tired." She couldn't tell him, not on the phone. He loved Cam, had taken him on like a son.

"Ah, well get a good night's sleep. Love you and I'll speak to you tomorrow."

The click told her he was gone and she stared at the phone for a few seconds, waiting for his voice to return. That was so unlike him. Usually, they'd chat for an hour or so, but tonight it was like he couldn't wait to get off the line. Maybe he had something on. Maybe there was something wrong. She chided herself. All of a sudden she was looking for problems everywhere. Perhaps she'd be better just dealing with the one she already had.

Talking of which, he'd be calling soon. She couldn't face it, couldn't stand to hear his smug, fake voice. Down in the kitchen she dashed off a quick text.

"Hi, darling, heading over to Tash's tonight." That would do it. He'd never call her when she was with Tash due to the small matter of their vehement mutual loathing.

"So don't worry if I'm not home when you call. Lo"…

Her finger stopped of its own accord, refusing to write the word. Her brain fought to overrule it, knowing that he'd notice if she didn't sign off the same way she'd signed off every text she'd ever sent him.

… "Love, Lanes xxx".

She pressed send with a disgusted groan and put her head on the kitchen table, her stomach churning yet again as she pictured him smiling as he read it, glad of a free pass. He wouldn't have to lie to her tonight, wouldn't have to hang up before midnight so he could go have Skype sex with Cara.

The urge to retch was almost impossible to quell. The mental image only made it worse and so did her next thought.

When was he coming back to Glasgow? Sure, he'd told her that he wouldn't be back until the end of the week. But then he'd also told her that he was going straight to Birmingham, went to bed at midnight and would love her to the exclusion of all others until death do they part. Prick. Bastard. Was he actually already back and shacked up with Cara? She thought back to his patterns over the last year or so. He was usually away Monday to Friday, but at least once a month, sometimes twice, he spent the weekend away, too, telling her that he was working with companies that preferred training time to take place out of the office in a relaxed weekend environment. Was that all nonsense?

There was no way she was going to spend another night in that café. She had already gone a whole night with no sleep, she couldn't do another one. Just couldn't. There had to be a way to overcome this. Perhaps nip out to the twenty-four hour pharmacy to pick up something to help her sleep? Or maybe go for a long bath. Or watch one of those programmes about people who buy up abandoned storage lockers at auction in the hope of finding a nugget of treasure in amongst tatty old golf bags and Great Aunt Hilda's sewing chest. Any of those would probably have her snoozing in no time.

Sleeping pills win out, she told herself, as she picked up her black leather cross-body messenger bag, threw it over her head and made for the car.

Sleeping pills. Bed. Sleeping pills. Bed. That was what was going to happen.

The mantra only stopped when she reached her destination and realised she wasn't kidding anyone, least of all herself.

The same friendly waitress as last night gave her a wink as she braved the fumes of sausages and the Calor gas heater, and took her place at the same table as last night. Centre of the window, with a perfect view of Cara's first floor window. Her heart beat a little faster as she realised that the light was on tonight. Oh God. Was Cam in there? Was he already back from London? Or Birmingham? Or wherever he was supposed to be? It was impossible to tell if he was lying to one of them or both. If he was back, was he with Cara right now, only a few hundred metres from where she sat?

The text message made her jump, hands shaking as she dug the phone out of her bag.

"No worries, darling. I'm turning in early tonight too. Exhausted. Miss you babe xx".

Laney's gaze returned to the window. She wasn't leaving. Absolutely no way. She was staying here until she saw him, or her, or both of them.

At that moment, the window in Cara's apartment turned dark.

17

Tash leaned forward, so her head was sticking through the tiny space between her two brothers' shoulders.

"Tell me again why you chose this car?" she asked, her disdain obvious.

In the driving seat, Jordan laughed. "Maybe because it's just a bit ironic."

He had a point. Two six foot four inch tall rugby players, each the size of a small garden shed, squeezed into a Mini.

"*The Italian Job* has lot to answer for," John interjected. He'd have punctuated the jibe with a friendly dunt to his brother's arm, but the space wasn't big enough to give his limbs freedom of movement.

The car zipped into a tiny space right outside Laney's building. "That's why I bought the car, OK smartarses?" Jordan said with a satisfied smile, before opening the door and slowly unfolding his limbs as he climbed out.

"Christ, I hope you don't ever have to get out in a hurry. It's like watching a bouncy castle inflate," Tash observed.

John roared with laughter, while out on the pavement, Jordan just looked heavenward, as if praying for gaffer tape to adhere to the gob of his smart-mouthed sister. Tash pulled up the seat release and clambered out of the back, clutching the huge bouquet that had been delivered to the office that morning. She jumped up to kiss Jordan on the cheek, said, "Thanks. Back in a minute," before darting through the doorway.

She boycotted the lift and ran full pelt up the stairs, glad to fit in some exercise to relieve her guilt over the night of excess that would no doubt follow. Any night out with her brothers ran the risk of injury to the liver, but tonight was a special occasion – the second instalment of the celebration of the cup win the Sunday before. Those rugby types liked to make the most of their victories.

She was breathless by the time she reached her floor, so she walked slowly along the corridor to give her lungs an opportunity to call the emergency services. *Must. Stop. Smoking.*

Her door was in sight when she stopped, turned, and banged on the one next to it.

Sy took so long to answer, she'd decided he wasn't in and was already mentally cursing him for the expended effort of running up the stairs. She could have just stood at the bottom and had a cigarette instead.

The "Must Stop Smoking" thing clearly wasn't sinking in.

"Hey," he said casually, leaning against the doorframe.

Naked. From the waist up. His bottom half clad in a pair of jeans. For Christ's sake, this guy was the wealthiest bloke she knew and yet he seemed to be unable to fork out the cash to keep the top half of his body covered.

Why did he do that? Why? And why couldn't she stop staring at the very point where the bottom level of his six pack met the opened top button of his jeans, a little trail of hair acting as a guide that took you down to his …

No! Back to the point. Focus.

She thrust out the flowers she'd carried the whole way. "Here."

"You don't like them? Allergic?" he asked, confused but obviously amused.

"I'm sure they're lovely," she replied. "But the thing is, they're not in the deal."

"The deal?"

"Yep. The deal is we swap the occasional pleasantries if we meet in the corridor, and have sex by mutual consent when mutually suitable."

He nodded, as his eyes did that cute crinkly thing again.

"Sorry, just didn't realise that was an actual deal. I don't think I got the contract."

"It was a verbal agreement," she shot back. "So flowers aren't in there. Flowers are for a different kind of agreement. Not the one we've got. But thanks."

She held them out again, gesturing to him to take them, but he didn't budge.

"But I don't have any requirement for these," he told her, still running with the official tone.

"Me neither."

Stand off. One that was only interrupted by a moment

SHARI LOW

of exquisite timing when, to her far right, the elevator pinged open and Giselle alighted, strutting towards them on her giraffe-like legs, with a swagger that came directly from the catwalk.

Tash turned to her and beamed. "Ah, just in time. Delivery for you. I took it in when it arrived because there was no answer here. Was just dropping it off."

Giselle's eyes widened as the blooms were thrust towards her. "Oh darling, they're beautiful!" she proclaimed. "Look, they match what I'm wearing. How perfect."

"Perfect," Tash agreed. "Great choice," she told Sy. "Anyway, I'll leave you two lovebirds alone. Have a great night."

Giselle had already suctioned herself to his face by the time Tash reached the lift. Back downstairs, Jordan and John were leaning against the car, arms folded.

"You two look like bouncers. Or gangland enforcers. Or the 'after' shot in a porridge advert."

Despite their irritation at being kept waiting, they both laughed, before Jordan stepped to one side, opened the door and let her climb into the back again.

Twenty minutes in traffic later they nipped into yet another space on Byres Road, directly across from their destination in Ashton Lane. Jordan raised a smug eyebrow to reinforce the fact that his point had been proven once again.

As Tash crossed the road, she slipped on a pair of sunglasses, despite the fact that it was seven p.m. and darkness had already fallen.

"Here she goes again. Who do you think it'll be tonight?" John laughed.

"I'm going for Jessie J. If I get Dannii Minogue again I'll go fucking mad," Tash retorted.

Covered eyes darting from side to side, she could see the wheels turning in the minds of the people who were stopping to stare. A raven-haired, red-lipped woman with dark glasses, walking in between two huge, stony-faced guys who were clearly her bodyguards. Their hands were reaching for their phones now. Their fingers twitching. She, John and Jordan played this game regularly and so far they'd had brilliantly diverse posts hit Twitter.

"OMG!!!!! Uma Thurman in #ashtonlane"

"Some famous burd in #ashtonlane with fckn huge bouncers"

"Is dita von teese in Glasgow? Swear just saw her n #ashtonlane #hot #stripperz"

And her very favourite …

"OMFG Dannii Minogue! Am gonna get autograph. Love!!!! #ashtonlane #whereskylie"

They strutted across the cobbles, each step accompanied by a hissed mantra of "Do not fall, do not fall, do not fall." Cobbles were no friend to eight inch stiletto heels and there was no way she wanted the starring role in the next viral YouTube video – the one where Dannii Minogue falls flat on her face in a busy street and bystanders have to duck to avoid being shot by her ricocheting teeth.

Relief and thirst popped up in equal measure when they crossed the threshold of the bar, followed immediately by rousing cheers from several men who were close in size to a Portaloo.

Tash loved the guys in the team dearly, but she was

glad she didn't have to foot the bill for their food or drink.

Jordan and Josh had been in the squad for five years so most of the other players were good friends who had long ago forgotten that she was female, five foot five and an occasional impersonator of B list celebrities. To them she was just one of the guys. Or a team mascot, without the furry animal costume and with a perpetual weakness for Mexican alcohol.

The fourth tequila shot had just burned down the back of her throat when a new voice filtered through from behind her.

"Are my testicles safe now or are there still conditions to me keeping them?"

The smile was already on her face by the time she turned around.

"Mark?" she said hopefully.

"Matt," he corrected her, his grin implying that he was unoffended. He reached out and grabbed a pint of lager that was being thrust in his direction from one of the other large gentlemen at the bar.

"Ah sorry." Bugger. She'd never been great with names. "Accountant?"

"Yep, but please don't let the sexiness of my job intimidate you."

"I'll do my best. Thank God you've got such a fascinating occupation. I'm sick of meeting stunt men and polar explorers."

Jordan overheard the last bit and leaned into the conversation. "Apologies for my sister. John and I got the looks and sparkling personalities and she got the bitter and twisted sarcasm."

To his credit, he didn't even flinch when she stood on his foot.

Back to Matt, who seemed to be genuinely enjoying the banter and was smiling between sips of his beer.

"So I believe I owe you thanks for seeing me home. I'm guessing I wasn't exactly hostess of the year."

"Your hospitality skills need work, but you've got potential."

"I really haven't," she corrected him. "That was as good as it gets."

"Wow. In that case, you might need to work on them."

"I'll bear it in mind," she said, reaching through two firmly toned torsos to put her drink down on the bar.

"I'll be back in a minute. Just off to order an etiquette book online."

His laughter followed her as she headed to the loo. In the cubicle, she put the seat down, sat on it and pulled out her phone, hitting Laney's number on the speed dial. Straight to voicemail.

She tried home.

Straight to answering machine.

She checked her watch: eleven p.m.. Where had the time gone? It felt like she'd just got there.

Speed dial 3. Millie answered on the second ring.

"Hello lovely, is Laney with you?"

"No. I tried to persuade her to come over or let me go there but she was having none of it. Why?" Millie's words came fast and oozed anxiety, which Tash immediately attempted to quell.

"Och, nothing. She's probably taken a sleeping pill and conked out. Or she just doesn't feel like talking to anyone."

"I think it's probably the second one," Millie agreed. "You know she's more one for analysing things than talking them through."

Tash didn't argue. Sharing and touchy feely stuff wasn't really Laney's way. She was more practical, task orientated and solution driven. And yes, she realised that did sound like a naff TV advert for a courier company.

"Look, I'll try her again in an hour and hopefully she'll pick up."

"Let me know. I can nip over to the house and make sure she's OK, but if she's sleeping I don't want to wake her," Millie said, and Tash could immediately picture her, face stricken with worry, chewing her bottom lip like she always did when she was nervous, concerned or anxious.

Ugh, she had never wanted to inflict pain on anyone quite as much as she did Cam Cochrane right now.

"No, it's fine. I'm sure she'll be OK. She just needs time to think all this through. I'll try her later and if I don't get her I'll call you. Try not to worry."

"OK," came the less-than-convinced reply. "By the way, where are you?"

"Sitting in the loo in the pub."

"There's a mental image I could totally have lived without." Millie laughed, before hanging up.

Back out in the bar, the crowd had thickened – four of the players were on top of the granite bar top singing "Love Machine", to the delight of at least a hundred revellers who were watching them with glee, some of them filming the antics on their mobiles.

Thankfully Jordan and John had all four of their size fifteen feet on the floor. They loved a good time, but they loved their sport more and had no intention of incurring the coach's standard one week ban for socialising mid-week. There would be hell to pay in the morning if they all showed up at training with hangovers or YouTube evidence of their errant behaviour. If officials at the rugby club saw this footage, they would be handing out fines like protein shakes.

Matt handed her back her drink and watched as she knocked it back in one. The sharpness of the taste made her cheeks suck in like she was chewing a lemon.

"So, where were we?" he asked.

"I think you were suggesting I wouldn't win an award for my warm welcome any time soon."

"Very true. But at least it was interesting. In a rude and obnoxious kind of way." The sting was taken out of his words by the wink that went with them. Despite herself, Tash smiled. Not a lot of guys could pull off a wink without looking like a prize dick, but he had just the right level of cheeky attitude to manage it.

A thought shot into her mind, interrupting the flirtatious exchange.

Laney. Where was she?

"Another drink?" he asked.

It was on the tip of her tongue to take him up on the offer, but her mind strayed again.

Why wasn't Laney answering the phone? Was she OK?

Her sharp, glossy bob fluttered against her chin as she shook her head.

"Thanks, but I need to go. I'll take you up on that next time though," she told him, surprising herself by the fact that she actually meant it. There was something of a challenge in the way he was totally up front about what he thought.

And the biceps that were oozing out of the sleeves of his Canterbury T-shirt weren't too shabby either. This guy didn't have the suave finesse of Sy, but he was definitely sparking up a curiosity somewhere in the general area of her libido. On any other night she would take him home and spend all night testing his general flexibility and stamina. Gotta love a great one night stand. It was like a sport. A hobby. One that was purely physical and made her feel great. Sure, there were many that wouldn't approve, but Tash genuinely didn't care. She loved sex, loved a great body, and as long as everyone knew where they stood – or lay – then she thought it was a damn sight more honest than pretending to care just so you could get into someone's pants.

Catching Jordan and John's attention, she motioned that she was going to head off. Jordan pushed through the crowd towards her, amused and aware that every step was being watched appreciatively by a table of young women next to them. Both her brothers had that effect, but thankfully along with great looks and sunny dispositions, they'd also got modesty.

"What's up?' he asked.

"Nothing, just want to get an early night. I'll get a taxi outside."

"You sure? I've only had one pint. I could take you home."

"Twice in the Mini in one day? I don't think I could take it," she teased.

"OK, well I'll walk you out."

Tash put an arm up to stop him. "No, I'm fine. If I

don't get a cab outside in five minutes I'll come back in. Deal?"

Reluctantly, he let her go. She was passing the table of adoring women when she stopped, turned and shouted back, "Oh, and darling, don't forget it's our anniversary tomorrow. Five years. Love you so much."

The rest of the team burst into hysterics at her blatant act of sabotage, as the table of adoring women immediately swivelled their attention away from Jordan, standing in the middle of the room, shaking his head at the woman who was walking away from him.

He leaned over to Matt. "You still want her phone number?'

""Yep," Matt told him.

"Then it's yours," he murmured, before shouting, "Bye, darling," to his departing sister.

Tash was still laughing as she reached the door, until a slurred, "Fuck me, is that Jessie J? She's no' bad looking in real life, is she?" took the gloss off the moment.

Ignoring the wide mouthed incredulity of the two drunk fans by the exit, she jumped into a vacant cab and tried Laney's numbers again.

No answer on either.

The best plan was to go home, let her sleeping pal rest and call her again in the morning, when Laney would no doubt reassure them that she just hadn't felt like talking the night before.

Yep, that was what she should do.

And yet, when she leaned forward to tell the cab driver her destination, it was Laney's address that came out.

18

Laney stared. Just stared. The window was still in darkness. There had been a brief moment of illumination about an hour before, and she'd watched a trail of lights go on from what she'd assumed was the bedroom, through the hall, and into the kitchen. A meander for a post-sex beer? Or a glass of water to make up part of Cara's two litres a day?

Not even a chorus of Oasis's "Wonderwall" from a drunk bloke in the corner could dull the severity of the pain that sliced her stomach at that thought.

She'd thought about going over, rapping on the door and demanding answers. Once she'd even risen to her feet to go through with it, but at that moment two cops had ambled in and she'd taken it at as a sign.

If he wasn't there, Cara would have her up on harassment charges. And if he was there, the outcome could carry a much longer sentence for her heart.

Stupid, she knew, but there was still a part of her that desperately hoped this was all a huge misunderstanding. Crazy, unbelievable things happened in the world every day, didn't they? So perhaps this was going to be one of them and they'd all look back on it with a giggle.

Yet, even in her desperation, she knew there was more chance of Noel Gallagher walking in here right now and joining the drunk guy for the second verse of "Wonderwall".

She lifted the coffee cup to her lips and then put it back down again, too nauseous to actually swallow.

Desperate for a distraction, something that would make the hands on the wall clock tick a little bit faster, she pulled her laptop out of her bag. She hadn't been able to concentrate on work for the last two days, but as she opened the computer, it felt like a relief to think about something else other than what her husband might be doing right now, only a hundred feet and a thick stone wall away from her.

A quick scan of the emails showed there was nothing urgent waiting to be answered, so she went back and worked through them one by one. The majority of them concerned the proposal taking place a few days later in Inverness, and the big one on the first day of next month at Queen Street station. One of the emails confirmed that the Transport Authority had given permission for the flash mob. She fired a copy over to Paul, the client who'd booked it and meticulously planned the vision he had in his head. Laney resisted her doubts about him. He'd seemed too calm. Too nonplussed. Almost like it was more of a technical performance than the most nerve-racking moment of his life. Some guys just hid their emotions well, she supposed, her eyes drifting upwards to the window across the street. Like Cam, for instance. He managed to hide the fact that he was carrying on a whole relationship with someone else.

Quite an accomplishment.

Another wave of nausea was deflected by focusing back on the screen in front of her. She ploughed through the correspondence like an industrial digger, grateful to be straying into other people's lives rather than staying in the hell that hers had become. When she was done, she flipped onto Facebook and was about to check her little-used account when a thought struck her.

CARA DEACON, she typed, terrified, but also fairly sure she'd find nothing. Didn't most people keep their profile private these days? She only used hers for promoting Personal Proposals. If she wanted to chat to a pal or show them a photograph, she much preferred to meet them in person.

Oh the irony. She'd always thought that was one of the advantages of Cam working away from home so much – plenty of time to spend with her friends.

How could she not have realised that he was doing exactly the same thing, but with one friend in particular? And why did every single thought she had end up with an image of Cam with Cara Deacon, in a double bed across the road?

Correction – king-sized bed. And she was looking at it right now. A massive, white leather sleigh style love platform, covered in a white fur throw and silver silk cushions, bordered by venetian mirrored bedside tables on both sides and watched over by a chandelier that Marie Antoinette would have regarded as a tad ostentatious. Totally glamorous. Totally over-the-top. Totally what she expected from Cara.

Oh my God, did Cam really go for this? They'd decorated their house together, all calm whites and dark Balinese woods that reminded them of their first trip abroad, to a beautiful but basic hut on Bali's Mengiat Beach. It seemed fitting that the drunk in the corner had now moved through his Oasis repertoire to "Don't Look Back In Anger".

Cara's photos were not protected by privacy settings and neither were the fawning comments that went underneath each snap of her stunning home. "Gorgeous babes". "In-fucking-credible". "Cara, I want to live there – that room is beautiful." And her favourite – a less charitable one that simply said, "Jammy cow".

One room at a time, Laney toured Cara's world until she reached the last snap in the "house" album. Lifting her eyes from the comments under the lounge photos, all of them proclaiming – admittedly correctly – that the room was stunningly decorated and furnished, Laney clicked on the next album, marked "All about me". Was Cam in there? Was she about to be faced with a snap of Cara's beautifully decorated boyfriend? Her stomach flipped with every click. Only when she was back at the beginning of the snaps, having glanced at all of them, did she breathe again. No sign of Cam, just photo after photo of Cara posing in different designer outfits, each one the same hand on hip, face to the side, self-satisfied pose. The urge to hate this girl was stronger than ever, but still tempered with sympathy because she was the other victim of Cam's lies and treachery.

She went through them again, this time really studying

the images for clues. In one, there was a laptop lying on a side table in the lounge. Same brand and size as Cam's but that proved nothing – there were thousands of them out there.

The pics of designer, "look at me" Cara were a little more enlightening. Cara on the beach. Cara in the airport. Cara riding a camel. Cara in front of the Jumeirah Beach Hotel in Dubai. Jumeirah Beach. Shit. Laney checked the date and then unlocked her phone and scrolled back through her calendar. Please don't make them match. Please don't make the dates tally.

It was last April. She remembered because it was her dad's birthday and Cam wasn't there, stuck, he said, on a job in the Middle East, working for a property company in their Dubai office. So that would make it April … Yep, there it was – the week commencing April tenth.

She checked the date on Cara's Facebook photo. April twelfth. Match.

With laser concentration, she worked her way back through the photos again, this time checking every one of them against the dates in her diary. On every occasion that Cara was pictured abroad, Cam was "away" on business. The locations didn't tie up, but then, how could she know where he really went? One mobile phone call sounded like another.

This wasn't good. Like a record stuck on repeat, she went through the images again, this time noticing different things. It was all absolutely perfect. A perfect home. A perfect figure. A perfect life.

Laney snapped, and was about to press the off button when she realised something else stood out. Cara was the only one in the images. No crazy friends photobombing the background. No siblings making cheesy faces. No boyfriend. If the images were a true indication of her life then it was flawless – but the only person in it was her. So the person she was with was the one not only taking the pictures, but staying out of them.

None of this made sense.

Closing the laptop, her head followed the direction of the cover, until her forehead rested on top of it on the table. Exhaustion seeped through her bones. Her head hurt. She felt sick. And drunk guy was now murdering "Stop Crying Your Heart Out".

Ironic, since he was a definite factor in her current urge to weep.

"Is this seat taken?"

Laney looked up but it took her a few seconds to focus. "Tash! What are you doing here? And how did you …?"

"Know? It's one of my superpowers. Along with walking in heels and making a man's balls wither with just a deadly stare."

Despite feeling worse than she'd ever done in her entire life, Laney laughed.

"Ah, sorry, I forgot about those."

All reticence to involve her friends moved to one side as Laney suddenly realised she'd never been so happy to see another person.

Tash slid into the chair across from her and smiled as she caught the waitress's eye and signalled for two more coffees. "I went to your house and you weren't there. But your car was, so I knew you hadn't gone to your dad's house. At first I thought you were home, so I climbed up your drainpipe and looked into your bedroom window, but you weren't there—"

"You're kidding!" Laney giggled.

"Nope. Safe to say, you can probably expect a visit from neighbourhood watch tomorrow. Anyway, so then I thought maybe you'd topped yourself, so I looked in all the other windows, but couldn't see anything suspicious …"

"Ah, right then," Laney nodded, never failing to be impressed by Tash's blunt manner and full-body tact bypass.

"So then I thought, where would I go? And then I realised – you'd be staking out the chick's apartment like a deranged stalker."

"Excellent. Very perceptive."

"Thank you," Tash replied, lifting her hands off the table to let the plump, cheery waitress put down two coffees. "So I came and here you are."

The mood dipped with the reminder of the brutal reality of the situation.

"Like a total sad but dangerous cow, staking out the enemy," Tash observed, deadpan, lifting the atmosphere back up to defiant amusement.

"Guilty," Laney admitted.

"Were you here last night too? And don't lie because I'll know. It's another one of my superpowers."

Laney spooned three sugars into her cappuccino. "Yes."

"Laney, why didn't you say? I'd have come with you."

Only the noise of the spoon stirring the hot liquid filled the pause. "Because I need to believe that there's a chance this isn't true. And I know that no one else could possibly think that. I just need to have hope."

Tash was looking at her with an expression that sat somewhere between understanding and concern.

"OK. I get it. So I won't judge and I won't say you're crazy for giving him the benefit of the doubt."

"Promise?"

"No," she admitted, with a laugh that woke up the drunk guy and launched him right back into the chorus of "Cigarettes and Alcohol".

Tash almost fell off her chair in surprise. "That guy's wasted in here. That's a talent that should be on a stage." She joined in, harmonising, to the amusement of the staff, and the smattering of other diners spread around a few other tables.

Laney's lips rose at the edges as she contemplated the absurdity of this situation. Only Tash would do that.

At the end, they both bowed – actually, Tash bowed and the drunk guy just slumped – as everyone else in the room applauded.

"So," Tash said, attention back on Laney. "What's the plan? Are you staying here all night?"

"If I say yes, will you try to talk me out of it?"

Laney watched as Tash thought about that for a moment, before answering, "No, because you need to know and I get that."

Tash reached over and put her hand on top of Laney's, her voice softening. "I do get it."

Laney felt her eyes fill, tear ducts ready to overflow.

Tash spotted it and reverted to bossy and pragmatic. "But if you're doing this, we're doing it together and in an efficient way that will work to our best advantage. Two hours' sleep each, you first, and I'll keep a lookout with the Oasis tribute act over there. We'll be through

(What's The Story) Morning Glory? by dawn."

Laney's first instinct was to object but the need for sleep took over.

"You're sure?" she asked gratefully.

"Absolutely positive. Now go to sleep. I promise I'll wake you the second anything happens."

Laney did exactly as she was told. As soon as her forehead hit the back of her hands on the table, she fell asleep, her first release in forty-eight hours.

Peace. Safety. Quiet.

Until morning.

19

Tash was bleary eyed and less than chipper when Millie gave her a coffee, with a side order of recrimination. "I can't believe you didn't call me! I'd have come over, too. So, then, what happened this morning?" she asked, now handing over a peppermint tea to Laney.

"Urgh, that stuff stinks," Tash moaned as Laney's cup passed across the area covered by her sense of smell. "Mint is supposed to be inside chocolate and served after dinner at Christmas. Why would anyone want to drink that in the mornings? It's vile."

Millie gestured to the complainant while addressing Laney. "Is she going to be like that all day?"

Laney nodded. "Yep, lack of sleep. She's cranky."

"Er, hello, I'm right here. And I'm not fucking cranky," Tash said. Crankily.

"But in fairness it's my fault and I do appreciate the

143

support," she told Tash, rubbing her knee. "But to get back to … sorry, what was the question?"

"What happened this morning?" Millie repeated, smoothing out the flowing contours of her skirt as she sat on the couch. Laney and Tash were both in dark skinny jeans, shirts and heels, but Millie had gone for a floral vibe today, a pale pink, ankle length skirt with cream flowers, a plain cream T-shirt and her long hair left messily around her shoulders. Tash decided she looked like she'd just stepped out of her mermaid costume and stumbled through a seventies wardrobe.

"Nothing. Cara left the flat about nine a.m., in full make-up, and jumped into a taxi. We waited another half hour but no one else appeared. I don't think he's there."

There was a moment of silence as the three of them pondered the ramifications of this.

"Look, I'm just putting this out there – do you think there could be an innocent explanation for all of this?" said Millie.

Laney blurted, "Yes," at exactly the same instant Tash spat, "No."

"OK, glad we got that cleared up then," Millie replied. She was interrupted by an incredulous Tash.

"Laney, I love you, but please don't get your hopes up because this isn't looking great. Let's pull the plug on it now. Let's just tell Cara she's going out with a married guy, get Cam in a room, force him to tell the truth and get the whole thing over with. Keeping it going will kill you."

Laney considered this for a few seconds. "But so will not knowing the extent of it. I know where you're coming from, Tash, but how can I move on when I would only have his version of the truth to base my decisions on? I need to see it. Need to know exactly what they have – because if I don't I'll always wonder if I've done the right thing, no matter how this ends up."

Millie nodded. "I get it, but I think it's a tough road to take, Lanes. I can't even imagine how it feels. Even contemplating Leo being unfaithful would be pure pain, so however you choose to handle this, we'll support you on it. Won't we, Tash?"

Tash grudgingly agreed, but not with the kind of conviction that would pass a polygraph test. She was grateful when she was saved by a buzz at the door. Millie reached it first.

"Delivery," she announced, pressing the button for the door release before heading out to the lift to meet the new arrival.

Inside, Tash yawned and shook her head to clear away the fog that was threatening to descend. In the café, she hadn't had the heart to wake Laney after two hours. Instead, she'd done the whole night watch, with just an Oasis tribute act as company – and he was way less fun as the night went on and he started to sober up. By six a.m., she was glad to be alone, watching the sun come up as Glasgow came to life.

The temptation to cross the road and bang on the door had been difficult to resist, but this wasn't her call, it was Laney's.

"Ooh, someone's getting spoiled," Millie announced as she burst back in, clutching a large box in the distinctive wrapping of Harvey Nichols. Since the department store had opened in Edinburgh a few years before they'd made an annual pilgrimage and, while

Millie was utterly unswayed by the designer labels, she knew Laney liked them, and for Tash it was like being called home by the Mothership.

"If that's from Cam, we're sending it back," Tash announced. "Unless it's fabulous, in which case I'll keep it."

"Actually, it's not for Laney. Or me. Again."

The surprise was tinged with glint-eyed anticipation and a touch of bewilderment.

The wrapping peeled away to reveal a white box with the words Jimmy Choo emblazoned in gold on the top.

Wordlessly, Tash opened it and gently, as if she was handling a priceless artefact, took out a silver strappy sandal with a beautifully carved six-inch heel. In all of her years, she'd never understood the concept of "love at first sight". Now she did.

"Holy fuck, they're gorgeous," she said, voice husky.

Laney required further information. "Who are they from? Hang on – there's a card," she said, pointing at the scalloped edge of cream peeking from the corner of the box.

Tash pulled it out and read it aloud. "'These wouldn't fit Giselle. xxx'. Arse," she said, with a sigh.

Millie was even more confused now. "Who's Giselle? Who are they from?"

"It's a long story, but they're from Sy. My neighbour."

"With benefits," Laney corrected.

"The one that sent you the flowers? So are you going to return these, too?"

Tash nodded her head. "I absolutely should. But I'm far too shallow, so no chance."

The other two dissolved into laughter.

"OK, so now that my day has been brightened by incredible footwear, let's get back to the less important stuff ..."

Laney threw a silver sequined cushion at her.

Millie interjected with some logistical input. "If we're going ahead with this then we need to get arrangements in place."

Laney pulled three identical sheets of A4 paper from the folder on the table in front of them and handed a copy each to the others.

"I've already mapped it out, so here's the game plan. Cara pretty much had the details down, so I've allocated tasks and listed everything that still needs done."

All eyes went down as they scanned the details. It was all pretty straightforward. They'd arranged a proposal in New York not long after they'd launched the agency, a beautiful Central Park event for a football player who was taking his girlfriend there on holiday and wanted to make it the trip of a lifetime. They'd proposed on a boat on the Central Park Lake with a Haribo jelly ring, and then whisked her off to Tiffany to choose her very own rock. Millie had cried on every stage of the journey and Tash had blown her whole commission on a Bulgari three tone gold ring in the duty free at JFK.

"Any issues?" Laney asked.

"None – I'll get on this straight away," Millie replied, still reading. "Oh, one thing – the travel. I think we might be able to get a good deal on that. The bloke that crashed into me came round last night and he's really keen to help. Guy. From Ocean Sky travel. He said he'd give us a discount."

"Brilliant." Laney nodded.

"Hang on," Tash was rewinding furiously. "He came round? To your house? Remind me to buy you a pepper spray."

"No, he was lovely. Just wanted to help get the car fixed."

"And what did the bold Leo have to say about the visit?"

Millie shrugged her shoulders. "Nothing. He's a bit … well, he's actually really, really happy just now because … Sorry, Laney, I didn't want to say anything because you're having such a rubbish time, but Leo got the part!" Her excitement took the last line to a screech.

The others burst into a round of applause. "Oh, Millie, that's incredible! I'm so happy for you both."

"And I'm so happy he can pay his way now." Tash giggled, earning another smack in the face with the sequined cushion.

"So when does he start?" Laney asked.

"Tomorrow. It's going to be really long hours and he'll be away quite a bit but it's what he's been desperate for all this time so he's over the moon."

Laney reached over and clasped her hand. "Congratulations, Millie, that's incredible. You both deserve it so much. Listen, we've got things here at this end. Why don't you head off and spend the afternoon with him? Sounds like you won't get a chance to do that for a few months."

"No, I couldn't …"

"Yes, you could. I'm glad of the chance to go over all the details for the proposals in Inverness and Queen Street station. I've got a million calls to make and I want to check on the dancers for the flash mob. Then I want to get stuck into the planning for this debacle. If you leave that bloke in the travel agent's details I'll give him a call and see if he's any cheaper than the company we normally use. Tash, you go home too. I love you for staying with me last night, but you've had no sleep and you look like a burst couch."

"No arguments here," Tash said, stifling another yawn.

Tired. Bed. Alone.

It was a vision of perfection.

Almost.

20

Millie realised there was no point in refusing. Once Laney decided something, especially something that made complete sense, she was impossible to budge.

"Thanks, Lanes," she whispered, as she reached down to hug her. Not for one minute had she ever regretted joining Laney on this venture and this was why – she was smart, loyal, caring and the most thoughtful friend. There she was, heart ripped out, and she was still thinking about her and Tash. That was some kind of woman.

Her laptop, notebook and pad were thrust into her bag, then she shared a ride down in the lift with Tash.

"Do you think she's going to be OK?"

Tash nodded. "I do, but she's going to need some help. I'll go by the café again tonight and see if she's there."

"No, it's my turn!"

"Millie, your feckless boyfriend is about to embark on

the biggest – perhaps *only* – job of his life. I think the least you can do is spend the night with him tonight."

Millie couldn't help but laugh. That was Tash all over. Laney was solid, consistent, smart and caring. Tash was evil on the surface, but underneath the caustic veneer, she had a huge heart and would do anything for her family and friends. Millie adored them both and felt an irresistible urge to share.

"I love you, do you know that?"

Tash snorted. "Oh God, you're going all Oprah on me. I'm not hugging you. I'm just not."

They were both still laughing when they got out the lift and said goodbye. Tash headed off on her five minute walk home, while Millie nipped around the corner to where she'd parked that morning. As good as his word, Guy's friend had arrived within half an hour of calling him this morning, taken her ancient Beetle and given her a replacement car to use until hers was fixed. It was way over the limits of her insurance cover, but he said Guy had insisted on it. Millie didn't argue, and that's why she travelled home in a very swanky Audi Q5 with full leather seats and a speaker system that sounded like the inside of a nightclub. She loved it – it was impressive, sleek and powerful – but it wasn't her. It was like going on holiday somewhere gorgeous, but looking forward to getting home to your cosy little house.

Less than half an hour later she glided into her driveway, after a brief stop to buy French bread, pâte, wine and Leo's favourite, tiramisu. As soon as she opened the front door, she heard music in the kitchen. Great, he was home.

Hands full, she kicked open the door with her feet.

The first thing she noticed was the smell of coffee. Strange. Leo never drank coffee. He was strictly a "water and occasional tea" kind of guy.

The next thing she noticed were the two shiny blonde heads on top of Lycra-clad bodies, both of them laughing, completely unaware that she was there.

It was like walking in to a scene from one of those really annoying workout infomercials that were invariably blaring when she woke up on the couch in the middle of the night, after falling asleep with the TV on.

Millie's eyes followed theirs to the point of hilarity. Leo, back turned to her, was pouring water into two cups while doing a stupid little arse-wiggling dance.

Like Miley Cyrus. Twerking. After three bottles of vodka and a stomach pump.

"Leo …?"

"Aw, fuck!" he screamed, as a slip in the kettle resulted in splashes of boiling water on his arm. Thankfully only droplets reached the flesh.

Horrified, the two strangers gasped, while Millie rushed over, grabbed his arm and thrust it under the cold tap. He winced again.

"Sorry, didn't mean to startle you. But I just … I just …"

What? The atmosphere crackled with tension as she eyed the two other women, hoping that at some point one of them would jump in and explain what was going on.

Leo put the tap off and shook out his arm. "I'm fine. Thanks. It's fine."

He didn't sound fine. He sounded agitated and defensive.

There was a pause, as no one rushed to fill the gap, before Leo realised it was going to be down to him.

"Sorry, Millie, this is DeeDee and Rianne. They're old friends from drama school."

"Oh, right. Hi. Pleased to meet you," she said, not entirely convincingly.

Friends from drama school? They certainly had the appearance of professional performers. They were both size six or eight, their hard, toned bodies unapologetically impressive in their tights and off-shoulder T-shirts. And leg warmers! When did they make a fashion comeback? These girls looked like they'd just walked out of an MTV video after spending three minutes draped over Snoop Dog. And if they were old friends, how come she'd never met them before and they'd never been mentioned? Millie would definitely have remembered these two. She noticed red marks appearing on Leo's arm. "Hang on, I've got some burn spray in the First Aid box."

"I'll get it," said Rianne hastily, before turning, opening the cupboard behind her and pulling out the large red box that contained a plethora of pills and potions.

All at once, everyone – Rianne included – realised what was wrong with this picture. How did she know where they kept the First Aid supplies? Who were these women? And how many times had they been here before?

For someone who'd been to drama school, she wasn't much of an actress as she stuttered, "Leo, erm ... got me an ... erm ... aspirin just a few minutes ago. For a headache. I've got ... erm ... a headache."

You're not the only one, Millie thought.

"Look, we'll head off," DeeDee said, her body language and tone cripplingly uncomfortable.

"Yeah, no worries. I'll see you around," Leo said, attempting casual but landing somewhere between mortified and shady. They both watched the departing shapes of the girls, pert bums, and toes pointing slightly outwards, like ballerinas.

Millie picked up the shopping bags she'd dropped at her feet and plonked them on the worktop. "Well, that was interesting. They seem like nice girls."

"Yeah, they … are." Millie didn't miss the tension in his voice. *Maybe he isn't much of an actor either*, she thought, before immediately chiding herself. He was a fantastic actor. But actually, at that moment, that didn't necessarily seem like a good thing.

"How come you're home so early?" he asked, as he sprayed his arm and then leant against the worktop to wait for a reply.

Millie didn't dare look at him because she knew she'd crumble, snog the face off him, and then this would all be forgotten. And she wasn't quite ready to let it go yet. Hang on, that was ridiculous. This was Leo. He'd never do anything behind her back. Or shady. Or dishonest. It wasn't the girls' fault that they looked so incredibly sexy in those clothes. Millie didn't often let her body insecurities rise to the surface. Leo had always said he loved her curves and his actions backed up his words, but there, red-faced and sweating after carrying in the bags, she was acutely aware that you could add the two twiglets who'd just left together and they'd still fit inside her panda onesie. *Note to self: maybe it's time to lose the bear-inspired nightwear.*

"It was Laney's idea – she thought we might want to spend your last day together. I kinda liked her thinking."

Leo shook out his arm, dismissing the pain as he nodded. "I kinda like her thinking, too."

His breath oozed across her neck as he came up behind her, snaking his hands around her generous hips in what would normally be a totally horny movement. Right now – call it concern, insecurity or even a tiny bit of jealousy – she just wanted to shrug him off. Wow. This was new.

He gently swept her waves of hair forward over one shoulder and placed a tiny kiss on the nape of her neck. Then another. Then another. Working his way up towards her ear, where he stopped for a moment, gently nuzzling it, before working his way back down again.

"And the girls? Why were they here?"

"I met them when I was out running this morning. We were halfway round Queens Park when I bumped into them. They just came back for a coffee and ended up hanging out for a few hours. I didn't think you'd mind."

"Of course I don't mind. Not at all."

I mind. I really mind. But I've no idea why.

Leo slowly turned her around, so that they were face to face, and then teasingly, provocatively, pulled up her T-shirt and eased it over her head.

"You realise what this means? We have all afternoon to ourselves and we can do anything we want."

His kisses were dotted along her collarbone now, from her shoulder to the centre of her chest, before moving downwards. She gasped as he licked the crease between her voluptuous boobs, then ran his tongue along the top edge of the cups of her cream lace bra. All insecurities were gone now, in their place, just delectable lust.

"And I might have brought a few of your favourite things home to celebrate," she said, her eyes going to the bag on the worktop. He reached in, pulled out the bottle of wine, grabbed a corkscrew and deftly popped the stopper out. He took a drink from the bottle, before slowly, carefully, pouring a tiny stream across the mounds of her breasts then sucking every drop until they were dry again. He unclipped her bra, before he poured again, the sensation of the dripping wine sending lightning shards of pure bliss to every one of her erogenous zones. Oh, this was good. This was so good.

Effortlessly, he lifted her on to the worktop, his hands going under her skirt to remove her cami-knickers. Her clothes might be hippy sixties and seventies, but her underwear was pure forties – always pale tones, cami-knickers and intricate lace bras. Millie reached forward and pulled off his T-shirt, patches stained dark where the wine had touched him.

He responded by pushing up her skirt, while deftly unzipping his jeans, allowing his erection to spring free.

Millie opened her legs wide and then gasped as he fell to his knees, pleasuring her with his tongue, before rising again and entering her, their torsos tight against each other, burning skin on burning skin.

He made sure she came first, then exploded inside her, making her throw her head back with the exquisite, incredible bliss of it all.

God, she loved this man. Loved every bit of him. Especially his heart.

Afterwards, as they lay entwined on the kitchen chair, covered with just a blanket, sharing a large bowl of tiramisu, she couldn't help but let her mind wander back to the fleetingly uncharacteristic bout of insecurity from earlier.

How bizarre was that? So strange and so out of her normal range of emotions.

This situation with Cam must be rubbing off on me, she decided.

As Leo splodged a large dollop of coffee mousse on her nipple, she laughed and dismissed the negativity.

Leo wasn't Cam. He wouldn't cheat. He wouldn't lie. He wouldn't hurt her.

But then, she was sure Laney had felt that way, too.

SHARI LOW

21

"Hey babe, how's your day been? Feel like I've barely spoken to you this week."

Laney pulled into the side of the road to continue the call. Even though they were speaking on hands free, she didn't trust herself not to have a heart attack and cause a ten-car pile-up.

"I know," she said, trying desperately to inject some kind of enthusiasm and brightness into her voice.

"You sound weird. Is everything OK?" Cam asked.

No, it's really not, is what she thought.

"Yeah, just think I'm coming down with the flu," is what she said.

"Aw, poor baby. I wish I was there to take care of you."

"I wish that too." This couldn't be right. He was saying all these things, being as lovely as ever, and yet she knew it wasn't real. It was like talking to a stranger, but trying to say the right things and sound the right way, and all the while her chest was threatening to shut down and make breathing impossible.

"How's Birmingham?"

"Yeah, fine. Faceless. Seen one hotel, you've seen them all. I'm working with a good group of execs, though, and they're really into what we're doing, so I think it'll make a difference."

It was there again – she wasn't imagining it. The slight pause at the beginning of the sentence, the almost imperceptible change in his voice that told her he was lying. How many calls had there been that she'd taken at face value when he was actually spinning her a whole load of crap?

"There's only one problem though – head office wants us in London this weekend to prepare for next week, so I'm not going to make it home. It's the Conser group, the new client I was telling you about. There's a lot riding on it and they just want to make sure we're at the top of our game and on the same page."

Three arse indicators in the one sentence. Two bullshit corporate speak phrases and one huge big fucking lie.

Laney wanted to scream, to rage, to smash the handset against the steering wheel until it was in as many tiny pieces as her life. How could he do this? How?

Somehow, using every ounce of strength she possessed, she managed to thrust her vocal cords into use.

"Babe, don't worry, it's fine. Look, I've just pulled up outside my dad's house so I'm going to go. I'll call you later unless I get home too late. Don't want to wake you."

Click. Disconnect. She was too battered and pained to even cry, but it took twenty minutes of sitting there, staring straight ahead, until she could stop herself from shaking. Home. She just wanted to go home. But she also craved the comfort of the one man who had never let her down.

Wearily, she drove for five more minutes until she really was outside her dad's house, and then grabbed the Marks and Spencer bag in the passenger seat and headed in to the West End garden flat she'd grown up in. It was in the middle of a Georgian terrace, in a curved street of homes that were once glorious townhouses, now converted into prime apartments that fetched way over the market value for a flat because they were pieces of history in one of the most desirable areas. Their home had always been her favourite place on earth. Down two steps to the original wooden front door, which opened to a beautiful hallway, wood panelled to half height and painted white, a gorgeous contrast to the light oak floors. Her mum, a keen decorator, had visualised, restored and created every inch of this apartment, and her dad hadn't changed a thing in the fifteen years since she'd left them. Walls had been repainted, scuffs had been repaired, but things always returned to exactly the way they'd been. It gave Laney a sense of security then, and that still remained today. Even though she was now an adult, her dad was retired from the force and life had moved on, some things were still absolutely the same.

She used her own key, and shouted "Hello," as she entered. No answer. Not unusual. Her dad was fastidious about keeping himself busy so he was often found out in the garden or the garage.

"Dad?"

She shouted again. Nothing. Except … There was a noise, a groan, almost like a strangled wail. Oh my God, it was happening. He was having a stroke. Or a heart attack. Laney sent a silent plea heavenwards. "Dear God, don't do this. Don't you dare. You promised you'd never take him away."

In more rational moments, she knew that wasn't actually true. The agreement had come about a year after her mum had left.

Laney, then fifteen, had been lying on her bed, doing her homework, when large pools of wet began to form on the page. That happened sometimes. She could be anywhere, doing anything, and the tears would start to fall. Her friends, especially Tash and Millie, had been sympathetic when her mother took off, but they'd eventually gone back to their normal lives, obsessing about boys and clothes and Westlife. (Although Tash would now deny the Westlife thing under all interrogation techniques including blackmail and waterboarding.)

Back then Laney tried to join in, but inside there was nothing, so she stopped making the effort and just threw herself into schoolwork instead. No matter how hard Tash and Millie tried to coax her out, she resisted. When she was studying, she wasn't thinking about anything else – but sometimes, it crept up on her and that's when the wet smudges would appear.

One day, there was a knock at the door and her dad came in and read the situation straight away.

"Do you want to phone her?" he'd asked. "You know she said you could call any time."

"Yeah, but she hardly bothers to contact us, does she?"

There was no arguing with that. Since Lana had gone, they'd had one or two calls a week, always uncomfortable, always brief. Her dad said it was the guilt, but Laney knew it was because Lana had a new life now, one that she loved and one that didn't include her and her dad.

She hated her. Right then, she absolutely hated her.

Fred's handsome face was a mask of sorrow. "I know, love, but we'll be OK. Sometimes people do things that no one understands. I can't explain this to you. I really can't. And I don't know that I'll always get this right, but I promise I'll try and I need you to try, too. You see, the only thing that hurts more than your mum leaving is seeing you unhappy."

That message immediately snapped into Laney's brain. She was making it worse for him and that was unforgivable, so she slapped a smile on her face, decided there and then that it was time to change.

After he'd gone, she stared at the ceiling. Only that week at school, she'd listened to her religious education teacher talking about God. Millie absolutely believed in heaven and angels. Tash said it was a pile of crap. Laney had yet to be convinced. She needed proof. Evidence.

So before she went to sleep, she made a proposal. "If there's a God up there, take care of my dad. I'll start trying to be happy again if you promise that Dad won't leave me, too. Promise you'll look after him." She took the calm feeling that swept over her as an agreement. From then until now, and despite the fact that she held no religious beliefs at all, God had held up his (or her?) end of the bargain.

Fred had been involved in some really dangerous situations as a cop, but had always managed to come home at night in one piece. He was indestructible. Invincible. Yet now he wasn't answering her and there was another groan, this time clearly coming from the back garden. Laney raced through the large, country style kitchen, and through the French doors that led to the back garden, a slate patio that joined a large stretch of lawn.

Nothing ahead. Shit, where was he?

"Laney!"

His voice made her spin to the side, at which point her jaw hit the French slate on the ground.

Her dad. Reclining. In a hot tub. With Mrs Crean from upstairs. Both of them clutching large flutes of champagne, which clearly weren't their first of the day.

"Dad!" she gasped. "And Mrs ... Mrs ..." It was a hallucination. Had to be. The stress must have caused it. Or pollution. Or the fact that she'd spent two nights this week in a café heated by Calor gas. Yep, it was the fumes. She'd been damaged for life. And right now that theory seemed a lot more attractive than the thought of her dad and Mrs Crean actually being in a hot tub together.

"Are you coming in, dear?" Mrs Crean asked, a definite giggle in her voice. She was a lovely lady, had lived upstairs for as long as Laney could remember. Her husband had been a fireman until he died suddenly, a heart attack in his fifties, maybe six or seven years before. When Laney was small, she'd thought Mrs Crean was the most beautiful woman in the world, after her mother, on account of the fact that she resembled Goldie

Hawn in *Private Benjamin*. But with shorter hair. And without the camouflage make-up.

Actually, seeing Goldie Hawn in her father's new hot tub wouldn't rack the surprise levels up any higher than they already were.

This wasn't actually happening. Her brain cells had been destroyed by an all-night café. Hang on to the positives.

"Erm, no. Thanks."

"Oh, well then. I'll head off and leave you two to it. Thanks for the champs, Fred. Same time tomorrow?"

Her dad leaned over and clinked his glass against hers. "Same time tomorrow, Maisy."

Mrs Crean's bare shoulders rose from the water as Laney's eyes widened in horror. Nooooo. This was her neighbour, a lovely retired nurse who had looked out for her, bought her Christmas presents and even taken her to a caravan in bloody Saltcoats, and she was about to see her naked.

Her hand went over her face, but when she peeked through her fingers, she saw to her relief that Mrs Crean was wearing a yellow bandeau bikini top, above matching drawstring bottoms. As the image burned into her brain, she realised it would be the first thing she saw every time she opened Mrs Crean's Christmas card, but at least it was better than nudity.

Mrs C pulled on a flowery robe that was lying on a nearby chair and minced off in the direction of the back steps that led to a communal hallway for the two flats above.

Laney waited until the heavy storm door had closed behind her, before turning back to her dad, eyebrows raised.

She'd come here for comfort, familiarity and perhaps even some reassuring affection. Instead she'd walked on to the set of *Naked OAP's Gone Wild*.

Hands on hips, she waited for some kind of reaction from Stud Daddy-ee-o.

"Sure you won't come in? There's some wine in the cooler. Or beer if you prefer." He motioned to the bar, the one that hadn't been there last week. A canopy, chiller, stools and wooden bar top that currently sported a bottle of champagne in a silver bucket.

Maybe it was her dad that had been affected by the pollution.

"Dad, are you OK? I mean, is something going on?"

A horrific thought struck her – he was ill. There was something wrong and it had sent him completely off the rails. He only had months to live. Or he'd lost the plot. Years of working in dangerous environments could do that to a person. She'd read about that somewhere.

"Actually, there is."

She knew it! Oh no. How much agony could she take in one week? Her dad stood up, and she yelped as she snapped her eyes shut. "Don't worry, I've got my swimming trunks on," he reassured her. Relieved, she raised her eyelids, only to clamp them shut again. "Dad! Those aren't trunks, they're Speedos! Oh, dear God, I'm scarred for life."

He was still laughing when, fully robed, he pulled out a bar stool and climbed aboard. Laney joined him on the other one, braced for terrible news.

"OK, go, Dad. Tell me. Don't sugar-coat it."

"You sure?'

She nodded, ready to stay strong for whatever it was he was going through. "Positive."

"Well, the thing is … I've decided to have a mid-life crisis."

It took a moment. Then further clarification was required.

"What?"

"Sorry, love, I know it'll come as a shock, but I've decided to have a mid-life crisis."

"A mid-life crisis," she repeated, hoping it made more sense if she said it out loud.

It didn't.

"Yes. Lanes, I've worked for almost forty-five years, most of it in a tough job. When your mother left, I was forty-five. We were just getting to the age where you were growing up and we had more time to enjoy ourselves, and then she was gone. Since then, we've done great and you've turned out incredible. We got through it all, Lanes, and I survived my full service. Now I've got a decent pension, my health is good, and every day I can wake up and do exactly what I want to, so it's time."

"For a mid-life crisis."

"Absolutely."

She pondered this revelation for a few moments.

"Can I ask you a few questions? I just have to know what to expect."

"Fire away."

"Is this going to involve a submissive mail order bride from a country where women are oppressed?"

He took the question with mock seriousness. "I'm fairly sure it won't."

"Sports cars?"

"Possibly."

"Will I ever be faced with nudity – yours or anyone else's – if I drop by unexpectedly?"

"I'll do my best to avoid that happening."

"Will there be drugs?"

"No. I'd lose my police pension."

"Good. Unsavoury characters?"

"Only Big Tam and Henry," he said, naming his two retired cop buddies. "I can't vouch for their personal hygiene regimes now that they've left the force."

"And the Speedos?"

"They're definitely staying."

"Oh, bugger." She laughed. "I think I'll take that drink." The relief made tears spring to her eyes and she blinked them back.

"So you're OK with this?" he asked, tentatively.

"Of course I am. You deserve it, Dad. But if Mrs Crean answers the door in a boob tube and thong, you're paying for the therapy."

The birds in the huge oak at the bottom of the garden bolted off as he roared with laughter.

"I'll bear that in mind, sweetheart," he said, leaning over and enveloping her in a hug. Why hadn't she gone for a man like this? Why hadn't she found someone solid and dependable, someone that would even put his obligatory mid-life crisis on hold to bring up his family? He was truly an incredible man. Even if he had spent the afternoon in a Jacuzzi with the neighbour.

"So you and Mrs Crean – an item?"

He shrugged, embarrassed. "We're just seeing where it goes. Taking it easy. You know, after your mum, there was no one for years and then just a few casual things."

"I know, Dad," she said, softly.

"So now I'm thinking maybe it would be nice to have someone … special. Someone around all the time. Would that be OK with you?"

"Of course it would, Dad. I just want you to be happy. Actually, I like the thought of you going off the rails. If you enjoy it I might give it a go myself."

Fred pulled a bottle of beer out of the chiller and snapped the cap off on the bar top. "Somehow I think Cam might have a couple of objections to that."

She stared at her shoes, determined not to give anything away. Fred was the happiest she'd seen him in years. There was a real aura of optimism and joie de vivre around him and she didn't have the heart to burst his bubble, to evoke the pain of what happened to him and tell him that history was repeating itself.

Too late, she realised he'd stopped and was staring at her.

"Something's wrong, Lanes. Out with it."

"No, nothing at all. Everything's fine."

He leaned over and gently lifted her chin so their eyes met. "Laney, I've spent forty years interrogating people. I could crack you in two minutes," he joked.

"Och, it's nothing, Dad, honest. Just Cam being a bit of an arse. Nothing we can't get past."

All hail the understatement of the year. She could see he wasn't convinced, but he decided not to opt for thumbscrews.

"So, want to phone in some food?" he asked. "There's a new Thai place on Hyndland Road that's supposed to be fantastic."

"Tell you what, Dad, why don't we just go there instead of ordering in? Then maybe I'll just stay here tonight so I can have a couple of drinks."

"Is this a cunning plan to keep me and Maisy Crean apart?"

"Absolutely," she laughed.

"Then I'll humour you and go along with it. Just this once."

He was half right. It was a plan, but one designed to stop her ending up at an all-night café, watching a window for signs of her husband.

Being here with Fred, even in the midst of his mid-life crisis, had completely altered her mood. Enough of the fear and the falling apart. He had lost the wife he adored and still had the strength to carry on, make a great life for him and his daughter. If Cam was cheating – and yes, she still started that thought with an "if" – then it might feel like the world was ending, but she'd survive.

"Can you just promise me one thing, Dad?" she asked him solemnly.

"Anything," he told her, still swigging his beer as he headed into the house to get ready for their night out.

"Can you lose the Speedos?"

He stopped, turned, aghast.

"Not even for you. Love me, love my unfeasibly small swimwear."

His laughter lingered even after he disappeared from sight and she vowed there and then that there was no way she was letting him in on this until it was all over. If she told him now, he'd be waiting for Cam with a SWAT team and several Alsatians. He still had friends that owed him favours.

Nope, she was a big girl now and this was her problem to deal with. It was time she manned up and got on with it.

If Cara was telling the truth, Cam had known about this situation for a long time. Laney'd had less than a week and most of that had been spent in a fugue of despair. If she was going to come out of this with even a shred of dignity and sanity intact, then she had to get ahead of the game. She needed a plan, a strategy, and she needed to get cracking on the details. But that was all for tomorrow. Right now, she couldn't think of anything she'd rather do than eat curry with her slightly bonkers father.

She took a stone and threw it at the window above her, the way she used to do when she came home from school and felt like company.

Mrs Crean opened the sash window and leaned out – not a great idea for a woman who was tipsy on afternoon champagne.

"Yes, Laney dear?"

"Mrs Crean, would you like to come for a curry with us? My dad's having a mid-life crisis so I can't promise we won't be getting there on a motorbike."

"Sounds lovely, dear. Give me five minutes to put my lippy on."

22

"Are you guys sure you don't want me to cancel tonight? We could blow the others off and just go out for a quiet dinner somewhere, just the three of us,"

Tash asked, almost hopefully. It wasn't that she didn't fancy a night on the town, but she was acutely aware that Laney and Millie weren't exactly blowing trumpets all the way to party central. Besides, the whole birthday thing didn't bother her. She'd have been happy to blatantly ignore the fact that her twenties were behind her and she was now heading directly to beige slacks and Botox, but her brothers had persuaded her that her thirtieth birthday demanded a celebration. In the end they'd compromised – just a few guys from the rugby club, Laney, Millie and their other halves. Of course, neither of the male partners would now make it due to the fact that one had gone into rehearsals for his first major movie role and the other had gone into a twenty-five year old stylist, penis first.

In response to Tash's question, Laney glanced up from her desk, which, as always, was an exercise in organised perfection. "Positive. Let's just get this meeting over and done with and then we can start getting ready."

"You sure?" Tash double checked, her head on a desk

that looked like a stationery store had met up with the MAC counter at House of Fraser, had a good old night together and then vomited all over her IKEA workstation.

"I am. I learned last night that it's better to keep busy. Although watching my father share lingering glances with his next-door neighbour is a mental image that I may never shake off. I ended up leaving them doing mai tai shots and headed home."

"Go, Fred." Millie whistled, ignoring Laney's disdainful glance.

"Indeed. Bye the way, Millie, I called that travel agent and he was great. Ten per cent cheaper than the company we normally used. Asked me at least a dozen times if you were definitely OK."

"Tell him only a fortnight in Bora Bora can heal your pain," Tash suggested, before being interrupted by the door buzzer.

A couple of minutes later, Laney returned with their client, Paul, in tow.

"Hey Paul, how's it going? Excited?" Millie asked him. He shrugged. "Yeah." If that was him excited, Tash decided she'd love to see him when he was playing something low key.

Paul had first come to them a month before, looking to propose to his girlfriend, Maggie. It had been the toughest meeting yet, almost a role reversal of the usual set up. When they probed him for ideas and concepts he had zero. Nil. Absolutely blank.

After half an hour of coming up with nothing that sparked any inspiration, he'd asked them what their ideal proposal would be. Laney described her own intimate experience at her favourite restaurant, surrounded by family invited there for the occasion.

Millie had described a windswept, utterly romantic encounter in the valleys of Glencoe, with a piper playing a lament in the background and the ring lying on a sacred stone in the middle of a stream. That girl had way too much time on her hands and way too vivid an imagination.

When all eyes turned to Tash, she'd had a minor panic. There was no way she could admit the truth to a client – that she'd rather spend the rest of her life listening to Coldplay songs while being lectured by the consciously uncoupled Gwyneth Paltrow on the bowel benefits of macrobiotic eating than get engaged. Firmly on the spot, she'd blurted out the first thing that came to mind. That morning she'd diverted into Queen Street station for a croissant and a coffee, and been jostled and crowded by the usual morning commuters. "A flash mob in Queen Street station," she'd said hastily.

"That's it!" he'd announced, to Tash's utter astonishment. In fact, they were all fairly stunned. Ideas and concepts weren't Tash's department. She was strictly there for logistical support and unlimited scorn.

Millie gently tried to talk him out of it. "The whole flash mob thing has been done so many times before," she told him gently. "Don't you want us to come up with something fresher? More original?"

He wouldn't be dissuaded, although he did allow them to add a few twists.

The planning for Paul's big moment had begun right there. Millie had intervened and added as many unique aspects as possible, layering on the romance and the wow factor, but it was still essentially a flash mob in a train station. *Been there. Done that. Got the one-day super-saver.*

Laney had sourced the dancers and musicians, Tash had nailed down the logistics, and it was all beginning to take shape. Paul had been working with the dance crew for a couple of weeks and they were confident that he'd got to grips with his part in the action.

Today, they had a quick run through of the details that hadn't yet been finalised. Costs? Tick. Video? Tick. Rehearsal schedule for the next fortnight? Tick.

When he left, Tash sat back in her chair and lifted her feet on to her desk. "Man, he's a cool customer. He doesn't bat an eyelid no matter what we throw at him."

Laney nodded. "Maybe he's just one of those really smooth guys who's confident he can handle anything."

"Or a psychopath," Tash suggested. "Wouldn't surprise me if we read about him in the papers. Storing dead fiancées under his garage floor, every one of them proposed to by a flash mob in a famous transport landmark."

Millie raised both her eyebrows. "Your mind is a truly sick place, do you realise that?"

"I do."

Millie giggled. "Then we're agreed on something. It had to happen one day."

Tash noticed that Laney had already switched her attention back to her screen. "What are you working on over there? I thought we pretty much had everything sewn up for this week?"

Laney slipped her glasses up into her pixie crop. "We do. I'm just ..." she stopped, thought for a moment.

"Please don't judge me."

"We won't," Millie said.

"We will," Tash countered. "OK, she won't, I will. Sorry."

Laney smiled, despite the concern that caused a band of worry lines across her brow.

"I'm looking into all Cam's and my financials. I feel like I have to get ahead of this and be ready for when it all goes tits up. When I got home from my night with love's young dream, I ended up staying up half the night, going through credit cards and bank statements and just trying to get a handle on what's going on."

"Did you find anything?" Millie asked anxiously.

Laney chewed on the end of her pencil as she thought through her answer. "A couple of weird things. We had an ISA that he's cleared out. And there have been a few fairly heavy transactions on his credit cards. All of them cash withdrawals, which I don't really understand, because why wouldn't he just take money from our current account? He knows I never question what he does with his cash."

Millie shrugged. "Perhaps he didn't want you to see them just in case you did wonder what he was up to."

"Maybe. But if he really has given Cara a credit card …" Laney's voice cracked and she paused to recover. Tash could see that she was struggling not to cry or crumble. "… then perhaps that's how he's paying it off. Moving big chunks of cash from one card to another. There's also another payment to a bank that I'm not sure about. Monthly. For about three hundred quid."

"What could that be?" Tash asked.

"No idea. Maybe a pension? I'm not sure what

arrangements he has with work. We've always had joint accounts, but we kept the ones we had before we met for long-standing stuff. I feel like I don't really know what I'm looking at. I'm going to track down a financial advisor tomorrow. Get some help."

Tash got to her feet, went over to the wall behind Laney's desk and pulled the plug out, making her screen go to black.

"Hey!" Laney objected.

Tash put up her palm in a "talk to the hand" gesture.

"Honey, I love you and I hate that your life has gone to shit. And I'm still available for acts of violence and tyre slashing. But you've had the worst week ever, so let's get out of here and take your mind off your woes, your fucker of a husband and your father's sex life. The issues will still all be there tomorrow. As long as your dad keeps taking his little blue pill."

"Tash, that's disgusting!" Laney blurted, horrified.

"I know," Tash agreed. "Horrific. It's their partners I feel sorry for. Apparently those hard-ons can last for hours."

Laney's expression morphed from outrage into incredulity into an irrepressible fit of laughter. "Tash, you're a disgraceful human being, do you know that?'

Tash nodded solemnly. "Indeed. Happy birthday to me. Now can we go and pretend to my brothers that I'm having a great time, then bail out at the first opportunity and head to a club where we can dance until dawn and pick up strangers for sex?"

"I'm in for everything except the last bit," Millie agreed, pulling her make-up bag out of a drawer and touching up her face, before shaking her glorious red mane out of its ponytail.

Tash slipped off her leopard pumps and replaced them with the Prada shoe boots she'd splashed out on as a birthday treat during a late night too many vinos splurge on Net-A-Porter.

She should have sent them back. But then, she should also have an appropriate savings plan and drink no more than five units of alcohol a week, and life would be no fun if she did those things, either. So the shoe boots stayed and, after all, they matched the rest of her favourite outfit perfectly. She pulled off the black jumper she was wearing, then replaced it with a metallic silver vest she extracted from the bag beside her desk. On went a short leather jacket, the perfect accompaniment to her body-skimming, leather-look jeans. A dozen silver bangles, six inch long silver tassel earrings, a slash of red lipstick and a rearranging boost of the cleavage and she was good to go.

"I have no idea how you do that. You just went from normal to goddess in five minutes."

Tash stretched over and planted a perfect red pout on Millie's cheek. "Yeah, but I'll look like I've been through a car wash and dried on a whirligig by midnight, so let's get going while I'm still presentable."

Tash glanced over to Laney, who was looking distant as she dabbed on some mascara. She absolutely didn't want Laney to be put under any more stress, so – despite her rallying speech earlier – she'd still rather change tonight's plan and make it a quiet one, with just the three of them. However, Laney was insisting they shouldn't cancel so Tash had decided to go along with it and just keep a really close eye on her. The first sign that her friend was toiling and they'd be out of there.

The taxi took less than ten minutes to reach their destination. It was actually a shockingly short distance that could easily have been walked, but not in brand new Prada shoe boots.

OK, Tash told herself, *this isn't going to be a crazy one*. She didn't want to spend the whole weekend in bed, dying with a hangover. Just a normal night. A few civilised drinks and home for midnight. Finely toned hunk for one-night stand optional. That was the plan.

The doorman held the heavy copper door open for them as they arrived at The Emporium, the chic bar chosen by Jordan and John because it had one of the city's top nightclubs in the basement. Tash was touched. The boys were more casual-west-end kinda guys, but they'd gone upmarket just for her. That was true brotherly devotion.

A rumble came from the back of the room, and Tash almost turned and headed back for the doors. There was no way she was staying all night in a bar with dodgy speakers.

It was only when she got closer and her eyes grew accustomed to the dim lighting that she realised it wasn't a sound system issue. It was an unruly sportsmen issue. The entire Glasgow Gore team, plus a couple of dozen others, were all staring at her with beaming smiles, hooters in mouths and glasses raised. They all blew at the same time, unfurling spirals of multi-coloured tubes and emitting a sound close to the mating call of a thousand ducks.

Tash wanted to curl up and die. Oh, God, a surprise party. The stuff of nightmares. Tash felt her elbow being clasped and realised Laney knew her well enough to intercept any bid for escape. "Smile and act like you're thrilled," Laney hissed and she propelled her forward, Millie laughing on the other side of her.

"Sometimes even those of evil nature need to accept that they're appreciated," she teased. Tash made a mental note to dye all Millie's bright flowery clothes black at the first opportunity.

As she reached Jordan and John, they enveloped her in a team hug and squeezed her tight. "I'm going to tell your next girlfriends you have syphilis," she told them through gritted teeth. They responded by sweeping her up and on to their shoulders, an act that provoked a barely decipherable chant that included the words "Tash" and "thirty".

It would have been far more accurate if it had included: What. An. Absolute. Embarrassment.

When they eventually returned her to solid ground there was a storming round of applause, before everyone eventually went back to their drinks and chat. Jordan handed Tash a tequila shot, which she downed in one. The replacement was already waiting.

Tash glanced around the room. Family members – cousins and a couple of aunts. Her parents had retired to Majorca five years before. They'd sent her tickets to go over as a gift for her birthday, but she hadn't booked the dates yet.

There were a dozen or so friends – a couple from uni, a few that had been pals since she was a teenager, Laney's dad, Fred, and the upstairs neighbour that looked like Goldie Hawn.

In the far corner, standing out like a lighthouse beam

against the granite walls of the club, Tash spotted a luminous yellow mini dress containing Gladys from across the landing. Tash raised her glass to her and the gesture was returned, then Gladys went back to chatting to … oh, fuck. Sy. What the hell was he doing here? The bloody man was everywhere. What bit of "neighbours with benefits" didn't he get? *Enough. Time to call that one a day*, she decided. He was crossing boundaries and she preferred those barriers exactly where they were currently positioned.

Talking of being everywhere, in her peripheral vision, she saw Matt the Accountant approaching and there was no way to dodge him. Not that she entirely wanted to – not when she could clearly see every one of his abdominal muscles through the thin cotton of his tight grey T-shirt. "Happy birthday," he said, taking her empty glass from her hand and replacing it with a full one.

She took a sip. "Thank you. We seem to be bumping into each other regularly these days."

"I know. I'm after another opportunity to nick your telly," he replied, making her laugh and come close to choking on a new tequila shot.

She could feel Sy's eyes on her and it was deeply irritating. It was also making her nipples hard and pert and she didn't want to give Matt the wrong idea, so she took evasive action.

"Laney!" she shouted, then grabbed her friend, who was deep in conversation with Jordan and John, and pulled her over. "Didn't you say you needed a finance expert earlier? Meet Matt. He's an accountant, but don't hold that against him," she added. Matt gave her a mock glare.

Laney went straight for the details. "What kind of accountancy do you practice?"

If Matt minded the grilling, he didn't show it. "Mostly corporate. I've set up my own company and we deal predominantly in dot coms and start-ups."

Laney was disappointed. "Oh. I was looking for someone who understood personal finance and division of assets. It's ... complicated."

"I can take a look, if you'd like me to. I spent a year in personal accounts when I was training, so it's not something that's alien to me. I'm working up north next week but perhaps when I get back ..."

Tash took that moment to back out of the conversation and leave them to it. At the same time, she noticed that Gladys had moved on to chatting to two scrum halves with thighs the size of buckets, so she decided to rip the Band Aid off the wound.

"Hey," she said, kissing Sy on both cheeks. She was nothing if not well mannered. He smelled so good. Whatever disgracefully expensive aftershave he was using was worth every penny.

"Thank you for the gift. I'd return them but when I like something that much my integrity gets battered to death by my shallow superficiality."

He nodded solemnly. "I like that kind of self-awareness."

"So. Nothing better on tonight? And how did you get to hear about this little gathering?"

"Gladys invited me. Brought me as her plus-one. She knows we're friends. Is it a problem?"

Tash shook her head, prepared to play nice, but

honesty hijacked her first thought. "No, it's just that …
actually, yes. It is. Look, you're a lovely guy and we
have a great time together …"

"Oh dear, this is beginning to sound like one of those,
It's not you, it's me,' conversations," Sy cut in, a smile
making those eyes crinkle again. Tash almost changed
tack and snogged the face off him instead. He was easily
the best looking guy in the room, despite being one of
the oldest and not in possession of watermelon biceps.
He was wearing black trousers, Italian leather shoes, and
a black, impeccably cut shirt, the top two buttons open.
Her pelvic floor muscles clenched in appreciation and
she realised a firm, internal conversation was required.
Stay strong, she told herself. *Commitment is not your
friend and he's coming dangerously close to being
demanding.* She knew the signs. They started turning up
unexpectedly. Making plans. Getting closer. Before she
knew it, their Y-fronts were in one of her drawers and
they were keeping a spare toothbrush in the bathroom
cabinet. The thought made her shiver.

"You OK?' he asked, calmly. That was another thing
she liked – he had that whole, utterly confident,
reassuring presence thing going on. He was a man who
was happy in his own skin and supremely confident that
he could handle anything. It was a quality that irritated
and turned her on in equal measure.

"I'm sorry, I just don't do the whole relationship
thing."

"I didn't ask you," he countered.

"I know. But even this – turning up here and sending
me stuff. It's too much. I'm just not into that level of
intimacy. I liked it better the way we were."

"And if I don't?" he asked, his face a mask of genuine curiosity.

"Then we go back to being neighbours. Without benefits."

"Tash," Millie grabbed her, "come and meet Kent. He's a right wing that doesn't believe in marriage, he's a fan of Jackie Chan movies and your brothers think he's completely insane. You have loads in common."

Tash allowed herself to be pulled away and placed in front of Kent, who was so huge that if she stared straight ahead she was on his nipple line. It would never work. She had no desire to spend her life looking upwards at an almost ninety degree angle. The bills at the chiropractor would eat into her "frivolous luxuries" fund.

They made small talk on the life and times of action movies, before she broke off and worked her way around the other guests, thanking them for coming to the most unwanted surprise party ever. Sy had gone, she realised. It was a good thing. Time to move on. Definitely. Absolutely. And if she'd had a couple more drinks she might have changed her mind. Damn the lack of willpower.

It was gone midnight when Jordan climbed up on to the bar, beer glass in hand, to propose a toast.

Tash, already a few more tequilas down, felt a surge of affection for her baby brother.

"I just wanted to say, thank you all for coming and really upsetting my sister because she hates surprise parties."

Cue chorus of laughter and a Richter scale tremor caused by the stamping of many large men's feet.

"And I'd like to say a few things about her."

Tash groaned and put her head in her hands, making the crowd laugh again.

"John and I just wanted to say thank you. Since our parents moved away, she has looked out for us, partied with us and kicked our arses when we stepped out of line. Which is often. She doesn't do the emotional stuff—"

"Really? We've never noticed that," Laney said, loud enough to make Tash roll her eyes and send another round of hilarity through the revellers.

"But underneath that skin like a cactus, she's got the biggest heart and we think there is no sister that can possibly be as badass brilliant as ours."

Tash felt a wave of heat rise from her stomach and colour her face and neck.

"So please, raise your glasses. To my sister, Jessie J."

"Jessie J," the others cheered. John handed Tash another tequila shot and she downed it in one, hoping the sting as it went down would take away the embarrassment of having sixty people staring at her.

Out of the corner of her eye she spotted Laney, still in conversation with Matt the Accountant. She was about to go rescue her when Millie slipped in to the space beside her. "Hey, it's midnight and you're still standing on those heels. Well done."

Tash nodded solemnly. "I know. If only wearing fuck off heels was a recognised sport, I'd get a Lottery grant."

Millie gestured in the direction of the door. "Laney and I are going to head off now, lovely. I want to get back and hear how Leo's first day went. And I'm going to head into the office in the morning and go over everything for the Inverness job. You stay in bed all day and think about how it feels to be thirty."

Tash put a hand to her head. "Old. Oh God, I'm old." She was about to follow up with a goodbye, when she changed her mind. "Actually, would you mind dropping me off on the way past? I'm ready to head home now, too."

It was Millie's turn to be surprised. "Sure, but don't you want to stay? I've never known you to leave a party. Especially your own."

Tash looked around the room. "It's fine, everyone's having a great night and I'm just knackered. There's been too many late nights this week. And I'm old now. Really old."

Reluctant to spoil the buzz of the party, Tash just whispered a goodbye to Jordan and followed it up with a kiss on the cheek and a hug of thanks. They'd turned out OK, her brothers – although, of course, she'd never tell them that.

Fifteen minutes later she was opening the door to her apartment. An attempt to persuade Laney to stay there with her had been valiant, but as usual, her friend had been adamant about heading back to her own house. After securing a promise that there would be no late night visits to all-night cafés, Tash agreed. She couldn't make Laney do anything – she just had to be there for when moral support and stakeouts were required.

It had been some week. Lows, highs and complications. Dropping her clothes on the way, she headed to the shower and stood under the hot jets for as long as her body could take the heat. Out and dry, she decided it was time for bed.

Not necessarily hers.

Outside his door, Tash knocked and waited for him to answer.

A few seconds later, the door opened and he leaned against it.

"I thought you might like to see how my birthday present looks," she said with matter-of-fact nonchalance.

Sy reached out, and pulled a woman, completely naked except for a pair of stunning Jimmy Choo sandals, into his home.

23

Where had the week gone? It seemed like every day just passed in a blur of twisted gut and anxiety, punctuated by an alternating roller coaster of rage and calm. In the days since Tash's party she'd made sure she was busy, had thrown herself into organising the details for the upcoming events: the Inverness spectacle and HHP, office shorthand for Her Husband's Proposal.

Contact with Cam had been minimal. At the weekend, she'd called Cara's number on the pretence of wanting to discuss some details with her. No answer. However, the message on her mobile phone had said she was away for a few days. Did that mean that Cam was with her? Was he genuinely in London or was he raving his loafers off in a nightclub in Ibiza? Or holed up in a beach house somewhere on the south coast? The thought of him doing his favourite things without her made her want to weep.

She picked up the phone again and dialled Cara's number by heart. Still no answer. Desperation rising, she fired off an email.

Hi Cara,

Have some details to discuss. Can you call me please?

Kind regards,

Laney Cochrane

Personal Proposals.

The email had only been gone for a couple of minutes when a reply pinged.

Hey Laney,

Sorry, in Marbella on a shoot. Photographer like, totally demanding. Will be back tomorrow. Will call ya! Cxx

Tomorrow. The same day that Cam was returning. The same day she was leaving for Inverness, her stay there brought forward a day by the utter conviction that she couldn't be in the same room as Cam without blurting out everything. And she'd gone too far now to back out. Flights were booked, hotels were reserved, dinner reservations made, petals ordered, butler sourced and musicians researched. The fireworks were proving to be an issue, but Laney was fairly sure they would be provided on the night – although not necessarily in the form of pretty lights and starbursts.

A question plagued her sleep and many of the conversations she'd had with Tash and Millie since she'd decided to go through with this. What was she going to do if it all played out according to Cara's vision? How was she going to react at the moment of truth? What would she say, what would she do, would she end up in jail and could they rustle up the bail money between them?

Laney had no answers. The plan was to stay cool, walk away with dignity, her head held high. It was a good plan. Great. And she could do that. Definitely.

Her cursor flickered over the "close" button on Cara's email when she realised she hadn't read it all.

PS: Just noticed you have the same surname as my honey. Like, total coincidence!

Laney slammed down the mug she was holding in her other hand so violently that tea splashed everywhere.

Oh, how she wanted to type: "It's not a coincidence, you daft tart – the symbiotic nature of our surnames is due to the fact that I'M MARRIED TO THE UNFAITHFUL FUCKER."

Only sitting on her hands stopped her typing, but nothing could halt the tears that were flowing down her face. Not tears of self-pity, but the kind that were far worse: the ones that came with frustration and the knowledge that there was nothing you could do to head carnage off at the pass.

The weird thing was, she missed him already. Missed their lives together, their closeness, and most of all, their future. How could he have taken that away?

Another thought struck her and she pulled her hands out from under her thighs and clicked the calendar on her PC, heart racing as she frantically scanned the dates. It couldn't be. Surely God wouldn't be so utterly cruel. Twenty-eighth. Twenty-ninth. Thirtieth. Heartbreak bingo. There it was in black and white. Her ovulation dates fell on the weekend they would be in New York. Cam had promised he'd be home for that. *Maybe he'll bring Cara and suggest a threesome*, she thought, with utter malice.

God, she hated him. Right at that moment, she truly despised him.

The door to her left flew open and Millie and Tash burst in, both flush-faced, their appearances in stark contrast to each other. Tash was in a forties power suit in dark olive tweed, with a nipped in waist, calf-length pencil skirt, and black patent leather kitten heels, while Millie was wearing a gorgeous pale yellow floaty jersey skirt with a white tunic over it, only a pleated yellow leather belt taking it from "religious robes" to "summer hippy". Laney, meanwhile, was more eighties, with tailored black Capri trousers, a white T-shirt and a jacket that sported shoulder pads the height of George Michael's Wham mullet. If their pictures were on the cover of the same novel, it would be a time travel fantasy that documented fashion through the decades.

They were both in visibly high spirits. Laney recognised the state immediately. There was something about watching people commit to each other that made the world just a little bit brighter.

That morning the girls had been on one of their more low key proposals, one that was to begin with them picking up the unsuspecting prospective fiancée – a budding singer – in a vintage car, then driving her to the Glasgow Royal Concert Hall and leading her on to the stage, where an orchestra awaited, ready for her to perform her favourite song to their accompaniment. It was Tash and Millie's job to persuade her to sing as a videographer recorded the performance. After the last chord of Etta James' "At Last" rang out her boyfriend would stroll on to the stage and get down on one knee with a sparkler.

It was the first proposal Laney had ever missed, but she just couldn't face it. The last thing the happy couple needed was a woman on her knees wailing, "Don't do it, he could turn out to have the morals of a traitorous prick."

So the office had been her refuge, her work had been her salvation and her thighs had saved her from typing out a big fat mistake. All in all, a win, she reckoned.

"Did everything go as planned?" she greeted them.

Millie nodded. "Oh Lanes, it was beautiful, really touching. She was an incredible singer and then when he walked on and proposed it was just magical."

Tash took a more pragmatic approach. "We need to get this one up on YouTube and our website today – it's marketing gold."

Millie butted in excitedly, "I think it will go viral, a record company will spot it, she'll get signed up, have a great career, find fame and fortune and it will all be because of us."

Beside her, Tash rolled her eyes. "And her new husband, Mike the tyre fitter from Paisley, won't be able to handle the fame and the impact on his marriage, he'll give her an ultimatum, she'll choose her career, and Mike will end up drinking himself into the gutter where he'll live, surrounded by broken souls, until the day he dies a lonely and miserable death."

There was a stunned silence, until eventually Millie found words.

"You know those old horror movies where an evil force bursts out of someone's stomach and wreaks bile and damnation on the world?"

Tash looked genuinely puzzled. "And the relevance is?"

Millie and Laney replied by shaking their heads, before Laney decided to intervene. "Anyway, glad it went well, and Satan, we'll get the footage up this afternoon."

Tash tutted and headed for her desk, muttering, "My talents are wasted here."

Laney moved straight on to the next point of business on her checklist.

"OK, so I'm heading on up to Inverness in the morning and I'll collect the client's van – I've arranged for him to leave it in my hotel's car park – and then go pick up the equipment. Tash, is the kit definitely ready?"

Tash nodded. "Yep, and they're expecting you at five p.m. to collect and test it."

"Great. They can help me load it and then I'll leave it in the van overnight, until you two arrive on Saturday morning."

"So what else are you planning on doing up there, apart from generally avoiding Cam?"

Laney shrugged. "That's the main thing, obviously," she said honestly. "But I've got a few other things that will hopefully slot in. I've put promos up on our Facebook and Twitter saying I'll be in the city for anyone in that area who wants to discuss making a proposal. There have been a couple of enquiries, so maybe I'll set up some meetings."

That was Laney's skill – turning up opportunities and capitalising on them.

"Oh, and my dad is coming up on Saturday morning,

too. He's bringing Mrs Crean. They've both volunteered to help us with the proposal. Apparently Mrs Crean did a scuba diving course in Puerto Pollensa last year so she now feels that she's qualified to advise on all things water related."

Millie visibly shuddered. "Please stop talking about it. That bit is still giving me nightmares. I hate the water. If you love me, change the subject."

Tash obliged. Over at her desk, she was chewing the end of her pen while she waited for her computer to boot up. "Laney, if Mrs Crean becomes your new mummy, do you think you'll finally drop the formality of her title?"

It was Laney's turn to shudder. A new mum. That reminded her – she hadn't spoken to Lana, her real mum, for weeks. She should really tell her what was going on, but at the same time, she had no particular urge to go running to Arran with her drama. Lana was a mother on her own terms and, sad as it was, they weren't about to win any mother and daughter affection awards.

"I haven't thought about it. I'll leave it up to her."

"They might make you flower girl at the wedding," Tash teased.

"Kill me now." Laney whistled, refusing to even contemplate the horror.

The ring of her mobile phone interrupted her thoughts and she snatched it up. "Hello? Oh, hi."

Laney could see the other two pretending not to listen while straining slightly towards her, trying desperately to overhear. Nothing was sacred in this office. "Yes, sure. Of course that's still fine, say six p.m? I'm staying at the Ness Town Hotel. OK, I'll meet you in the bar. See you then."

Hanging up, she immediately turned back to focus on her computer, wondering who would crack first.

"New client?" Millie blurted, only a split second before Tash offered her suggestion: "Male escort?"

Laney shook her head. "Neither." That would drive the other two nuts. Sometimes this relationship was definitely on the *Friends* side of normal. They'd known each other since primary one, they worked together, spent every day together, watched each other's every move. For others it would be claustrophobic, but for them it was comfortable. The only "normal" they knew.

"It was Matt," she revealed, putting them out of their misery.

"Matt who?" Millie asked.

Tash answered with another question. "Matt from the rugby team, Matt? The one with the body of a Greek god and the mind of a geek God?"

Laney laughed. "Did you just make that up? You're wasted here. You should be writing tag lines for crap advertising companies."

Tash bowed. "I totally agree. Wasted."

Millie was in fully-fledged confusion stakes. "Who's Matt?"

"He's an accountant that plays in the Gore team with Jordan and John. I got talking to him at Tash's party and he offered to help me out with my finances. Turns out he's working for a company in Inverness this week, so he's going to come over and meet me and go through Cam's and my accounts. Dreading it, to be honest. Feels like I'm totally violating our privacy. But I need to know what I'm dealing with and do what I can to protect myself. Is that totally selfish?"

In rational moments, she knew it wasn't, but still, years of loyalty were hard to shake off.

"We don't need to answer that," Millie said gently. "The loyalty is already broken, but not by you."

Of course, she was right. But knowing that gave Laney no satisfaction at all.

Cam had changed the road they were on. And right now, her path led to Inverness, where a large man with an expertise for numbers would put yet another nail in the coffin of her marriage.

24

The elastic strained just a little more than it should as Millie clipped the two sides of her bra together in the centre of her cleavage. There was no escaping the fact that she'd gained a couple of pounds. That was the problem with being an emotional eater. She ate when she was happy – Leo finally getting his chance of a lifetime. She ate when she was sad – her heart broke for Laney and everything she was going through. And she ate when she was bored. Thus two bars of Galaxy and a homemade Victoria sponge had somehow evaporated over the last few days spent waiting for Leo to come home at night. Invariably, he'd got back at close to midnight, tired but excited, the adrenalin rush caused by the thrill of the new job cancelling out the lethargy caused by late nights and early morning starts.

She'd never seen him so happy, and it was brilliant, so she refused to burst his bubble by telling him how much she was missing him.

Tonight, though, she knew he was finishing at seven, so she'd prepared a perfect evening. His favourite homemade carbonara was simmering in the oven. The aroma of thick chunks of garlic bread permeated every inch of the kitchen. The Rioja had been uncorked and there were two Bond DVDs ready and waiting on the coffee table in the living room.

Her favourite Jo Malone Wild Bluebell body lotion had been lavished on after her shower, her hair left to dry naturally into deep red curls. A brief glance at the reflection in the mirror made her wince slightly. The too-tight bra was causing a definite double boob spill-over, so she leant forward and attempted to shoogle them into a better position. Standing up again, she realised she'd just about managed it. To be on the safe side she swapped her white strappy vest for a T-shirt with a deep V at the front. Hopefully Leo would be so transfixed by her cleavage that he wouldn't notice it was like a valley surrounded by the anatomical version of the Pyrenees. As she tugged on the button of her pink ankle length skirt she made a decision. Diet. Monday. But then, didn't she say that last Monday? Or was it the one before?

The old grandmother clock in the hall, bought from a second hand shop a few months after they'd moved in, chimed to mark the arrival of seven o'clock as she opened the oven door to check on the food. All perfect. The first Rioja of the night splashed into the glass while she chopped the tomatoes, onions and peppers for the salad. This was her idea of bliss, preparing a gorgeous meal while waiting for her love to arrive home. Another noise made her finish that thought with *even if he does forget his keys and then ring the doorbell.*

The buzzer was still going as she dropped the chopping knife and headed into the hall. "One of these days you'll remember your k—' She cut off when the door was halfway open and she realised that the man standing there bore no resemblance to Leo.

"Oh, hi. Sorry, I thought you were Leo."

"Nope, just your common, pain in the arse stalker," Guy replied, his self-deprecating grin making Millie chuckle.

"Ah, I don't know if you qualify as a stalker now that you've gone days without turning up at my door. You might have been relegated to 'some bloke I know who once crashed into my car'."

Guy nodded. "I'll take that. It makes me sound like less of a saddo. Your face is looking great."

"Thanks. Took a while for the yellow to go. For a few days there I bore a disturbing resemblance to Bart Simpson."

Their laughter mellowed into a moment of silence, before Guy suddenly realised it was his turn to speak, or at least explain what he was doing there.

"Oh, right, anyway …" he stuttered, and Millie thought again how endearing his slightly bumbling ways were. A bit Hugh Grant in *Four Weddings and a Funeral.*

His hand emerged from his pocket, dangling a set of keys. "I brought your car back," he told her, then stepped aside so that Millie could see her spectacularly transformed Beetle. The damage was completely fixed, but as she walked towards it she could see it was more than that. The rust was gone. The scratches had vanished. The chrome gleamed. It was like a brand new car.

Her hands flew to her mouth and – bizarrely – she felt tears spring to the back of her eyes. If Tash were here, Millie had absolutely no doubt that she'd be telling her to get a grip.

"It's so … so … beautiful," she whispered.

"Sorry it took longer than we'd expected. There was a delay in getting a part for the bumper, so I asked my mate to re-spray it while they waited for it to arrive. Just an apology from me for all the pain and inconvenience I've caused."

"It wasn't exactly a hardship," Millie replied, still stunned, unable to take her eyes off the shiny vision of motoring perfection in front of her. "The Audi was lovely to drive. I'm thrilled to have this back, though. I can't thank you enough."

"No worries. I just need the keys for the Audi and I'll take that one back for you."

"Of course! Come on into the kitchen. Have you got time for a coffee?"

"I think I've interfered in your life enough," Guy countered hesitantly.

"Not at all. Actually, I've just opened a bottle of wine. One wee glass would be fine, wouldn't it?"

"I'll stick to coffee thanks. Just in case I hit another car."

In the kitchen, the aromas from the food made Millie's stomach rumble.

"Wow, it smells amazing in here. Are you some kind of Nigella? Only every time I'm here you have something in the oven."

Millie flicked the kettle on and took a pink and blue spotty mug and an instant cappuccino sachet from the cupboard. They didn't taste exactly like the real thing, but they were close enough.

"Hardly. I can rustle up a great bowl of pasta but that's about it. Plus it's a bit of a special occasion tonight. My boyfriend has been working really long hours this week so it's the first time we've had together in ages."

"Then please don't worry about the coffee – I'll go and get out of your hair."

"No, it's fine, honestly," Millie countered, lifting the boiled kettle and pouring. "Everything's ready and he's not back yet, so you can keep me company until he gets here."

"Are you sure?"

"Positive," she assured him, placing the steaming mug in front of him.

"And before I forget, I'll find those keys." A quick rummage in her handbag located the keys for the Audi. "Thanks again for arranging everything."

Guy shrugged. "It was the least I could do. I suppose in hindsight a rubbish situation has had positive results for both of us. You have a revamped car and I have a new client. Laney booked the New York trip through us and she's asked me to look at a couple of other events in the next few months. Although why someone wants to propose at the top of a roller coaster in Disneyland is beyond me."

Millie switched the oven off, eyes flicking to the clock on the wall. Twenty past. If Leo didn't come home soon the food would be dried out. Damn.

"So how would you propose, then?"

Guy laughed, took a sip of coffee, obviously buying time to come up with an answer.

"Actually, I did propose once," he said. "In Paris. Under the Eiffel Tower. Not much of an imagination."

Millie immediately felt a pang of sympathy. During their previous chats, he'd definitely said he wasn't married so that meant ... "And she said ...?"

"Oh, she said yes. But then a few months later we realised twenty-one was far too young to tie the knot. I broke it off. It was for the best."

"I bet she was heartbroken."

Guy shook his head. "Not particularly. She went off to be a tour rep. Within a year she married the owner of a Greek taverna and she's got six kids now. If we'd stayed together I'd have had to buy a people carrier."

Millie laughed. "It's a nice image though. Romantic. Greek sunsets in the garden surrounded by a brood of children. I think I'd like that. Although I'd have to stop at three. That's how many children I've always wanted. "

Saying that out loud gave her a pang of ... what? Expectation? Excitement? Apprehension? Whatever it was, it came with the realisation that if she didn't get started soon, she wouldn't have time to get to three. Sometimes she wished they'd started trying as soon as they'd met, but there always seemed to be a reason not to. They'd just moved house. They were skint. Leo was still searching for his break into acting.

Well, those reasons were all gone now. Baby-boom here we come.

The thought made her smile as she cracked open a new

packet of Jaffa cakes for Guy.

"Why three?"

"I suppose it's because I've got two older sisters. They both moved to London. Three children each. We're a bit predictable." *Note to self, call sisters this week.* It was her turn to arrange the monthly group Skype that kept them all in contact with each other, and with their dad.

"And where do your parents live?"

"Parent. My mum passed away a few years ago. My dad moved back to Cork. That's where he was from originally. Met my mum on a holiday here when he was twenty and never left her. But after she died he decided to go back to his hometown for a holiday. He's still there. And he's happy, so that's all that matters."

Millie had a vision of her dad, guitar in hand, sitting in an Irish bar singing his heart out. He was a free spirit, but he belonged back with his seven brothers and sisters. She tried to nip over every couple of months for a visit. He was slowly but surely getting over the loss of her mum. Every time she saw him his shoulders were a little higher and his beard was a little longer.

Perhaps, like Laney's dad, he was due a mid-life crisis. Sad that the two men both lost the loves of their lives – one through death, one through betrayal – but it did show that you had to make the most of every day you had with someone you loved.

Talking of which, if the one she loved didn't get his arse back soon they'd have to phone out for a pizza.

Pulling out a chair, she sat at the table directly across from Guy. Wasn't it crazy how the universe just plonked people into your life sometimes? If she hadn't been at the same school as Laney and Tash, they'd never have met. If she hadn't gone to that gallery that morning, she'd never have met Leo. If she hadn't been sitting at those lights, she would still have a healthy stock of Jaffa cakes in her cupboard.

"So anyway, back to you – what about now? Someone special?"

Guy nodded. "I've been seeing one of the girls that works in the office for a few months. Jorja. She's lovely."

"I know a great agency that could help with a proposal," she said with a giggle. "And can also get you cheap flights and accommodation if you want to travel abroad."

His eyes crinkled with amusement. "Sounds like an excellent service, but I'll pass for now. I'm not sure that we're quite at that stage yet. But I'll let you know if the situation changes. Jeez, you're hard sell."

"I prefer 'passionate about the product'. So do you live together?"

Guy waited until he'd swallowed before he spoke. "Not yet. We both still kind of like to do our own thing. She's away through to Edinburgh tonight with her girlfriends to see a show."

Before she could ask him anything else, her phone buzzed. Yay. That would be Leo saying he was on his way.

She picked it up and opened the text.

"Sorry babe, been held up. Won't be home until late. Soz again. Love you xxx".

Millie sighed as she tossed the phone on the table. Bugger. She'd been so looking forward to seeing him, to having a night together.

Now she was all dressed up and nowhere to go.

What a bummer. She would call Laney, she decided. Or Tash. But then, Laney would be packing and Tash would probably be busy at Pilates. Or with Jordan and John. Or sucking the face off the next-door neighbour.

So perhaps …

"Guy, do you have plans for tonight?" she asked.

"Only to take back the Audi."

"Can it wait until later?"

He looked at her quizzically. "Sure, but why."

"Because Leo isn't going to make it home for dinner. How would you like some carbonara?"

He picked up the Jaffa cakes, closed the box and slid it across the table.

"You sure this isn't just a ruse to make me stop eating your biscuits?"

"Oh it definitely is." Millie smiled.

"Then it worked," he said, shrugging off his jacket. "And I might have that glass of wine, too."

25

It had seemed like a good idea at the time. Coming up to Inverness, avoiding Cam, giving herself some space to breathe. Laney just hadn't thought through the fact that having no distractions would send her anxieties soaring. Her heart felt like it was beating faster than normal. Wild scenarios were going through her mind. Cam and Cara's wedding. Cam's face when she confronted him. Tash doing a flying rugby tackle and taking him down. In one of her many fitful dreams last night, he'd pulled off a face mask and revealed that he was actually the serial killer from the episode of *Criminal Minds* she'd watched before bed.

The sad truth was that going over her accounts had become something to look forward to just because it gave her something to focus on.

The last two weeks had been both brutal and exhausting, yet Laney almost felt like she'd been in a bubble of surrealism. Right on cue, the phone in front of her in the deserted hotel bar started to ring and Cam's number flashed up. His screen image used to be a pic of them windsurfing in tandem off the coast of Crete. After Tash had borrowed the phone for five minutes last week, it was now a picture of Freddy Krueger.

"Hi," she answered as brightly as she could. Strangely it took less effort now than in the first couple of days when her heart had been freshly ripped out. Now it was more like a constant throb. The kind of pain that wouldn't render you completely incapacitated, but would definitely require a trip to A&E.

"Hey, babe, I'm home and you're not here. The house is so empty without you. I'm bored already."

"Oh, I'm sure you'll find something to fill the time," she said, then immediately regretted it as an image of Cara straddling him in their bed filled her mind. No, surely he wouldn't. Their house had too many personal things in it, too many feminine touches. Any girl coming in to it would realise immediately that a woman lived there and it would give his philandering game away. After thinking about it night after night, she'd decided that Cara had definitely never been in her house. It was a small comfort, but in a week in which she would grasp on to any positives that she could get, she'd take it.

"Sleep, that's what I'll be doing. I'm knackered. It's been a tough couple of weeks."

Please stop talking. Please stop. With every word something inside her died.

Yet, the masochist in her couldn't resist prodding the monster.

"How so? Have you been working out more than

usual?"

"Not particularly. Just juggling too many things, I guess."

DEAR GOD! What was he doing to her? It was like he was leaving it wide open for her to wade in and call him out. But she wasn't doing it. Absolutely not. No matter how tough this got she was going to see it through.

"Well, you take it easy this weekend then, darling. Lots of lying down, lots of rest." As she said it, Laney was painfully aware that in the world she'd discovered Cam inhabited, those two actions weren't necessarily linked. Especially if Skype was involved.

She rang off and contemplated what he'd said. Was it still possible that she had this all wrong? That there was another Cam Cochrane at MindSoar? No, Cam's lunch with Cara cancelled that theory out. Was she some mad fantasist? Didn't *Criminal Minds* regularly feature psychopaths who were convinced they were in a relationship with an unsuspecting acquaintance? How many times had she driven past Cara's house, sat outside, called her, and never once had there been a hint that Cam was with her? Maybe he really was at work all this time. So maybe that meant there was still a glimmer of hope that she had this all wrong? Then why was she sitting in a hotel bar waiting for an accountant to give her advice on the best steps to take to protect herself if her marriage faced the death penalty?

"Hi Laney, sorry I'm late – held up with my client. Can I get you a drink?"

Matt looked so different, it took a few moments for Laney to process it. The unruly black hair was swept back and styled – there was definite use of product there.

The suit trousers were deep navy and matched with a blue and white striped shirt, open at the neck, tie pulled down as if he couldn't stand the constriction on his larynx. He looked like he belonged in a movie about Wall Street.

"I've got one, thanks," she said, motioning to the gin and tonic in front of her. Not her usual choice of drink, but she'd felt like a change – and besides, every wine seemed to remind her of a place and time spent with Cam.

Matt ordered a bottle of Bud from a bored-looking waitress at the bar, then sat across from her and pulled a notepad and pen from his brown leather briefcase.

"How are you doing?" he asked – and that's when it happened. It was an innocuous question. A standard greeting. He was clearly just expecting the automatic reply of "fine". Maybe even "great". But the dam that held Laney's emotional reservoir burst, her eyes filled with tears, her face puckered and she managed to squeak out a strangled "Not good."

Matt's expression immediately turned to fear and alarm, proving he was a stereotypical West of Scotland man for whom women crying incited feelings of deep discomfort and borderline panic.

Laney dipped her head, but hiding her face didn't mask anything given that big fat tears were splodging down on to her pale blue jeans.

The waitress either didn't notice or ignored her as she put Matt's bottle down on a white coaster napkin and departed without so much as a cheery endearment.

Matt swiftly passed the napkin to Laney, who used it to dab her eyes.

"Look, we can do this another time," he said. "I really don't want to upset you."

Laney blew her nose noisily. "It's not you," she croaked, stating the obvious. "It's … it's …" The heaving shoulders and the uncontrollable sobbing kicked in again, in tandem with the sheer mortification of crying in front of a virtual stranger. Oh, the embarrassment. Crying wasn't her thing. She'd never been one of those women who turned on the tears at the drop of a sympathy-seeking hat. Yet here she was, terrifying this poor guy who had been kind enough to do her a favour and help with her finances.

"It's OK, just take a moment to get your breath back," he said, reaching over and putting a comforting hand on her arm. Oh bollocks, nice man alert! The concern just made the tears come even thicker.

Several minutes – which felt like an hour and a half – passed before she could speak without choking. "I'm so sorry," she eventually stuttered. "If you want to run for your life, I'll totally understand."

Matt shook his head – the hair didn't move an inch, definitely good product. "That's fine. The bar staff have probably already called the cops so it would look like I'm fleeing the scene," he joked. It was the right thing to say, made her feel so much better than any well-meaning but useless platitudes.

"Let me explain," Laney said, tossing the shredded, mascara-stained napkin into her handbag.

"You really don't have to …"

"I know, but it's relevant. The reason that I need advice on my finances is because my husband is … is … having an affair."

SHARI LOW

She steeled herself this time. Do not cry. Do not. The poor man is already traumatised.

"Oh. I'm sorry. What a dick."

"Thanks – for both sentiments."

"You're welcome." He paused. "So have you separated?"

Laney nodded. "Yes. He just doesn't realise it yet."

Matt's confusion was obvious.

"He works away most of the time. I only found out at the beginning of last week that he was cheating. He's been away ever since, so there hasn't been an opportunity to confront him."

"Can I ask how you found out?" Matt immediately qualified that question. "But only if it won't make you cry again. Sorry. Male. I'm officially hopeless in emotional situations. I think it's genetic."

"I think you're doing OK," Laney corrected him. "If Tash had been here, she'd have told me to get a grip and threatened to leave if I didn't pull myself together."

Matt laughed. "Yeah, I've had the 'Tash' experience."

"And how did that go for you?" Laney was teasing now.

"She threatened to remove my testicles with a spoon."

"Yes, her humanitarian side needs work. Listen, are you sure you want to help with this? I promise I won't be offended if you don't."

"Absolutely," he reassured her.

"Right. Sorry what was your question again?" Either the sobbing had flooded her brain or the gin and tonic must have been stronger than she realised.

"How did you find out about his affair?"

Laney sighed, drained her glass and motioned to the

barmaid for two more drinks.

"That's the most bizarre part of it all. His girlfriend came to us and asked us to plan her proposal. To my husband."

It took a moment to digest.

"You're kidding."

"If only I was."

"So what did you say?"

Laney really wished those drinks would hurry up.

"I said yes. She's proposing to him next weekend in New York. We've arranged it all."

"And he doesn't know?"

"Nope, he knows nothing about it at all."

Another stunned pause, until …

"Then you'd better make sure Tash and her spoons are nowhere nearby."

Laney tried her very best to smile. "Do you think I'm crazy?"

"Completely," he admitted honestly, finally discarding the tie altogether and rolling up his sleeves to reveal very brown arms. "Why not ask him about it? Confront him before then?"

"Because he's done such an incredible job of lying to me up until now, that I'm pretty sure he'd attempt to lie his way out of it. Or at least minimise what he's done. I want to see it because … because I love him, and that's the only way I know for sure that I'll absolutely never go back."

Matt leaned back in his wooden chair and exhaled. "That's either incredibly brave or incredibly crazy."

Laney appreciated his honesty.

The waitress brought the next round of drinks, then

wordlessly put them on the table and walked away. This was an American-themed sports bar that the hotel literature promised was a "fun experience". Someone should probably notify them that no one had informed the staff.

"So what do you need me to do?" he continued.

Laney took a deep breath. She'd thought long and hard about this and decided that she had to deal with this in a fair way. Then she thought again and decided that if he'd been using their joint cash for his private entertainment, she wanted to claw back every dirty, disloyal penny.

Opening her laptop, she booted it up and then turned it to face him so that they could both see the screen. Matt picked up his pen again and prepared to take notes.

"There are loads of inconsistencies in our accounts. Fairly small sums being taken out, I guess because he hoped I wouldn't notice. And I didn't. Most of our finances are handled through a couple of joint accounts, and to be honest, I didn't pay particularly close attention to anything except the one we use for day-to-day stuff. He's emptied an ISA, and there's a regular payment of three hundred quid going out of an account that's in his name only. I knew the password, so I checked it, too. Also, his girlfriend says he has given her a credit card that she can use for anything she wants. That's how she's paying for the proposal."

"Ouch. So in effect, you're paying half of it."

Laney hadn't quite thought of it like that, but now she saw the truth of it.

Bastard.

"So I guess what I need you to do is protect me. I want to know everything about his finances – I'll give you our account details and passwords – and I want to know what he's done with the money he's spent. And what all the other payments are for. And then I'd like you to find a way to shield me from any further exposure. I'm not paying for his future with her, Matt."

"I'll do everything I can to make sure that doesn't happen."

"Thanks. I like to get everything out up front, so can we talk about your fee? I'll pay whatever your going rate is for this."

Matt shook his head. "Don't worry about it. If I ever decide to propose to some unsuspecting girl, you can return the favour."

26

Tash heard the thud of the music as soon as she opened the door to the dance studio. "Hey Baby" by Bruce Channel thundered from the speakers.

She slipped to her left and stood against the wall, the dancers, facing away from her, toward the mirror, completely oblivious to her presence. This was the third or fourth time she'd dropped in on them and they were getting better with every rehearsal. Pretty much flawless now, she realised, as she watched the run-through. Paul, her seriously underwhelming client, was at front and centre, busting some impressive moves. He'd told them he could dance, but – in the land of the deluded and the *Britain's Got Talent* wannabes who claimed they were the next Beyoncé but couldn't move in time if their hips depended on it – he was a revelation. There must be some professional training in there somewhere along the line. Maggie was a lucky girl if that rhythm extended to the bedroom.

The team of dancers that she'd hooked him up with were doing a great job, too. It had been a fortuitous coincidence. The leader of the dance team had just emailed Tash a video of their work, sterling references and a request to be kept in mind for any future events an hour after Paul had walked out the door.

Tash had decided to give them a try and it seemed like it was paying off.

When they stopped for a break, Tash whistled to get Paul's attention and called him over.

"Hey, I didn't see you there," he said as he sauntered towards her.

"It's coming together really well," she told him. "Are you nervous?"

He shook his head. "No, it's cool. Looking forward to it."

Tash marvelled at his calm steadiness. They'd done dozens of proposals now and on every single one the client had shown some degree of nerves, ranging from mildly anxious to complete meltdown.

"OK, so we're ready to go, then," she told him. "Two more rehearsals next week for you and the dancers, but other than that, everything is arranged."

"Cool," he repeated.

Actually, his complacency was getting irritating now. She tried not to let it show.

"The only thing that we haven't covered is the ring."

For the first time, she noticed a slight chink in his veneer of control.

"The ring?" he repeated, a question now.

Tash pointed to her finger. "Yeah, you know – a round

thing, commonly given from one person to another to mark the occasion of an engagement."

"A ring," he repeated. Was he stoned? That was it – the guy was completely wacked out of his head. At least that would explain the comatose approach to the biggest event of his life.

"I haven't … thought about it," he admitted.

"So what were you planning to do after the dance?"

"Just … ask her to marry me."

"With a ring. You need a ring," Tash insisted.

"Oh."

He looked so perplexed, Tash decided to step in and help.

"So what type of ring would she like? We can help you arrange it. Even go buy it for you if you don't have time."

Paul shook his head. "No, it's fine – I'll get it sorted. Not sure what she'd like though."

"She's never hinted? Never stopped you outside a jeweller's window and pointed to a fuck-off big diamond in the window?"

"Never," he answered. "What's the best style to get? I mean, what would you want if you were getting engaged?"

Oh bloody hell, here we go again, Tash thought. Asking her opinion was the reason he was now doing a pathetically unoriginal bloody flash mob in a train station. Why would anyone want her thoughts on this stuff? Why?

Yes, she was choosing to overlook the pertinent fact that she did indeed have "Proposal Planner" on her business cards. She decided to channel her inner woman and answer honestly.

"I suppose I would want something really simple – just a silver band. White gold, maybe. But that's because I'm not much of a jewellery person. The more understated the better for me."

Paul nodded thoughtfully. "Yeah I guess my chick is probably a bit like that too. Understated."

"Then I'd stick to something plain and classy," Tash told him.

"Cool," he said. Again.

His expression then completely changed, as if a light bulb of an idea had been switched on over his head.

"We're just about to do one more run through, but then, could you come with me to the Argyll Arcade? It's just across the road and it won't take long. I'd just appreciate a woman's advice."

Tash checked her watch. Bugger. She'd been hoping to go squeeze in something vital – a quick diversion to her flat for a cigarette, a coffee and last night's episode of *Nashville* – before heading back to the office, but this was a client in need and, however grudgingly, she knew she had a duty to help.

Twenty minutes later they were in the Argyll Arcade, an emporium of treasures that was home to the widest collection of jewellery stores in the city.

Even being in there made Tash feel slightly claustrophobic. What was the point of all this? Wearing a piece of metal to show that you'd decided to devote the rest of your life to someone who may or may not turn out to be a complete knob?

Urgh, the very thought made her itch. People often thought her aversion to being married must be due to a bad relationship experience, but it truly wasn't. In fact, the opposite was true. She'd always got exactly what she wanted from every coupling she'd ever had, while watching those around her suffer because of commitment. It simply wasn't what she wanted. Never had been. She was once again reminded why she was in the wrong job.

Tash decided to make it quick, painless and straightforward.

She spent a few minutes contemplating the smaller shop windows then moved Paul on to the large store in the corner. Row upon row of sparkling promises, stones waiting for hard earned cash to be splashed on them.

"Do you have a rough idea of your budget?" she asked Paul, who stood back, showing no particular interest in proceedings.

"Erm, no, not really."

"Ballpark?"

"Definitely under a thousand," he decided.

Tash scanned the window. That made it easy. Nothing she liked was much more than a couple of hundred pounds anyway.

After perusing the red velvet pads for enough time to make it seem she wasn't just going for the first thing she saw, Tash pointed to a pad of white gold bands. In the centre, was a ring similar to the only piece of valuable jewellery she owned – the tricolour gold Bulgari band she'd bought in duty free last time she was in New York.

This one had two layers of white gold, sandwiching a yellow gold band in the middle. It was probably closer in style to a wedding ring than an engagement ring, but it was exactly her taste – simple, classic and definitely not ostentatious. The only time she broke those rules was when it came to designer footwear. Somehow, she didn't think Maggie would appreciate being proposed to with a pair of Manolo Blahniks. Fool.

"That one," she said pointing it out. "But Paul, I need to emphasise, that's not what most women would like. The majority would prefer at least one diamond, the bigger the better."

Paul pondered this. "I'll have a think about it," he said. "Thing is, Maggie likes simple things …"

Tash bit her tongue to prevent blurting out the obvious.

"… so maybe she'd like that one best, too. I'll have a think about it and come back when I've decided."

"Good move," Tash agreed. "But try to do it within the next couple of days, because then that's another thing ticked off the list. You don't want to be running around at the last minute."

"I hear you," Paul told her.

"Oh, and try to bring another ring from her jewellery box with you – that will give you an idea of her size."

"You're good at this," he told her earnestly.

"I try," said Tash with a wink.

She put her hand out and shook his. "OK, well, I'll pop in on you again at final rehearsal next week, but in the meantime, if you want help with the ring or you have any last minute questions or worries, just call me. I'm heading up to Inverness tomorrow to stage a proposal up there, but I'll have my mobile with me the whole time."

"Will do," Paul agreed, before sauntering off, the epitome of calm, in the other direction.

Tash flicked to her default setting of mild irritation.

There was something strange about that guy. She just

hoped that his girlfriend, Maggie, knew what she was getting into.

27

"Are we ready?" Fred asked, teetering precariously on the banks of the Ness. Laney had travelled fourteen miles south to Drumnadrochit to meet the others at eight a.m. It was now noon, and her head still hurt as she nodded an affirmative in answer to her dad's question.

"Are you OK?" Millie asked her. "Are you coming down with something? Tash and I can handle this part if you're feeling rough. And you know Mrs Crean said she would stand in for you."

Laney shook her head. Which made it hurt even more. Too much gin followed by physical activity the next morning did not make for a good match. In fact, there was absolutely no form of activity that made a good match for the amount of gin she'd consumed last night.

The last thing she remembered was …

"Tell me you didn't shag Matt last night," Tash hissed, out of earshot of Fred and Mrs Crean.

Laney jerked her head around. *Ouch.* "Of course I didn't. Some of us have morals," she replied in the same hushed tone.

"Shame," Tash shrugged. "That would have taken your mind off Cam. He's got buttocks that could crack walnuts."

Millie pulled a mask down over her face and shuddered. "God, it's freezing in here. I hope these wetsuits heat us up soon. Still, at least it takes my mind off the terror. Have I mentioned I hate water?"

"Only a dozen times," Tash replied.

"You'll be fine when you start swimming," Laney assured her. "Dad, you can let go. I've still got a grip of the rope. I just need you to check if they're out in position yet and then give us the thumbs up."

Fred scrambled to his feet, Maisy Crean hanging on to his belt in case he had a slippage issue that ended with a large splash. Laney, Millie and Tash, all in wetsuits, life jackets and snorkelling masks, all up to their chests in water, looked at him expectantly as he raised his binoculars and scanned the mass of water to his right.

Loch Ness was a breathtaking sight. The second largest loch in Scotland, it stretched for twenty-two miles at its longest point, almost two miles across at its widest. Surrounded by undulating green hills, on a dry day like today, the view was magnificent.

This was their most challenging proposal yet – requiring stealth, the construction of elaborate, specialised equipment, and a taste for danger that probably demanded the intervention of a health and safety officer. However, they'd decided against bringing in safety experts – mainly because they knew that what they were about to do was definitely foolish and possibly illegal, but utterly magnificent. If they didn't meet a watery end first.

"OK, they're there. Go, go, go!" Fred urged them, like a SWAT commander rushing his troops into a hostage situation.

On command, Laney, Millie and Tash took a deep breath through their snorkels, as instructed at the week-long course they'd all undertaken in preparation for this moment.

They then dipped under the edge of the polystyrene shell, designed and manufactured specially for the occasion, collected by Laney yesterday and driven in four pieces in the client's transit van to the edge of the loch that morning. They'd then built it from four parts into one, behind an area of trees that shielded them from view. It was now twenty feet long, ten feet high at its tallest point, painted in scarily realistic shades of grey, and an impeccable replica of the creature commonly regarded as Nessie, the legendary Loch Ness monster. They'd carried the surprisingly light structure to the water's edge, carefully lowered it in, and hopefully their client was about to realise his vision.

Stewart, a crofter from Thurso, on Scotland's far north coast, had met his love, Elma from Virginia, on a Nessie fan forum, and they'd immediately connected over their mutual obsession with the large, prehistoric beast that may or may not exist. They were both certain that she did.

Over the following months, their communications had gone from monster-related to romantic, until the moment they finally met, when Elma made her pilgrimage to

Scotland and they went on their first date to Nessieland – the world of all things Nessie.

It was a meeting of minds, hearts and strange obsessions, one that had convinced Stewart that he'd met the woman of his dreams. Thus, right now, the three partners in Scotland's first proposal planning agency were casting off from the side of a loch, hidden under a giant polystyrene monster, in the hope of making Elma's wishes come true. If the shock didn't kill her.

Although it wasn't Elma's long-term health that was concerning Tash at the moment. Able to take out her mouthpiece now that they were in the middle of the polystyrene shell, with air holes punched along the side and apertures at the front to let them see where they were going, she expressed her latest fear.

"I swear to God, we'd better survive this. I am not having an obituary that reads, "Tash O'Flynn died suddenly and tragically, with her head inside a monster's arse."

Laney and Millie both spat their mouthpieces out as they laughed, before Laney took charge.

"Right, so I reckon we've got a hundred metres to swim and push this thing. Ready?"

The other two nodded. They'd spent a couple of months swimming four times a week preparing for today. The training showed – especially in the case of Millie, whose fear of water had been contained enough to allow her to take part.

Laney at the front, Millie in the middle, Tash at the back, they slipped one hand into the straps placed to their requirements on the inside of the shell, then used their legs and free arm to push out of the camouflage of the trees.

Stewart had been advised as to the direction of their approach, and Laney just hoped he'd fulfilled his part of the plan – to make sure Elma's back was to the approaching amphibian. Or should that be dinosaur? Or mammal? Laney wasn't sure which category was relevant when the creature was constructed purely of materials that were usually used for packing electronic goods.

They covered the first fifty metres with relative ease, and through the peepholes, Laney could see Stewart, sitting in a rowing boat, facing Elma, and over her shoulder, the approaching Nessie.

Forty metres. Thirty. Twenty.

What if she gets such a shock, she falls in the water? Laney suddenly thought, her breath becoming laboured now with the exertion. Oh shit, they'd be accomplices to murder. Or would it be manslaughter, because they didn't mean it to happen?

No, she'd save her. She'd done her lifeguard badge and passed it. She was twelve at the time, but surely the rules hadn't changed much.

Fifteen metres.

Stewart would prepare her, wouldn't he? There was no way he'd let the love of his life be faced with something so shocking it could lead to serious injury?

Ten metres away. *OK, Stewart, start preparing her now, before the ripples in the water give it away.* She could see the back of Elma now, her black padded oilskin jacket, her long flowing grey hair, with a … oh shit, what was that round her head? He'd blindfolded her. Oh fuck, that wasn't in the plan!

When had he added in that not-so-insignificant detail?

"He's blindfolded her," Laney told the others.

"Always thought he looked kinky," Tash retorted, completely unhelpfully. "Is he wearing a gimp mask? If he is, we're reversing out of here, arse first."

Millie spluttered as the combination of giggling and water went wrong.

Hearing inside the shell wasn't a problem, but the polystyrene blocked all sound outside. When they'd arrived, there were very few tourists along the bank, but Laney had no doubt that there would be some spectators on the shore watching this with utter astonishment. Hopefully Fred and Mrs Crean had carried out the instructions to go to the main area where most tourists were gathered and assure them this was a hoax. Still, there was a fair chance that a) there would be shouts and hollers coming from the bank around now and b) this would make it to the front page of the *Daily Record* tomorrow. It was a calculated risk. It would either give them the kind of publicity you couldn't buy, or it would land them in jail. Possibly forever, if the shock killed Elma.

"Here lies Elma Flangbucket, killed by the Loch Ness Monster," Tash wittered.

Just a few metres away now, she saw Stewart reach over, and gently remove Elma's blindfold.

Then he went down on both knees in front of her, a wise move as the one-kneed traditional approach would risk a capsize situation.

Nessie was still moving forward, five metres now, four, three, when Elma turned around, her face a mask of wonder and awe.

"Oh thank Christ, he must have said something that stopped her from being scared for her life," Laney whispered, her cardiovascular system totally under pressure now. Two months of training hadn't been enough. She could see from Millie's pink face and Tash's heaving chest that they both felt the same.

Peering through the peepholes, only two metres away now, Laney watched as Elma's hands flew to her face, her eyes wide with wonder.

"She's loving it! Brake, brake, brake!" she ordered, and six legs shot forward, pushing against the movement of the vessel, forcing it to slow and then stop with a gentle thump as it bumped the edge of the couple's boat.

"What's happening? What can you see?" Millie asked urgently, moving to the front so that she shared Laney's prime position and had a view of events through the left aperture. At the back, Tash had a hand through a strap on both sides of the inner monster and was lying back, recovering her breath. "She'd better bloody say yes after the state my hair's in," she muttered. Laney and Millie weren't listening.

They were watching as Elma slowly, in a haze of disbelief, reached over and placed her hand into the little basket that was tied with a red ribbon around Nessie's neck. From there she pulled out a green leather box, opened it and gasped.

The ring had been custom made, too. Nine carat Scottish gold, shaped into the emblem of their love: a tiny, amphibious, monster-type, prehistoric creature.

Millie thought it was romantic. Laney thought it was bizarre. And Tash thought they should be seen by a member of the psychiatric community.

227

But Elma clearly disagreed as she passed the ring to Stewart and he slipped it on her finger.

"She said yes!" Millie gasped, tears flowing.

"How can you cry?" Tash demanded to know. "We're up to our necks in water, you're in the approximate position of a dinosaur's intestine and it's fucking freezing in here."

Laney and Millie ignored her, both watching with true happiness as Elma bent over, kissed her new fiancé, with tongues, then reached over and hugged the polystyrene neck of her new best friend.

Laney and Millie instinctively pulled back, then returned to their viewing positions as Elma released Nessie, and sat back on the wooden plank that was her seat.

Now that they were stationary and right next to the apertures, Laney and Millie could hear what sounded like a loud chorus of cheers from the shore. Laney hoped that was the case, and not the police in a motorboat, with a loud hailer, telling them to put their prehistoric paws up in surrender.

"Our job is done here, girls," Laney announced. "Back to shore."

Reverting to their original positions, Laney kicked to the left, Tash kicked to the right, and the beast started to turn. "And Millie, if the police are waiting, we're relying on you to go all feminine and get us out of trouble."

"Or distract them by pointing them in the direction of someone else." Tash suggested. "Tell them there's a bloke with a gimp mask in the middle of the loch."

28

Only the kitchen light was on when Millie pulled the
Beetle into the driveway at eleven p.m. It had been a
long but ultimately unforgettable day.

As soon as they'd got Nessie back behind the
camouflage of the trees, Fred joined them and they'd
quickly unsnapped the clips holding her together,
dismantled her back into four pieces and loaded her back
into the transit van.

Out of their lifejackets and wetsuits, Laney had
jumped behind the wheel and headed – followed by
Millie and Tash in one car, and Fred and Mrs Crean in
his swanky new mid-life-crisis Range Rover – to a
nearby car park. There, she'd left Stewart's van in the
prearranged spot, with the keys under the wheel arch.
Millie just hoped that no one stole it. Or that if they did,
there was footage of their faces when they opened up the
back, expecting a haul of flat screen TVs or golf clubs,

and found a polystyrene Nessie.

They'd then convoyed south, calling Stewart on the way to check all had gone according to plan.

Elma had answered.

"Hi Elma, congratulations – we're so happy for you."

There was a pause that made Millie's heart leap. There was always a risk that proposees didn't enjoy their moment or would react negatively. Thankfully not this one.

"Oh my gosh, that was amazing. I never expected such a thing in all my life. Y'all are quite special. Quite special indeed," she enthused in her Southern drawl.

"It was our pleasure," Millie said, ignoring Tash who was shaking her head in the passenger seat. "Did you pick up the van?"

"We did indeed. We're heading north now and we'll be putting Nessie in the garden. My Stewart says she'll look over us forever."

Tash put her head in her hands. Millie ignored that too.

"That's lovely, Elma. So, congratulations again and we hope the two of you are very happy together. Please send us a photo of the wedding and take care."

The goodbyes were cheery, with all parties on loudspeaker at both ends contributing.

"Aw, see, this is why we do this job."

"To meet crazy people and encourage them to think their actions are normal?" Tash asked.

"To bring soul mates together," Millie countered.

"Just wish that it came with repeat business," Laney interjected. It was a good point. Theirs was one of the few industries, along with funeral directors and astronauts, in which the chances of repeat business were slim. People were more inclined to go overboard on their first engagement, but even – or especially – if it didn't work out, they tended not to go for lavish plans the second time around. Even if they did, chances were there would be many years between the proposals so the girls had yet to get the benefit of seeing clients a second time.

That's why every single client mattered, and that's why they were miles from home, risking life, limb and a criminal record in the name of a happy new beginning.

They'd decided to take the scenic road home, down the A82, a sometimes perilous road but one of unequalled beauty. They passed Fort William, travelled through the wondrous Glencoe, then further south, before stopping for a break at the Lodge on Loch Lomond, a hotel and restaurant with incredible views across Loch Ness's big sister, the largest mass of water in Scotland.

Refuelled on oysters and the restaurant's famous beef cheeks, they drove on home, parting ways with Fred and Maisy's vehicle when Laney's dad peeled off on Great Western Road, and Millie headed straight on to the city centre, depositing Laney and Tash at the entrance to Tash's building.

Twenty minutes later she was home.

As she opened the door, the scent of lilies enveloped her. Throwing her bag on the hall table, she headed into the kitchen, hoping that Leo was waiting.

He was.

"Hey baby," he said, glancing up from the pages of script in front of him. He was sitting in the huge pink arm chair in the corner, illuminated by the lamp behind it, wearing the glasses that he only used for reading, despite Millie's request that he wear them more often because they made him look damn sexy. The baggy white linen shirt and ripped up jeans only added to the effect. From the waist up, with his long black wavy hair pulled back into a loose ponytail, and his sallow skin stretched over perfect cheekbones, he belonged in a period drama. Or an advert for some manly aftershave.

"Hi love," she replied, walking towards him, her body already yearning to be wrapped in his.

There were no words to describe how she loved this man and she was fairly sure he loved her right back, although lately there hadn't been much time to show it.

Now, though, it was just them, in the same place, with no interruptions or distractions.

"You look exhausted," he told her. "And pretty wild."

Her hands immediately went to her hair. "Oh. I was swimming in Loch Ness this morning, so I just left it to dry in the wind."

Cue astonished expression. "Swimming in Loch Ness?"

"Under a polystyrene monster." Folding herself into him on the chair and loving the feeling of his arms going around her, she gave him the bullet points of the event, up to the point where the newly engaged couple drove off into the sunset in a transit van.

"You've got the craziest job I've ever known," he decided, his face only inches from hers, their breath mingling in the middle.

"You're pretending to be a junkie gangland enforcer who kneecaps anyone who crosses him," she argued.

"Good point."

He leaned over and kissed her, ending when his teeth gently trapped her bottom lip and hung on to it just a fraction longer than necessary. Laughing, she grabbed a chunk of his chest hair and pulled until he let go.

"Ouch."

"Now you know how a bikini wax feels," she told him tartly. "So anyway, tell me how it's going."

Her head rested on the back of the chair, her knees up at her chest and her feet curled under his thighs as she listened, looking into his eyes as he spoke.

"I'm not sure. They seem to be happy with me – the director is being really positive – but I still feel like the new kid at school. I keep waiting for them to tell me I'm crap and let me go."

It was such an uncommon moment of vulnerability that she struggled, but just managed, to hide her surprise. Leo had always had absolute faith in his abilities and a real conviction that the future he wanted was out there and he'd get it one day. It was what drove him, helped him work in café after bar, cleaning job after warehouse packer, knowing that it was only temporary until the big break came. No wonder he'd been acting weird lately. And how selfish did she feel, mentally chiding him for his lack of romance and engagement action when he was dealing with the biggest crisis of confidence he'd ever faced?

What kind of crap girlfriend was she?

"Leo, you'll be great. You're a fantastic actor and they must see that, so don't doubt yourself."

"I think I just wanted it so much and now I've finally got it I'm a bit freaked out in case I lose it."

Millie nodded. "I see why you would feel that way." Wasn't it exactly the same way she felt about him? "But it's not going to happen. You'll do a brilliant job, they'll think you're terrific and it'll just be the start of great things."

"You're the start of great things," he told her, "and I'm sorry if I've been a bit distracted lately. Just had a lot on my mind. I love you, though."

Millie leant in and kissed him again.

"I love you too," she murmured, before pulling back. "So here's what I think you should do. You should take your girlfriend to bed and let her take your mind off your worries."

He gestured to the pile of paper resting on the right arm of the chair. "But I need to learn that for tomorrow."

Millie unfurled herself from the chair and stood, pulling him up.

"Then I'll be quick with you," she said, laughing.

When he was standing, he pushed his hands through her hair and curled them around her neck. "I'll make this all up to you, you know that don't you?"

"Oh, you'd better," she agreed.

"I will," he said. Kiss. "Definitely." Kiss. "Just tell me how."

Her body screaming for him, Millie decided that this wasn't the time for pragmatic discussions about future plans and commitment. Or weddings and families. Or anything else that didn't involve one or both of them being naked.

29

"I never want to have sex again," Laney said as she exhaled, and then doubled into a choking fit. "I also now remember why I never took this up. It's a bloody vile habit."

Stretching over to the other end of the sofa, she passed the cigarette back over to Tash and sipped her Prosecco to get rid of the taste.

"I agree on the second, and think you might come to regret the first. It's the only truly enjoyable thing you can do without consuming calories," Tash replied, flicking the cigarette into the ashtray that was balanced on her abdomen, careful not to let burning embers flip over on to her Clash T-shirt. "Why would you want to give that up?"

There was a pause before Laney said quietly, "I'm ovulating next weekend. We were going to try again."

Tash took a long drag on the cigarette, obviously

searching for the right thing to say. Laney knew she'd be wishing Millie were here. Emotional trauma and comfort weren't Tash's department, but at the same time she had enough of a sensitivity chip to realise that she really shouldn't say something crass and glib here. She really, really shouldn't.

"Are you lying there trying to think of something to say that isn't crass and glib?" Laney asked.

"Aaaargh," Tash exclaimed, "it's a sad day when I'm not just crap, but *predictably* crap. I'm sorry, Lanes. You know I love you and I'll do anything for you but I just don't have the skills to make you feel better."

Laney smiled. "You do make me feel better," she told her, moving her legs into a crossed position and pulling her cream jersey cardigan tighter around her.

"Excellent. Even if you're lying. I like to be humoured. So where does he think you are tonight, then?"

Another sip of Prosecco. "Still in Inverness. I told him I would be getting back tomorrow afternoon. He's leaving at seven a.m. to catch the shuttle down to Manchester. I can't face seeing him, Tash. I just don't trust myself not to go into full scale meltdown."

Tash pushed herself up on one elbow, looking serious. Laney instinctively knew what was coming.

"I'm only going to ask once and I promise that I have no feelings either way – but are you really sure you want to do the whole New York thing?"

"You've no idea how many times I've thought this through," Laney told her, "but I'm sure. I need to see it with my own eyes, but most of all, I need to know what he'll say when she presents him with the whole fait accompli."

"Thank God, because I'm packed already and there's a brilliant sale on at Macy's next week. I checked. Does that make me a bad person?"

"Absolutely."

"Sorry. But I'll be a bad person that buys you something wonderful at forty per cent discount to make up for my failings."

Their laughter was only interrupted by a thud from the other side of the wall. 'What's that?" Laney asked.

"A signal. It means Sy is home and he's checking if I'm in and alone. If so, I bang the wall and he appears at the door within ten minutes. Usually topless. It's a system. I'm trying to wean him off it, though."

"He's too keen?"

Tash nodded. "Getting that way. I don't understand why guys just can't keep it casual and non-committal. What's wrong with them?"

"I think you might find that other women have the opposite experience."

Tash agreed. "Maybe. But that's the thing – I know that in most cases, it's the thrill of the chase. It drives guys nuts because they become so sure that I'll give in eventually, when they really don't understand that I truly do not want to have a relationship. I'm not just doing it to be the ultimate tease."

Laney registered that her left thigh was going numb and unfurled her legs. This morning's swimming had left her with a dull ache from the waist down.

"Anyway, enough about my relationship-avoiding woes. I'd rather talk about your sad life."

"Thanks," Laney retorted with a bow.

"You're welcome. So. Have you started wondering where he is tonight and having thoughts of staking out your place in case Miss Perky Tits shows up?"

"Since the minute we arrived home. But I really don't think he'd let her go to our home. It has me all over it."

"So you think he might be at her place?"

"I have no idea and I don't want to know."

Tash thought about that for a moment, before saying, "Are you lying?"

"Absolutely."

Tash jumped up and a pulled a cardigan from the back of the sofa. "Then let's go."

"Are you sure?"

"Definitely. I've only had half a glass of wine so I'm still fine to drive."

Two minutes later they were out the door and on the way to the lift. Tash banged Sy's door as they passed it and then kept on walking. By the time he answered, looked right and then left, they were already in the lift and the doors had begun to close. Tash waved and he shook his head, laughing.

"I thought you said you were cooling that one off," Laney reminded her, one eyebrow an arch of cynicism.

"I know, but sometimes I can't help myself."

Even at the last hour on a Sunday night, the city streets were still busy with revellers falling out of pubs, packs of girls walking along the streets in bare feet, clutching their stilettos as they linked arms with their pals and sang along the way.

"God, I miss that," Tash announced.

"You still do it," Laney corrected her.

"I'll ignore that. So where are we going first? Your

house or Perky Tits?"

"Hang on." Laney pulled out her phone and texted him. "Hi darling, just wanted to say goodnight."

The reply was immediate.

"Goodnight babe. Miss you. Will call you from Manchester tomorrow. Hope the proposal went well today."

She turned to Tash. "He replied immediately, so he's either texting me in front of her and pretending I'm someone else, or he's at home alone."

"That doesn't really help me in my route planning responsibilities here.'

"OK, her flat first."

Tash screeched round a ninety-degree corner like something out of *The Fast and the Furious*. If this street was covered by CCTV, a visit from the local constabulary would be imminent.

Ten minutes later, they pulled into a space outside the all-night café, facing over on to Cara's flat. In synchronicity, their eyes went up and across, and they both shook their heads when they spotted the darkness within. "No one there. Or they're already in bed," Laney decided.

"Yep, so what next? Your house?"

Laney paused. Did she really want to go there? Was she not just taking this to ridiculous levels, staking out her own house? This was stupid. Crazy. Totally irrational.

"Yes," she decided.

"Hang on." Tash bolted out of the car and straight into the café, returning five minutes later with two steaming cappuccinos and two ginormous blueberry muffins.

"I love you," she told Laney, "but I can't do this without food."

They drank as they headed along the Expressway, then onto Crow Road, up to Anniesland Cross and on to the Switchback, which took them almost directly to Laney's house. Out in the suburbs, the streets were almost deserted. The occasional dog walker. A few guys in tracksuits, grouped outside a chip shop, swigging from bottles and cans.

In Laney's street the only movement was their car as it crawled along, heeding the twenty miles an hour speed limit, thanks to the speed bumps that were placed every fifty metres. Tash spilt her coffee and cursed when they thudded over the first one.

They stopped outside her neighbour's house, the uncontrollable Leylandii at the front providing perfect cover for a military operation. Or two chicks in a Suzuki Jeep clutching blueberry muffins.

"What now?" Tash asked.

"I don't know. I hadn't thought this far ahead."

"Wow. First time ever."

Tash was right. Every moment of Laney's life had been planned, thought through and strategised. Unfortunately, those skills seemed to have been rendered redundant in the face of extenuating circumstances – i.e. a faithless dick.

"I'm going for a look," Tash announced, opening the car door.

Laney grabbed her arm. "Wait, I'm coming too."

The both climbed out and crept along the front of the ridiculously large hedge. Laney made a mental note to stop badgering her neighbour to get it cut.

At the end of her driveway she scanned the windows. All in darkness, but there was a faint glow in the bottom left one, the lounge, which meant that there was probably a light on in the kitchen behind it.

"Do you have security lights?" Tash checked.

Laney shook her head. "No."

"That's your Christmas present taken care of then. Right, come on."

Praying that none of her neighbours happened to be looking out of their windows at midnight on a Sunday night, she followed Tash, half running, half creeping up the side of the house.

They were midway along when Laney realised they were right – there was definitely a light on in the kitchen.

Underneath the side window they stopped, and Laney grabbed Tash's arm and pulled her downwards so she could whisper in her ear. "Right, here's the plan ..."

"Knew it wouldn't take long for you to revert to type."

Laney ignored the jibe.

"If he spots us, I'll just say I came home early and forgot my keys."

"Good plan. So what next?"

"Climb up and look in the window," Laney told her.

"Me? You do it!"

"You're taller."

"It's your husband."

"I'm emotionally devastated."

"Fuck." In the darkness, Laney could still see Tash's eyes roll as she realised she was beaten.

There was a bench under the window and Tash used that to get the height she required to see in over the row of flowers Laney had put along the windowsill.

Slowly, like a praying mantis, Tash stretched up until Laney could see that her eyes cleared the obstacles to achieve a full scan of the room. After staring inside for a few seconds, she crouched back down again.

"Well?" Laney asked, her stomach swirling so much she felt sick.

"He's at the breakfast bar, alone."

Relief. Oh, thank God.

Tash wasn't finished though.

"He's got his laptop open. And Laney, I can't get a proper look at it because it's too far away, but from what I could see, he's watching porn."

Laney closed her eyes and let her head fall back against the wall behind her. That didn't sound right. Porn had never been Cam's thing. But then, as far as she knew, affairs with blonde perky stylists hadn't been his thing, either.

A thought, a glance at her watch, a gut-twisting revelation.

"It's midnight," she said, her voice thick with pain. "I don't think it's porn, Tash. I think it's Skype."

30

It was one of those nights where Tash really didn't feel like going out, but knew that once she got there she'd enjoy it. Monday was her regular jaunt with Jordan and John to the watering hole of their choice, usually in the West End, usually in whatever bar had a promotion on lager or shots.

Tonight they were back on Byres Road, this time in Crimson, a new bar that already had a reputation for cheap drinks and raucous behaviour.

Tash had dressed down – skinny jeans, boots, and a black T-shirt, thick leather belt with a steel buckle. It wasn't exactly slobbing around, but it was as close as she got.

Jordan and John spotted her over the heads of the other people in the pub and beckoned her, giving a round of applause as she approached.

"God, I really need to get other social life options," she

told them when she reached them, compelling John to lift her up, kiss her on both cheeks and then return her to solid ground.

"I absolutely understand why neither of you two has a girlfriend," she muttered. Actually, that was only partially true. On the one hand, they were definitely a catch. Even now, in jeans and rugby shirts (non-matching – they'd stopped that when they were twelve), they were definitely seriously attractive. But while they didn't quite share her opposition to relationships, the combination of a heavy training schedule and the love of a social life with their mates left them pretty averse to tying themselves down to one relationship.

It was a good life strategy – although it did get monotonous when Tash repeated the condom conversation every time they went off with someone new.

She was swapping frivolities for vodka cocktails when she felt the arrival of a new presence.

"Hey, how's things?" she said, turning to the newcomer. "I owe you a thanks for looking out for Laney the other night. She said she was a wreck and you were great, so thank you."

Matt grinned and Tash couldn't help but mirror the smile. He was cute. Definitely cute.

"No problem. She's great. The husband sounds like a prick though."

"Good analysis," Tash confirmed.

Yes, he was cute. It would be the easiest thing in the world to flirt a little here, maybe a snog, then take him home for a night of wanton lust. She was almost going to go down that road when she remembered Laney had told her she'd enlisted Matt's services to help her during the split. That meant he'd be around. Maybe even at the office. So if the sex wasn't great, or she didn't want to see him again for any other reason, he'd still pop up in her day-to day-life.

That put him in the "to be avoided" category.

Anyway, she had a heavy week this week. Starting it off with an all-night session of wanton bendiness probably wasn't the best idea. Pace. Stealth. Energy conservation. That's what she needed this week. Especially if she was going to require her optimum strength to punch Cam Cochrane in the face at the end of it.

Lifting her drink, she took a sip through an orange bendy straw. God, she hated those. What age was she? Eight?

"Well, listen, thanks again anyway. You're getting to be a regular superhero – taking drunk women home and swooping to the rescue of damsels in distress."

He laughed, a little bashful, and she remembered the other reason he didn't put her hormones on high alert – he was way, *way* too nice.

Where was the challenge? The danger?

Talking of which …

Behind Matt, she spotted a former hand-to-hand combatant approaching.

Shay Dixon, businessman, bar owner, man about town, hot, funny and a dead ringer for Daniel Craig, circa blue shorts emerging from the ocean phase. He was also an unreliable nightmare if you happened to be going out with him. Thankfully, Tash had never done that. She had, however, had several nights of glorious passion with him last year before he hooked up with a former WAG and went off the market.

"Shay Dixon. Long time no see. I thought you were in jail." She teased him, taking in the sharp suit, his navy shirt left open at the neck, the short styled hair and the brilliant white smile. Almost certainly veneers, but even up close – very, very close – she'd never been able to establish that for certain.

"I probably should be," he joked. "Right next to you. I'm guessing your lot had something to do with that stunt at Loch Ness yesterday?"

Tash laughed and said, "Absolutely not," in a voice that made it fairly obvious the opposite was true. That was still a slightly dodgy subject. The night before they'd been on the road, having a lovely dinner on the shores of Loch Lomond, when the TV news bulletin ran, carrying the story of a proposal that had sparked 161 calls to police and media websites reporting a sighting of Nessie. Thankfully, someone on the shore had captured the whole thing on a shaky video camera, so it was clear that it was in fact a stunt, and not the first modern day, full Technicolor sighting of a Scottish legend.

The daily papers had all run the story today, too, accompanied by pictures that were thankfully too grainy to identify Stewart and Elma's faces, but reporting that it had been a marriage proposal stunt and speculating as to the elaborate set up. Each report came with the tag line that police would like to speak to the drivers of a transit van seen departing the area; however, they were still looking at whether or not a crime had actually been committed as there had been no official complaints. There had been a few fishing phone calls to their office from the press, but they'd gone unreturned.

Hopefully it would all blow over and be forgotten by the middle of the week. Or at least until a twenty foot long Nessie popped up in a garden in Thurso. Or until police confirmed that there would definitely be no charges pressed, in which case they could load the top class footage taken by Mrs Crean on to their website and milk it for as much publicity as possible.

"Then – purely hypothetically – if it was your lot, it was a cracking idea."

"One you'll consider when you marry your lovely girlfriend."

Shay shook his head. "Ah, I'm afraid you're behind the times. Ex-girlfriend. We broke up a couple of months ago."

"Oh no! And it had so much potential. I thought as soon as you got those matching tattoos that you were mated for life."

He took the ribbing in good spirits, aware that half of Glasgow had seen the photos his semi-famous girlfriend had plastered all over Facebook, Instagram and Twitter of the heart containing their entwined initials etched on her right breast.

"I have no idea why I like you," he laughed, "no idea at all."

Tash shrugged. "Me neither. Anyway, what brings you in here? Not a little down-market for you?"

"I own it," he said, not boastfully, just matter of fact, although in an impressive spot of timing, a barmaid appeared at his side and handed him a clear drink. Tash knew it would be tonic water. Shay never drank alcohol. Said that when you were in the bar trade there was too much temptation to make it a normal part of your life, so he abstained. Tash liked that kind of discipline, but refused to share it.

"What about you – what brings you here?"

"Neanderthal brothers who will go anywhere that has cheap drink and videos of Beyoncé on the TVs," she said, gesturing to the flat screen on the wall on which Beyoncé was demonstrating her flexibility in unfeasibly skimpy outerwear.

"Ah, I remember them," he said, raising his glass to Jordan and John, who eyed him with blatant suspicion. They'd never liked him – too suave and smooth for their taste.

"I see they're friendly as ever," he remarked, utterly unfazed by their disapproval.

They both recognised the moment – when they decided either to make a night of it or not. Tash was undecided. What had she been thinking earlier about conserving her energy, pacing herself? On the other hand, he was looking mighty fine and many years of casual acquaintance had given her ample proof that he was as sharp as his suit in bed.

"I'm going to head off and get dinner," he informed her. Good, he'd made the decision. He had other plans. Was moving on. "Fancy joining me?"

Bugger.

To do or not to do …

The "no thanks" was almost out – almost – when her inner hedonist took over. "Sure. But only because I'm concerned for your safety. If you stay here much longer talking to me my brothers will start growling and it'll all get messy."

With a beaming smile, she gestured to Jordan and John that she was heading off. They didn't return her enthusiasm. The phone call in the morning would be frosty and contain at least one reprimand – going one way, from them to her. Sometimes, it was difficult to tell which of the siblings was supposed to be in possession of good judgement born of extra years of wisdom and experience.

In the car, Tash chose the destination and he didn't object. Park Circus. The nineteenth century crescent of townhouses that formed the boundary between the city and the West End, beautiful sandstone buildings, many of which had been converted into offices over the years, but now reclaimed and returned to their former level of luxury housing.

His home was just as she remembered it from her last visit, maybe two years before. Back then it had been newly decorated in muted greys and creams, the entrance hallway and sweeping staircase adding enough drama without elaborate wallpaper or ostentatious chandeliers.

"No feminine touches?" she asked him, surprised, as they made their way from the hall, through the lounge and into the black and white gloss kitchen. Gleaming units, marble worktops, top end appliances.

"All removed when she went screeching off to live happily ever after with a Wigan player. The sheen of my lifestyle soon wore off. Said she didn't want a life with someone who worked nights instead of gracing the city's highspots with their presence. I didn't object."

Tash could see the issue. "I can see her point," she acknowledged, opening the huge Smeg double fridge-freezer and staring at the contents – or lack thereof.

"There is absolutely nothing to eat in here," she declared disapprovingly.

"There is," he said, coming up behind her. "There's fruit. And, er, fruit. And some butter. And more fruit. I think there might be a stick of celery in the box at the bottom."

It jogged a memory. He had his food sent in daily, already prepared, by one of those meal delivery companies.

"There are take-away menus in the top drawer there."

His hands rested on the sides of her hips, as a very light kiss on the nape of her neck sent shock waves ricocheting to all the right areas. Oh, this felt good. The familiarity of him, the smell and ...

She pulled off her T-shirt and let him unhook her bra, leaving a trail of kisses from one shoulder blade to another, before she turned to him.

... the taste. He tasted so, so good.

His jacket already discarded, Tash deftly, flicked open the buttons of his shirt and pushed it off before he picked her up and groaned with pleasure as her legs went around his waist.

He turned and she knew he was headed for the door, and to the bedroom on the first floor. Tash decided she didn't want to wait that long.

"There. Right there," she told him, motioning to the long, gleaming black glass table that filled the cavernous space at the other side of the granite kitchen island.

It seated sixteen. Tash just needed it to have horizontal space for one.

Understanding what she wanted, he placed her down on it, and watched as she curled up to her feet and removed her jeans and boots. To her left, a window, too high for passers-by on the street below to see in, but wide enough to give a glistening view of the lights of Glasgow below.

He caught up with her, shedding his clothes, happy to let her take the lead and call the shots. She knelt down on the table top, waited for him to come to her, gasped when he did.

"I've no idea if this table will take our weight," he said, as he climbed on board.

She liked that – meant he hadn't had sex on here before. It was always good to be first.

"Well, let's test that then, shall we?"

They did. Twice. And should the manufacturers ever have cause to ask, yes, it did match up to the customer's needs.

As they sat in bed much later, eating Thai food from cartons with chopsticks, she felt that blissful ache from her head to her toes, the one that stopped on the way and checked in at her thighs, her hips, her shoulders.

"Why did we stop doing this?" he asked.

"Because you went for the pretty girl with the penchant for sentimental yet trashy tattoos," Tash replied.

Shay playfully poked her on the naked thigh with a chopstick. "I seem to remember that only happened after you point blank refused to do anything more than treat me as your occasional plaything," he teased. "The scar on my ego may never heal."

"Super glue. The rest of my exes tell me that works," she told him, punctuating the sentence with a kiss.

"Stay the night," he asked. "I know it's not in your

usual terms and conditions, but just tonight."

Tash liked him. Liked the way he gently mocked her. The way he said the right things. His humour. His charm.

"No. I'm sorry. I could give you lots of reasons, some of them true. I need to get up early for work in the morning. I've got a lot on this week. I'm allergic to jacquard duvet covers …"

"Are you?" he asked, eyes immediately darting downwards to the silver and black Paisley pattern jacquard on which they sat.

"No," she answered. "That was one of the ones that wasn't true."

His hearty laughter pre-empted another prod with the chopstick.

They finished dinner, made love again, this time on the non-allergenic duvet,

before Tash headed into his spectacular black marble en-suite for a quick shower.

When she came out, a thick, white towel wrapped around her, he eyed her with a mock sad face.

"You're going to go now, aren't you?"

"Yes," Tash said, giggling at his expression.

"I can't persuade you to stay?"

"No."

"So I'll see you again?"

It was a question, not a statement.

"Sometime," she said, leaning over to kiss him. "My clothes are in the kitchen so by the time I retrieve them the taxi will be here."

He swung his legs around and slid off the bed, grabbing a robe from the overstuffed chair in the corner before following her downstairs. Her timings were correct. She'd just pulled on the second boot when a buzzer told them the taxi was waiting outside.

Tash stretched up to kiss him, and then headed out the door with a wave behind her.

In the taxi, she sighed.

It had been her perfect kind of night. Good food, great company, incredible sex.

Why then, she wondered as the taxi cut through the deserted streets of the city, did she feel nothing at all?

31

"Are we ready? Are you sure we're ready?" Millie mumbled to no one in particular, which was just as well because Tash was attempting to ignore her and Laney was on her computer over at the other side of the office, concentrating on paying bills. It was the distraction she needed to take her mind off the next couple of days.

"Maybe we need a signal we can use if we can see it's all going wrong or it's too stressful and we want to close it down. A code word! We need a code word. What can it be? How about … about …"

"Chill!" Tash said, lounging back, crossing one skinny-jean-clad leg over the other.

"Nope, too simple," she replied.

"It wasn't a suggestion, it was an order," Tash countered. "Millie, you're more strung out than Laney and it's not helping."

At the mention of her name, Laney finally looked up

from her computer, having been blissfully unaware that Millie's chatter had been aimed in her direction. "What isn't helping?"

Tash sighed. "Millie, being so bloody frantic. Apparently we need a code word, so that if you get too stressed out you can utter it."

"And what will happen?" Laney asked, intrigued.

Tash already had the answer. "An armed response unit will storm the building, but they'll be too late because Tom Cruise will have already come crashing feet first through the window clutching a rope that's suspended from the roof," she told them, deadpan.

"In that case I might try it," Laney said. "Would be worth it for the entertainment value."

Laney recognised that they were all acting absolutely to type this morning. Millie was fretting because someone she loved was about to face a painful situation, Tash was trying to wisecrack her way out of it, and Laney was maintaining an absolutely cool veneer, concentrating on tasks, details and strategies.

Inside however, she only had one plan: get through the next hour without cracking. She had nothing to prove. Nothing to compete with. Yet she was wearing a beautifully cut, pale cream wrap dress that made her look and feel great. At least on the outside.

It had been her idea to bring Cara in for a pre-proposal meeting. She still wasn't sure why, other than a tiny, unfathomable, desperate hope that she would say something that would make them all realise that this whole thing had been a huge misunderstanding.

When the buzzer rang, Millie simultaneously jumped and yelped.

Tash ignored her. "It's Tom Cruise. He decided to save on repair costs and use the door."

Despite her determination to stay cool and calm, Laney handled the phone like it had the stability of high-grade plutonium.

"I'll go get her," Tash offered, already out of her chair and heading for the lift.

Laney let her go and moved to the edge of one of the sofas. If she was already sitting down it eradicated the possibility of her legs collapsing.

Too soon, Tash was back, with Cara teetering behind her. The new arrival's appearance was every bit as impressive as it had been the first time around.

The blonde locks were pulled back into a high ponytail that fell down her back in a slick, straight line. On her banging body a dress this time, skin tight, round neck, grey, reached down almost to the ankles and looked decidedly like a Victoria Beckham one she'd seen Jennifer Lopez wear on the cover of one of the celebrity mags. Or was it Gwyneth Paltrow? Or Madonna? Focus, Laney, focus.

A black tailored jacket and high gladiator shoes accessorised the look to perfection. Laney hated her just a little bit more.

Hang on, this wasn't fair. Cara wasn't the one in the wrong here. She'd been betrayed as much as Laney and she had no idea what was really going on. The thought transformed her emotions immediately, and she stepped back from the ledge of fury into the land of understanding and concern.

"How are you?" she asked Cara, motioning for her to sit down at the other end of the same plump sofa, only the glass coffee table separating them from Millie and Tash.

Actually, Laney realised, she had no need to ask the question. She could see how Cara was. The knot of tension on her forehead, the slight dart of her eyes, the anxiety in her mouth – all characteristics mirrored by almost all of her clients in the days before the proposal.

The planning stage was done, the reality dawned, the moment of truth drew closer – and the clients suddenly took stage fright and started to panic. It was textbook.

"I'm great!" Cara lied. "Totally, like, buzzed for the weekend."

"And you've gone through all the updates that I've been emailing over? You're happy with the details?"

"Yeah, it's all so exactly as I pictured it," Cara confirmed, her pale blue nails tapping on her thigh as she spoke.

Wow, she was definitely getting nervous. For a moment, Laney doubted her plan. One of the many niggling doubts she'd been struggling with since day one of this debacle bubbled to the surface again. Was she being heartless, letting this play out at Cara's expense? To an extent, she probably was, but not because she wanted to hurt the girl sitting in front of her. She still felt that Cara deserved to know the truth – the whole truth – too. And if she was going out with a guy who would promise to marry her while he was still married to someone else, that was a fairly significant nugget of information that Cara should be aware of.

Besides, another thought had occurred to her. What if Cam was actually in love with Cara and genuinely did want to marry her? What if he just hadn't told Laney that he was leaving her yet, but already had that on his To Do list?

The skin under her arms started to heat to a temperature that could possibly defy the lashings of antiperspirant she'd applied that morning.

The others kept quiet and let Laney take the lead, a consideration she knew must be killing Tash. Millie, meanwhile, looked like she was about to burst into tears.

"Do you think he has any idea? Does he have any suspicions that you're planning to do this?" Laney asked, the forced levity in her voice making it come out a few notes higher than normal. Shit, this was so hard. These were all questions she would normally ask, yet in this case each word was like a sucker punch to the gut.

Cara shook her head, making the sleek ponytail wobble. Laney was transfixed by her perfect pink mouth, immaculately outlined and filled with gloss that gave her the kind of pout normally seen in cosmetic ads. Did Cam kiss that mouth? Did he run his fingers along those tanned cheekbones, gaze into those huge blue eyes framed with sweeping lashes? For a second, Laney wondered what Cara would look like without the hair extensions, the false eyelashes and the make-up. Still beautiful, undoubtedly.

"Not at all! He works away so much, and I've been, like, so busy over the last couple of weeks that I've barely seen him. At least in person," she added with a suggestive giggle. Too much. Way too much. Laney experienced a visceral reaction to the boast and suddenly it took every ounce of strength she had not to blow it all wide open there and then. In fact, she should. Enough. Time to end this charade. Her glance went to Millie and

Tash and she knew them so well she could see exactly how they were reacting. Millie felt the same as her, desperate for this to be done, and Tash looked like she was about to explode.

"Cara …" Laney began. How to tell her? What words should she use? This wasn't an occasion she could ever have prepared for, not one she'd ever encountered, but she knew, just knew that she had to come clean.

However Cara hadn't paused for breath and was now working up to full flow on the wonders of her relationship with her future fiancé.

"The thing about my Cam is that it doesn't matter. Even if we, like, don't see each other for a week, we've still got that … *connection*. He says that's what makes us special. You know, because we don't spend every minute together. We totally make it our priority to see each other. Do you know what he did last week?"

Nope, Laney didn't know. She absolutely had no idea what Cam Cochrane did last week.

Cara was doing that "welling up, fanning the face with her fingers" thing again.

"He flew all the way to Marbella to see me for just one night. One night."

Fan, fan, fan.

"Oh, I don't know why I'm getting so emotional – must be all the excitement of next weekend. He always says I'm the softest, sweetest woman he's ever met. He's always telling me I'm beautiful on the outside and inside too. Says I'm perfect," she finished, trailing off wistfully, her hands now going faster than a wind turbine in a hurricane.

Silence. Utter silence. Laney had no words at all, and

even if she did, her brain had exploded so she'd have no idea how to put them in the right order. Her jaw was clenched shut. Her throat closed. Her whole body trembling from top to toe.

Tash jumped to her feet. "Laney, are you OK, darling?" She turned to Cara. "The flu," she explained. "We told her not to come in today, but would she listen? Of course not. Dedicated. Committed."

Laney knew that right here, right now, was her only chance to explain and call the proposal off. That's exactly what she had to do.

Tash handed her the mug of tea that had gone cold on the table in front of her, using the moment of contact to peer at her searchingly, trying to guess what Laney wanted the next move to be.

In an instant, Laney decided.

"Thanks, Tash," she said, taking the tea gratefully. "Don't know what came over me there – I felt a bit faint." She wiped the dampness off her forehead with the back of her hand and pulled it together. "That's so lovely, Cara. He sounds like quite a guy."

"Oh, he is. I'm so, so like, lucky. I've known it since the moment we met."

"How *did* you meet?" The injection of Millie's voice into the conversation for the first time made them all turn to look at her.

Cara grinned widely, eyes glistening. "Well it was the funniest thing."

"I doubt that," Laney said – but fortunately not out loud.

"We were both at in the VIP lounge at Rome airport. I'd been doing a shoot there and he was at some meeting

or other. The flight was delayed for twelve hours.
Remember that ash cloud from Sweden, or somewhere?"

"Iceland," Laney corrected.

"Yeah, well, wherever it came from it was the best
thing that ever happened to us."

Laney's mouth went dry as she scoured her memory
for a reference point that would remind her of the date
that happened. She'd yet to set up the company, she was
still in pharmaceuticals, there had been a sales
conference in Paris and she'd just got home in time
before they grounded all the flights in and out of the UK.
Cam hadn't been so lucky. He'd ended up stranded in …

"So we ended up stranded together in Rome and …"

For four days, Laney remembered. He stayed at the
airport hotel at first …

"Well, when we got chatting at the bar we just clicked,
so we ended up staying that night in an airport hotel and
then …"

The city. Cam had gone into the city and stayed at …

"So we moved to the Hotel …"

Raphael. The same hotel Laney and Cam had visited
on their honeymoon. Please don't say it. Please don't.

"… Raphael, and had the most incredible few days.
And the weird thing was, although we'd only just met it
all felt so familiar. Like it was, totally, meant to be."

Laney was still stuck back at the Hotel Raphael. He'd
taken Cara there. To their hotel. To one of the few places
in this world that held special meaning for them. If Cam
Cochrane had walked in that door right now she would
quite happily have killed him.

But wait. She'd studied Cara's information
questionnaire – hadn't she said they'd only been together

for two years? The ash cloud was in 2010. So, what …
was she making this all up? Was this a vile trick? A
deranged woman?

Cara was still in full flow. "But Cam was, like in a
relationship at that time and he felt torn. That's my Cam.
Such a huge heart. So we went back to our lives and
didn't see each other until … You'll never guess what
happened!"

Tash was the only one, other than Cara, who still had
the power of speech. "You're right. We'll never guess,"
she said dryly.

Cara didn't detect the negativity. "We met again in an
airport! Two years ago. Gatwick. Oh, it was magical.
There he was, in Mulberry, buying a bag for his sister
…"

Laney's eyes went to the Mulberry Mitzy tote that was
sitting at the side of her desk.

"… and our eyes met and that was it."

"Aaaaw, that's so lovely," Tash told her. "And the
relationship he'd been in when you first met?"

Cara waved her hand dismissively. "Oh that was all
well over. He said she was a boring cow anyway."

Laney spat her tea out.

"Sorry," she stuttered. "Went down the wrong way. I'll
just … I'll just …"

"Get a cloth!" Millie exclaimed. "Right, I'll help you
look for one."

She grabbed Laney's hand as she was passing, pulled
her to her feet and they headed towards the kitchen,
stopping just inside the door when she heard Tash say,
"Lovely story. But listen, can I just check with you – are
you absolutely sure you want to go ahead with this?"

"Why wouldn't I?" Cara exclaimed, her offence clear.

Tash back-pedalled. "No reason at all – it's just something we ask all our clients the week before the big day. We just want to make sure you don't have any reservations at all?"

Cara shook her head. "Not, like, a single one. Cam and I are meant to be together. And I can't wait until he's officially mine. Cara Cochrane. It's got a ring to it, hasn't it?"

In the kitchen Laney slid down the wall and didn't stop until she reached the floor. No tears. They were way past that now. Instead a weird numbness descended.

It definitely had a ring to it.

And Laney needed to see the moment when her husband slipped it on to the third finger of his girlfriend's left hand.

32

Millie had tried to work the rest of the day, she really had. Aside from the flash mob in Queen Street station, there were two proposals on the board for the following month, both awaiting lightning bolt concepts that would create life-defining, priceless moments. But somehow, conjuring up romantic ideals was a tad challenging when your best friend's heart had just been ripped out and battered to death by the love of her life's girlfriend.

Every time Millie envisaged the distraught expression on Laney's face that morning she felt physically sick. Hate had never been a familiar emotion to her, but right now she really hated Cam Cochrane. If he was guilty, that was. There was still a tiny part of Millie that thought it was so horrific, it had to be a huge misunderstanding.

Had to be. She just hoped they sussed it out soon because in two days' time they'd be boarding a plane bound for New York that could very well be a one-way ticket to divorce.

Oh God. The D word. The very thought of it made her shudder.

Infidelity. That was another word that made her tremble.

After Cara had left, thrilled to pieces with every detail of her forthcoming event and still wittering about how great Cam was, Laney had been stoic as ever. Or at least, she had been after two large glasses of wine and a scream that threatened to shatter the office windows.

Millie still thought there were all insane to go through with this, but she was doing it anyway. There was no way she'd leave Laney to face this with only Tash for support. That would be like going into a peaceful protest with a cruise missile.

She turned the Beetle on to Pollokshaws Road and made her way along, stopping at the lights opposite Guy's travel shop. Sitting on the opposite side of the road from where she'd crashed, the memory did make her fleetingly wonder if the pros of meeting Guy outweighed the cons. She was now driving a totally revamped car. The company had secured an ongoing discount arrangement that would benefit their bottom line. And he was a lovely guy who she was sure would remain a friend.

For the sake of a minor facial injury and a couple of weeks of inconvenience, it was worth it.

Late afternoon traffic was nose to tail so it took another half an hour before she turned into her street. It was almost deserted, as always. Most of the houses had large grounds around them, so although they'd been converted into three or four flats, there was enough room to park several cars off road.

It was just as well because the roads were all double yellow lines around here and the traffic wardens were lethal.

That was what made her notice it – the one car, stopped about fifty metres past the gates to her drive, on the other side of the street.

Red. Nondescript. Maybe a Ford Focus or an Astra? Millie knew nothing about cars and cared even less – except for a rather dashing, gleaming Beetle.

OK, red car. Someone inside. Probably just a mum on the school run stopping to take a phone call. Or a rep updating their paperwork.

She was almost at her drive now and as she glanced over, she could see neither of those scenarios was accurate.

There was a woman in the car, but no child, so that ruled out the mum theory. And the driver wasn't head down, buried in paperwork, but looking out of the window.

Blonde hair, escaping from a baseball cap. Huge, over-sized sunglasses. That was it. As far as she got.

Except for one other small detail.

The driver's sightline was fixed on Millie, and when she approached, indicated left and then turned her car into her driveway, she noticed that the woman's gaze followed her every step of the way.

Who was she? Why was she sitting there?

Millie felt the familiar itch of anxiety and then immediately shrugged it off. Obviously the woman would watch what Millie was doing, because there was absolutely nothing else to do in a deserted street.

A niggle. There was something vaguely familiar about her, but Millie had absolutely no recollection why.

Closing the car door behind her, she was tempted to walk back down the drive, and look to see if the woman was still there. She'd never been prone to paranoia, but there was definitely some curiosity there. Before she even reached the gate, the noise of an engine told her the car was on the move. At the pavement, she realised she was right, when it drove straight past her.

That should have been it. Story over. Nothing to tell.

But why, as it drove past her, were the driver's oversized sunglasses focused on Millie's gate?

33

So what exactly did one wear to one's husband's proposal?

Laney scanned the row of clothes hanging in the wardrobe in front of her and didn't know where to start. They'd be in New York for three days – unless of course it all went horribly wrong and they ended up detained there for the foreseeable future. However, if that was the case, she was fairly certain that the New York State penitentiary had its own dress code. Natty orange jumpsuits could be the way forward.

Jeans, a couple of T-shirts and her trusty Converse were already in the suitcase, next to toiletries, underwear and pyjamas. The three of them would be sharing a triple room in a small but gorgeous boutique hotel in the Upper East Side – within walking distance of both the Met and the Carlyle. It was good of Cara to pick easy, convenient locations in which to destroy Laney's life.

Always a bonus.

A pair of tailored black Capri trousers, a black polo neck and flat patent shoes went into the case next – very Audrey Hepburn and perfect for the unpredictable weather that came with April in New York.

One dress, a Next crepe shift in burnt copper that looked far more expensive than it actually had been. Everything in Laney's wardrobe was understated, neat, with straight lines and no fuss. *Exactly like me*, she mused. And the opposite of Cara.

Was that the problem? Had Cam grown bored of her? Did he need someone more exciting, someone that came with a side order of over the top glamour and a show stopping presence?

That had never been their dynamic. He was the larger than life half, the socialiser, the live-for-today kinda guy and she was the solid, steady one that took care of all the groundwork so that he could have complete freedom to do and have anything he wanted. She just hadn't realised that extended to a replacement model in the partner department.

Meeting Cara, and the wave of sympathy that had evoked, had propelled her to make a decision – she wasn't going to reveal the truth to her on the night of the proposal. She, Tash and Millie would watch from a distance, then – no matter which way it went – they would retreat and fly home the next day. It was enough to see it – she didn't need to cause a huge scene that would just make it more painful for everyone. Patience. Stealth. Let them have their moment. Then fly home, change the locks and decide what to do next.

Actually, there was no decision to make. If it was true,

they were over.

If. No ifs. Ifs were for the hopelessly optimistic and the deluded.

Laney was neither.

The ring of the doorbell broke into her thoughts. A charity collector, probably. Perhaps the kids from the local scouts selling macaroon bars and home baking. The last time they'd stung her for a fiver and she'd told them she'd have a job for them in sales when they were adults.

Feet bare, she padded downstairs, hoping it was no one she wanted to impress, as she had on her oldest grey yoga pants and a baggy pink T-shirt that belonged in an eighties pop video.

The caller had just followed up the ring of the bell with three loud thumps on the door when Laney opened it with one finger on the panic alarm on the wall to her left. Cam had had it installed because he was away so much and worried that an intruder might hurt her. Oh the irony.

"Tash!"

"Correct. You'll do a great job in a police ID parade. Just thought I'd drop by and see how you're doing," Tash informed her, already propelling herself inside. "I brought dinner."

Laney laughed as she checked out the produce in Tash's arms.

"Honey, two bottles of wine and a large bag of Doritos do not constitute dinner."

Tash looked offended. "They absolutely do! Throw in a couple of cigarettes for dessert and you've got a three course meal."

Laney was still smiling as she reached the kitchen, surprising herself. Her heart was broken, rage consumed her, yet Tash still made her laugh.

Tash pulled a stool out from under the breakfast bar as Laney retrieved a couple of wine glasses and a corkscrew from the chrome drying rack on the sink.

"I'm going to have to detox my liver after this month," Laney said, popping the first cork. "I'm usually a couple of glasses a week chick, and lately it's been a couple of glasses a day. More, sometimes."

"You're right, it has to stop before we have to scoop you out of gutters and drag you in to work."

Tash broke open the Doritos, and then from her satchel bag, produced two large tubs of dip, one sour cream, one salsa

"Don't double dip – it makes me crazy when we end up with salsa in the sour cream." For someone so haphazard, Tash's little foibles were highly amusing. *It's fine to live on nothing but tequila and convenience food, but don't dip your Dorito into more than one substance because that completely freaks me out.*

Laney was tempted to do it just to see her reaction, but she wasn't that brave. Sarcasm would hopefully incur less of a life-limiting backlash.

"Yep, I can see why that would be a tragic event. Have you ever considered you might not have enough to worry about in life if that's what you consider a crisis?"

Tash responded by crunching her nacho as loudly as possible, then swooping up the glass that Laney slid across the breakfast bar.

"So. How's the packing going?"

Laney sighed. "Just about done. As long as I've got

flat shoes for a speedy exit, I'm good to go." It was an admirable attempt at light-heartedness, but she was kidding no one, least of all herself. "How about you? Packing done?"

"Laney, look at me." Tash gestured to her own outfit. Ancient ripped jeans that Laney vaguely remembered her wearing to an Oasis gig at the Barrowlands sometime in the last millennium, and an Enrique Iglesias T-shirt from the era when he had that ballad out that got stuck in your head and wouldn't shift.

"I can be your hero ..." Aaaaaaargh!

"This is the outfit of a woman who has half her clothes in the washing basket and the other half in a suitcase, waiting to go. I'd usually never be seen dead out in this outfit, but it was this or my *South Park* boxer shorts and a T-shirt declaring my love for Iron Maiden." She took a large gulp of wine. "It feels weird, doesn't it? Usually, when I go anywhere I get really excited but this is like setting off for the trip from hell."

Laney understood completely. "I know. I feel sick every time I think about it, yet it doesn't quite seem real. Does that make sense?"

"Not at all," Tash answered cheekily, taking another large sip of wine before placing the glass back down on the granite. A deep exhalation followed and Laney could see that she was working her way up to saying something important. She wasn't wrong. "Laney, call it off. It's crazy. Let's just get on a train or a plane and go to wherever Cam is now and confront him. Don't do this to yourself."

"I have to. I know it's insane, but I have to. Is that why you came over – to talk me out of it?"

Tash shook her head and Laney marvelled at how the black gleaming, chin length bob returned to exactly the same position every time. "No, but – aside from the bonus that this engagement will earn ten grand for our company's bottom line, I just can't see the upside."

"Ten grand isn't enough?" Laney replied teasingly, aware that she was just deflecting the issue.

"Oh, I'll take Cam Cochrane's money any day of the week, but not at your expense."

To her horror, Laney felt a large lump form in her throat. A large sip of wine only partially dislodged it. "I've got this, Tash. I know it's a brutal way of letting it play out, but if I'm going to say goodbye to my marriage, then it has to be unequivocal and it has to hurt so much I could never find a reason to let him stay or take him back."

"Fair enough. But I'd like it on record that I tried to talk you out of it."

"So noted." Laney opened a jar of olives and tipped them into a bowl beside the Doritos. "So anyway," she started, desperate to move on to easier territory. "It's the night before we head to New York. Why are you here and not out stocking up your sexual reserves by doing filthy things to some poor unsuspecting bloke?"

"Ach, just didn't feel like it. Don't know anyone who shares my past love of Enrique Iglesias." Tash's eyes never left the olives during her explanation or the pause that followed it.

"Right, out with it," Laney demanded.

"What?"

"Come on, Tash. You have a free night yet you're here babysitting an emotional wreck instead of hitting the bars and copping off with someone with less than twenty-five per cent body fat. Either you're ill or … or …"

"Or what?"

Laney shrugged, pretending to pause for serious contemplation. "Nope, got nothing else. You must be ill."

"I've no idea why I have to put up with this. I need new friends," Tash said, repeating a mantra she'd been quoting since they were thirteen and Millie and Laney teased her mercilessly about taking to dressing in cargo trousers and singing All Saints songs at the youth club.

"So are you going to tell me?" Laney persisted. "Because you know I'll just keep asking until you do."

"There's nothing. Honestly. I think maybe I'm just … Oh, I don't know … maybe getting a bit bored with the whole one night stand thing."

The shock made Laney freeze, olive halfway to mouth. Only when her motor skills kicked back in did she manage a stunned, "I never thought this day would come. Authorities should be notified."

Tash rolled her eyes, but Laney wasn't letting her off the hook. She topped up both their glasses.

"When, exactly, did you start feeling bored?"

Tash shrugged. "Don't know. I hooked up with Shay Dixon the other night."

"He was on my list," Laney blurted. Must have been the wine. "You know, the hypothetical fantasy list that everyone has if they had to have a last shag before a nuclear apocalypse. He was one of them. Always thought he was gorgeous."

Tash couldn't hide her surprise. "You have a list?"

Laney feigned outrage. "Yep, Miss Boring had a list. I would never have acted on it, but at least I had one."

Tash pointed out the obvious. "You can act on it now."

She had a point. Laney felt a cold rush of blood under her skin. Sex. With someone who wasn't Cam. Other than the list, which included a couple of wealthy entrepreneurs and three Hollywood A-listers, she'd never considered having sex with anyone but Cam for the rest of her life. The thought of someone else touching her made her shudder. That was another one to be filed under the banner of "too painful to consider". Switching the subject back to Tash was so much easier.

"So. Shay Dixon. Did something go wrong? Did something upset you?"

Tash shook her head. "No, it was great. He's funny and smart and the sex was awesome."

"So the problem was …?" Laney prompted, confused.

"I don't know. It just felt odd afterwards. Weird. A bit pointless."

Laney took it all in, considered it from every angle. "Has this happened before?"

"No."

"Are you sure the sex was good."

"Yes."

"Did he say anything to annoy you?"

"No."

"Did he ask you to stay afterwards?"

"Yes."

"You refused?"

"Yes."

"Do you regret it?"

"No."

"And who else have you been with lately?"

"Just Sy next door."

"And did that feel pointless too?"

Laney watched as Tash frowned, clearly trying to revisit a moment in time and come up with a truthful answer. Her expression swept through confusion, to surprise, to incomprehension, before she finally revealed her answer.

"No."

34

Millie finished the last drop of her tea and rinsed out her mug, before putting it on the draining board to dry. She'd bet her worldly goods it would still be there when she got back. Leo had never been a paragon of efficiency in the housework department, and was even less so now that he was working such horrendously long hours.

He'd been filming for the last couple of days, most of which, he revealed, had been spent hanging around, waiting hours to shoot a two minute piece of footage.

Not that he was complaining. Millie had never seen him so happy, so absolutely full of life and enthusiasm. His crisis of confidence seemed to have passed and now he was just so engrossed in it all, leaving the house sometimes before dawn, and usually coming home, exhausted long after dark.

"Hey babe, ready to go?" he asked her, strolling into kitchen in shorts and a T-shirt that was soaked with sweat. The five-mile runs in the morning were a new addition to his regime. Every morning at five thirty he set off, then was back, showered, and away by six thirty a.m. Not that Millie witnessed any part of this exertion as, on normal workdays, her alarm didn't go off until seven thirty.

This morning, however, was far from a normal day.

"What time have you to be at the airport?" he asked her.

"Seven o'clock check in. The taxi should be here any minute and I'm meeting the others there."

He moved towards her and she leant forward, puckering up for a kiss. She adored him, but sitting for seven hours on a flight with the scent of his sweat on her mint green T-shirt was a token of love too far, even for Millie.

"I'll miss you," he murmured, meeting her lips and moving in further. Sod it, she decided, arms snaking around his neck – she could just spray perfume on the way.

"I'll try to call you while I'm away," she told him between kisses.

Leo pulled back, then turned to take a bottle of water out of the fridge.

"Yeah, erm, cool. But I know we've got four long days ahead, so don't worry if you can't get a hold of me. You know, with the time difference and stuff."

"Well, tell you what – you call me when you can. It doesn't matter if it's during the night, New York time. You're worth it," she joked.

"OK, but I know you're busy, too, so don't worry if I don't."

Millie felt a flutter of disappointment, but brushed it away. Had he been less affectionate and attentive since he got this part? Absolutely. But it was only because he was under so much pressure to deliver and was finally on the cusp of his lifelong dream coming true. Anyone in his Adidas running shoes would be exactly the same.

The noise of a taxi crunching over the gravel snapped her back to the present and a sunny smile immediately settled on her lips. She slid her feet into white wedges, a springtime contrast to her deep, bottle green skirt, popped a white floppy hat on her head and grabbed her straw tote.

"I'll miss you babe," she told him, lifting her chin so that she could kiss him without assaulting him with the brim of her hat.

"I'll miss you, too. Here, let me take that." He lifted her suitcase and followed her out. "Are you sure you've got everything? Passport. Tickets. You don't want to have to come tearing back because you've forgotten something."

"It's fine; but I love the fact that you're being so conscientious," she said with another kiss, desperately wanting to just go back inside, go to bed and show him just how conscientious she could be too.

The jaded taxi driver, bags under his eyes after a hard night shift in the city centre, bumped her case into the boot, banged it shut, then jumped back into his seat just as Romeo and Juliet finally parted ways. Seriously, who could be arsed with all that slushy stuff first thing in the morning? He'd been about to clock off when this call came in, but a fare to the airport was too good to pass up. Now he just needed to get her there and get home before rush hour. Which would be helped immensely if these two lovebirds would hurry it up.

Millie banged the door shut and waved as the taxi started down the driveway. She was still waving when they reached the gate and she realised that Leo wasn't standing there any more. Oh well – it was pretty cold out and he'd be dying to get in the shower.

Reluctantly, she turned her mind to the days ahead. No good could come of this, and the thought depressed her. Wasn't this the opposite of what they were supposed to do? They specialised in making dreams come true, in romance and in bringing people together for the rest of their lives. At no point did she ever think they'd be planning an event that was designed to break someone's heart. It was so wrong, and yet – despite begging and pleading – Laney refused to change her mind. That left Millie and Tash with two choices. Refuse to participate, or go along with it under duress. Actually, Tash claimed there were three options but kidnapping Laney and holding her in a padded room while Tash and Millie blew Cam's cover could seriously damage their friendship.

So engrossed in the mental image of that scenario (Cam tied to a chair, forced to confess all, his words taped and then shown to Cara) that she almost missed it.

The traffic as they pulled onto Pollokshaws Road was light, so visibility was good. That's why, as they approached the same spot that she'd crashed at only a few weeks before, she was fairly certain that the car she could see coming towards her on the other side of the road was the one that had been sitting outside her house earlier in the week.

Goosebumps popped up on her forearms as the two cars passed and the blonde in the other vehicle turned the other way, blocking Millie from getting a good look at her face.

Rubbing her arms back to normality, she chided herself.

This whole bloody thing with Laney was making her see suspicion everywhere.

The sooner it was all over, the better.

35

"Ladies and gentlemen, can I have your attention, please?" Laney's stomach flipped and she was grateful that she'd refused the bacon rolls that Tash and Millie had tucked in to in the restaurant before they made their way to the gate. Now, as they sat in uniform rows with the morning sun streaming in the floor to ceiling windows on either side of the concourse, she just wanted to get on that plane and do this.

"It has come to our attention," the nasal ground stewardess continued, "that flight 162 from Glasgow to Newark this morning has unfortunately been over-booked. We politely request that, if your travel is non-essential this morning, you would allow us to transfer you on to an alternative flight."

Tash sat forward in her seat. "This is a sign. An omen. We're not supposed to get on this plane," she announced to the others, her fear of flying kicking up a level to borderline anxiety.

"It's not a sign," Laney argued. "It's an administrative error."

"Remind me you said that when we're in the brace position," Tash retorted, making a woman in the row behind them visibly pale.

The nasal stewardess bing-bonged again.

"We would also like to offer any passengers that would be prepared to switch to another flight, compensation of an eight hundred dollar flight voucher per person."

Tash jumped to her feet and Millie had to grab on to the bottom of her leather biker jacket to stop her charging towards the desk.

"Tash, no!" Laney hissed, just as the pale woman behind them stood up and made her way towards the flight official behind the microphone. Laney wasn't sure whether it was the financial enticement or the prospect of being stuck on a plane with Tash that had made her opt to be bumped to a later flight.

Every fibre of her being wanted to do the same, to put off the inevitable, to wind back the clock and make a different plan, but she knew that, like ripping a Band Aid off a wound, this had to be done. And it had to be done right now.

Twenty minutes later they were on the plane, in a row of three leather seats in the middle. "Business class?" Millie had asked, one eyebrow raised in disbelief.

Laney clipped her seatbelt into position. "I decided it was the least Cam could do."

Neither of them said a word as they taxied out on to the runway, then stopped to await clearance. It was only when the plane started to move forward, increased speed and Tash's nails dug into her arm, that a horrific thought floated to the front of her consciousness.

She was going to New York married to the love of her life.

If this all went according to plans and predictions, she'd be coming home single.

36

The driver holding up the name COCHRANE looked like he'd just stepped off the set of a New York musical playing Danny Zuko in *Grease*. Tall, dark and "Holy fuck, who sent him?" Tash exclaimed under her breath, but loud enough to make the other two roll their eyes. Actually, they might not be rolling their eyes – it might just be her head that was rotating. Lack of sleep combined with eight Jack Daniel's and Cokes, four coffees, and a spectacularly ineffective sleeping pill was having a strange effect on her.

Granted, given that Laney had issued strict instructions to say they were here for leisure purposes – something to do with Homeland Security being way uptight about visas – she probably shouldn't have told the bloke on the desk with the general demeanour of someone whose mother didn't like him as a child that she was here to audition for Broadway. As a cat. And then purred.

Christ, she was pissed.

Laney and Millie were absolutely humouring her while trying to keep her moving in a straight line as they followed the hubba hubba guy out of the terminal building, through to the parking area and, finally, after what seemed like the same distance as a half marathon, to their waiting car. Tash jumped in the front seat, then realised she was sitting behind the wheel. "Oops, forgot about the whole 'opposite side of the road' thing. Damn. One JD and a sleeping pill too many." Sheepishly, she headed around the bonnet of the sleek black Mercedes to the front passenger door.

"Sorry about her," Laney apologised. "We've no idea who she is. She just tagged along with us and we're far too polite to report her to the police."

The driver's expression, which had been a mask of concentration as he focused on the cadence of her accent, broke into a wide grin.

"Ah, the same thing happens to me every time I go out. I now have twenty strangers living in my garage."

"I saw that on an episode of *Criminal Minds* once." Tash was inordinately chuffed to see that made him laugh, too.

It was just before one o'clock and the lunchtime traffic was heavy as they headed along the Lincoln Highway towards the Holland Tunnel, Tash keeping up an incessant chatter with the driver. Seemed like a nice guy. All his own teeth. All his own hair. By the time they crossed into Manhattan she knew he was single, thirty-two, from Hoboken, called Todd, and a jobbing actor whose career highlight so far had been an advert for deodorant foot spray.

That one sparked Millie's attention, compelling her to lean forward from the back seat.

"Oh, my boyfriend is an actor too," she said brightly.

"S'cuse me a second, so that I can give my interrupting friend a stare that would make a cactus wither," Tash said, as she turned and carried out the threat.

Todd laughed and Millie got the message, sat back and returned to her conversation with Laney.

This was Tash's favourite thing. The flirting, the chat, the testing the waters and reeling them in. Currently, it seemed like Todd was happy to be reeled.

As they alighted from the car on East 78th Street, Todd helped them out with their cases then waited until Laney and Millie had already headed for the awning over the front door of the cute boutique hotel.

"It's really unprofessional, but can I give you my number?' he asked, and Tash watched how the sides of his eyes crinkled up when he smiled.

Damn.

She was looking at his face, but suddenly it wasn't Todd, the limo driver from Hoboken that was looking back at her, but Sy, the neighbour who was becoming more irritating than an over-tight thong.

Definitely too many JDs.

The realisation made her even more determined to shake him off. How dare he be thousands of miles away and yet somehow still intrude on her life?

"Absolutely," she told Todd, picking the mobile phone from his hand and typing in her number. "We've got work to do here – please don't repeat that if you're related to anyone who works in security at Newark airport – but maybe we can catch up for a drink sometime."

Todd leaned towards her and for a second she thought he was going to kiss her. Whoa – he was fast. She was about to adopt a full pucker position when she felt something being placed into her hands. Her handbag. Shit, he hadn't been going to kiss her at all.

She was never drinking Jack Daniel's again.

He was still laughing when he jumped back into the car and pulled away.

Inside the sparse, minimalist lobby, Laney and Millie were standing at the window waiting for her, both of them with amusement in their eyes.

"We've already checked in," Laney said, shoving a wad of paperwork into her Mulberry Mitzy.

"Did you see all of that?" Tash plonked down her case, gestured to the street outside and put her hand to her forehead like a forties silent screen star about to swoon.

"We did," Millie confirmed.

"Did I just make a total arse of myself?"

"Not total," Laney told her honestly, "but there were definite shades of mortification. Did you think he was about to kiss you? You look like you braced yourself for a full scale snog."

Tash shook her head sadly. "I know. Fuck, what's happened to me? I'm bored with casual sex and my 'come on' signal radar is completely buggered."

Only then did she spot that the fifty-something, grey haired, concierge behind the desk to their right was listening with amusement to every word.

"Sorry, didn't see you there." Tash felt her face flush for the third time in ten minutes. Jeez, she was a mess. "Can I ask you something?"

The nice man behind concierge desk nodded. "Of course, madam. Anything at all."

"If you see me acting in anyway inappropriately that could lead to a date with a stranger, can you send me to my room immediately?"

"Of course, madam," he said, with a chortle that lasted until the lift doors closed behind them.

37

The room wasn't huge, but contained two double beds, a wardrobe and a dresser with a TV on top.

"This is great," Tash declared. "As long as we always walk sideways."

Laney conceded that she did have a point. It was definitely going to be a bit of a squeeze, but let's face it, she'd already gone overboard on expenses with the business class flights and the car service from the airport.

"It's three hundred dollars a night," she told the others. "And even that rate had a thirty per cent discount because Guy at the travel agency pulled some strings."

Tash remained indignant. "Laney, who's paying for this?"

"Cara – with Cam's credit card. But …"

"No 'buts'," Tash ordered. "Do you want to spend the most devastating time of your life in a hotel room in which you're so close to me you'll be able to check when I last waxed my top lip?"

Despite the gnawing in the pit of her stomach, Laney couldn't help but giggle.

"I'd rather not, to be honest. Point taken."

The receptionist answered on the second ring with a cheery, "How can I help you?"

Laney took a deep breath. "We just checked in and I know we requested a room with two double beds – and please don't think I'm complaining about the room as I knew the square footage when I booked it – but do you have anything a little larger?"

She picked up on the furious hand gestures Tash was making and amended that last question. "Sorry, a *lot* larger?

"We do, madam. There's a penthouse suite available, but I'm afraid there is a price difference."

Tash, listening in, gave an immediate thumbs up.

"Can I ask how much it is?"

"It's normally six hundred dollars more per night, but as it's not booked for the next three nights, I could discount that to a flat rate of seven hundred dollars per night." Laney did a quick calculation. Seven hundred dollars. Almost five hundred pounds. It was a lot of money, but if they stayed where they were they would have to cope with Tash bitching all day long. Any amount of money would be worth it.

"That would be lovely, thanks."

Ten minutes later, the nice gentleman from the concierge desk showed them to a lovely corner suite with three huge floor to ceiling windows on each of the two walls that bordered the street. Millie immediately spotted that the middle windows on each wall were actually French doors with little Juliette balconies. She pulled open the first one she came to and stuck her head out. "If you stretch right over you can see right down the street to Central Park," she reported back.

The thought alarmed more than impressed Laney. "In which case, close that before Tash tries and ends up in a splat on the street."

She needn't have worried. Tash had already flopped down on one of the two king-sized beds, melting into the thick white duvet that was gorgeously accessorised with a red velvet throw and matching pillow shams.

The rest of the furniture was in the same minimalist style as the reception, and in a dark wood that coordinated with the bed frames. White walls, oak floor. A desk in the corner. A double wardrobe that opened to reveal a drawer and hanging system that would amply accommodate their possessions. In the other corner, a unit with a fridge, a kettle and a docking system for mp3 players.

On the wall opposite the beds, a fifty inch plasma TV. Running perpendicular to that wall, two white leather sofas, with a deep oak coffee table in the middle. Stark. Classy. Luxurious.

It was like the kind of New York loft you saw in the movies, Laney decided, and they bloody deserved to be here. Cam should count himself lucky they hadn't checked into the Plaza.

Millie had crossed the room again, opened the mini bar and extracted a diet coke. "What would you like?"

Laney thought for a minute. On top of jet lag and dehydration from the flight, she was starting to feel her heart race, so she should definitely stay away from alcohol.

"I'll have a gin and tonic," she announced, deciding, for once, that she wasn't going to do the right thing. It wasn't a pattern that had served her well up until now, was it? Maybe if she'd been a bit less responsible and a bit more "gin and tonic in the afternoon" she wouldn't be in this bloody position now. Cara was definitely a wine with lunch chick. A life on the wild side, with a bit of "who gives a fuck, it's all about me" thrown in. Clearly, that had more appeal than someone who stayed on the sensible side of the rules.

"Are you OK?" Millie handed over the drink and flopped onto the end of the other bed. Laney joined her there, kicking off her boots before climbing on. See! She even removed her shoes for fear of marking the duvet – that's how fucking responsible she was.

"I don't … I don't know," she said, lying back, her body propped up with two over-stuffed pillows. "Sometimes I feel like I'm going to throw up and other times it's like the worst kind of sadness. But today I just feel … furious. So angry. And I keep asking myself what she has that I don't? I mean, apart from the way she looks. But Cam was more than that. He wasn't a guy that went for the obvious beauties. He liked a laugh. Liked our conversations that would last for hours. Loved … loved me." Her voice was a whisper by the time she got to the end of the sentence and Millie moved up the bed to hug her.

"Honestly, Lanes, he's having some sort of messed up mid-life crisis. This isn't about you, it's about him. And he's going to spend the rest of his life regretting this because he'll have lost the best woman he could ever have had."

Laney returned the hug. "You're biased because you're my friend," she said, a large tear making a wet mark on the shoulder of Millie's T-shirt.

"I am. But I'm also speaking the truth," Millie continued. "He's an idiot. If this is all true, that is."

The hope in Millie's voice made Laney pull back and look her in the eye. "Do you still think there's a chance that this is all some huge, confused mistake?" Laney asked, realising that it didn't even sound in anyway believable.

"Maybe," Millie told her. "I just can't imagine Cam doing this."

"But that's because you only see the good in people. I'm beginning to think we should all become cynical and jaded like Tash. It would be easier on the heart."

Right on cue, Tash let out a soft snore.

"Let's see how this plays out before we go over to the dark side. But remember, you can bow out of this at any time. Tash and I can handle it all – as soon as she sobers up – so if it's too hard, just say, OK?'

"I will." Laney released Millie from her embrace, and pulled her legs up and crossed them, so that she was sitting in the bed in a yoga position.

After shuffling back down to the end of the bed, Millie lay across the bottom, facing her friend.

"So what's the schedule? Talk me through it."

Laney didn't need to consult her notes. She knew every single step off by heart.

"OK, so Cara says that Cam is staying with her in Glasgow tonight, and she's persuaded him to take the day off tomorrow on the premise of flying to London with her for some awards show. I don't know. Best gusset in a pair of knickers or something."

"See, you're getting more like Tash already," Millie teased.

Laney acknowledged the compliment with a bow, before continuing.

"So then at the airport tomorrow morning, she's going to reveal that they're actually flying to New York, and whisk him here, first class. They're getting picked up by the same company we used today, but this time it's in a big flash limo instead of a regular saloon. Then they'll head to the Carlyle. First thing tomorrow morning, we need to go there and check their suite before they arrive – I'm putting rose petals on the bed – Cam hates that. When we went to the Maldives last year, the hotel gave us the romance package – full-scale petals everywhere. His hay fever went into overdrive and he was choked up for a week." She paused to savour the memory, before continuing. "Cara also wants there to be champagne on ice and extra Budweiser for Cam. Which is weird, because I always thought he preferred Miller Lite. But then I always thought he preferred me to a vacuous twenty-five year old."

"Stay on track," Millie urged her, "don't make it personal."

Laney wanted to state the obvious – it *was* fucking personal – but she knew Millie meant well so pulled back.

"They should arrive at the same time tomorrow as we did today – so around one o'clock – and then there's a gap until eight that I don't even want to think about, before the car will pick them up and take them to the Met. We'll already be there. I've arranged to meet the musicians there at seven, but I've spoken to them on the phone several times and checked out their references and seen footage of their work, so I'm trusting they'll be there and organised."

"Did you find a harpist? And a string quartet?"

"Not quite, but I'm sure my stand-ins will have just as much impact. It'll be beautiful. I've organised candles for the stairs, and more rose petals, but that needs to be set up just minutes before they arrive because the authorities might have something to say about that."

"What about the ring?"

"We'll collect that on the way there. Cara is leaving it at the reception of the Carlyle, and we'll pick it up when we head over to meet the band. A butler is also booked – or actually, an actor dressed as a butler – to do a grand handover of the ring, and then the limo will whisk them off to the Mandarin Oriental. If Tash hasn't ordered a gangland execution."

Millie pushed herself up on one hand, and Laney could see how unhappy this was making her. It went against every fibre of Millie's romantic soul.

"Still think I'm nuts?" Laney asked, knowing the answer.

Millie smiled sadly. "Yeah, but I just hate that this is happening to you, Lanes. You're the strongest out of all of us, but I'm devastated that you're having to go through all this."

Laney threw back a hefty measure of the gin and tonic. "Me, too. But hey, it could be worse …"

"How?"

"We could be Cam Cochrane right now."

The words were barely out of her mouth when her phone started ringing, the surprise making her jump.

When she leant across to the bedside table to fish it out of her bag, the image of Freddy Krueger flashed on the screen.

"Shit," she said, before pressing the "accept" button, her tone immediately switching to sunny.

"Hi darling, how are you?" she answered, wanting to retch with every word. Perhaps the gin and tonic hadn't been such a smart move after all.

"I'm good, honey. Having a great day. The directors at Anderston have already called back into MindSoar and told them they're thrilled with the way the last week has gone, so I'm looking at a lovely little bonus. I think it's time to book a holiday, Lanes. Somewhere hot. Bali? We've always said we'll go back one day."

Their first holiday together, then their honeymoon. The pain of the memories was like a physical blow. Bastard.

"Yep, I'm all in for that," Laney told him, voice cracking.

"Are you alright darling? You sound ... odd."

Laney attempted to shake off the agony. "I'm fine – just a bit of a cold, I think."

"OK, well take some paracetamol and you'll feel better in no time."

That one nearly made her flip from devastation to hysteria. Hark, at the guy who – playing up to the male stereotype – took to his bed for three days with a hot water bottle and a confection of pills and potions every time he had so much as a hint of a sore throat.

"I'll do that," she assured him.

"So anyway, how's Paris? I wish I was there with you, Lanes."

She ignored the second part of the sentence, going for, "It's beautiful." It had been her master stroke – telling him that she was going to be in Paris for a couple of days, so that if he called, he wouldn't be suspicious about the difference in her ring tone. "I always forget how gorgeous this city is. What about you? How's the weather in Manchester?" If that's where he was. Without the aid of some form of tracking device, she couldn't be sure.

That pause again. The one that told her he was thinking through his words before he shared them with her.

"Yeah, great. But God, it feels like it's been ages since I last saw you."

At least he noticed.

"It *has* been ages – almost three weeks. The longest ever." It was impossible to disguise the sadness in her voice, the wave of utter despondency that was washing over her.

"Yeah, well, let's not ever let this happen again. I've missed you."

Really? Have you really, Cam? Again, her thoughts went unsaid. But how could this be? How could he sound so plausible and loving, and yet she knew that he was having a full-blown affair with someone else – one that had been going on for two years? How could he sail through this double life so easily? There had to be some kind of fundamental flaw in his psyche that allowed him to do this. Or a recognised affliction. *Infidelitus Optimus.* There – she'd given it a proper name.

"I've missed you too," she told him, and over at the window, she saw Millie wince.

"But hey, it's only for a couple more days," he bounced back, catching her off guard.

"You're coming home this weekend?" she checked.

"Of course! You didn't think I'd forget, did you?"

"Forget what?" Her mind was whirring now, going through a database of previous comments and plans, desperate to throw up the correct one.

"Lanes, have you been drinking?"

"I wish," she laughed, mind still whirring.

"You're ovulating this weekend. I've cleared my schedule and I'm all yours."

Oh. God.

Ovulating.

She'd completely pushed that out of her mind.

And oh, how hearing him mention it notched the pain up another level. Two years they'd been trying and nothing. They'd agreed this was going to be their last attempt to conceive naturally before they were to go back to the doctor with a view to discussing IVF.

It was fairly certain that chance was gone.

"So there's a final dinner here tomorrow night and then I'll be home Saturday morning, darling."

But hang on – how could he be coming home to her on Saturday, when he'd already be here in New York? She hadn't even told him that she wouldn't be home this weekend because she'd assumed he would come up with some excuse to stay away again. Cara had already said he'd be with her tonight, Thursday night, yet here he was blatantly lying to her about staying longer in Manchester. She checked her watch and made a quick calculation. Eight p.m. He was probably on his way up to Glasgow now. Perhaps at the airport. And, according to Cara, he was spending tonight at her place, before they headed to the airport tomorrow morning – which was Friday. Argh, it was so difficult to keep track after a large gin and tonic and a time difference.

Back to the plan and she realised why he thought he would still see her this weekend. As far as he knew he was only going away for one overnight to the fashion dinner with Cara. Was he planning to jump off the London shuttle on Saturday morning, drop Cara home and then dash to their house and slip into bed for ovulation sex? And what would he do when he realised that Cara had very different plans?

That would be his last moment of choice. When he got to the airport and realised Cara had planned a whole weekend in New York, what would he do?

Would he go along with it?

Or would he refuse, and honour the commitment he'd made to Laney and to the child they'd dreamt of having?

And if he did the latter, how much of a shock was he going to get when he realised his wife was in New York, on his credit card, planning the rest of his life with his girlfriend?

38

"Bugger! I can't believe I fell asleep and missed all of this. So then what did you say?" Tash asked, desperate to get the full picture.

"I said I'd see him Saturday. Couldn't wait. Told him I loved him and hung up."

"Then she cried," Millie added.

"Then I cried," Laney repeated. "But only for a few moments, before blind fury kicked in again. Then confusion. Then ... oh, I don't know Tash. He was so definite. So ... normal. He'd be home on Saturday. We'd make a baby. Life goes on as planned." The last two sentences were understandably steeped in bitterness.

Tash pulled her T-shirt over her head to reveal a tartan bra and started to unzip her jeans. A hot shower and she'd be feeling great, considering it was now seven p.m. New York time, so midnight at home.

Laney's mobile buzzed and she picked it up and then

visibly sighed.

"Cara. She says he's home with her now. So there's the first lie. He told me he was staying in Manchester tonight."

"Then the first moment of truth will be at two a.m. our time here," Tash told them as she headed in the direction of one of the two bathrooms.

"How do you mean?" Millie asked, but Laney immediately grasped the significance. "Because that's when he'll check in at Glasgow airport and realise he's going to New York. And that's when he'll have to choose."

Laney picked up her phone and spoke the words she was typing in the text to Cara aloud.

"Great. All ready to go at this end. Text me as soon as you've checked in and let me know all going according to plan."

En route to the shower, Tash paused at the bed to give Laney a hug, her heartstrings tugging with sympathy for the utter devastation that was written all over her friend's face.

If this was what relationships did to you, she was glad they weren't her thing.

"OK, so I'm going to get a shower. What do you feel like doing tonight?" Tash asked.

Millie shrugged. "I'm easy. Happy to go with whatever."

Tash knew she meant it, but at the same time she could see her looking wistfully at the street lights outside.

Laney spoke, despite the fact that she was still staring at the screen on her phone, waiting for something to happen. "Just something easy. Maybe call some food in and then chill out with a movie."

"Good idea," Tash responded, "but absolutely no chance. We're going out. We're going to get in a cab, we're going to head to Chinatown, get some great food, then do a bar crawl all the way home again. And I'm not accepting objections."

"But …" Laney, of course.

Tash threw up a hand to shush her. "You've clearly not understood the term 'no objections'. Look Laney, I get it. It's shit. And yes, I want to kill him. But if we stay in here tonight every minute and every hour is going to drag past so slowly that there's a good chance you'll go insane. If we go out – on expenses, of course – then at least we'll be busy, the night will pass quicker."

A subtle change in Laney's tense body language told Tash that she was getting through to her.

Good. Score one for the serial hedonist.

An hour later they were downstairs and dressed for a smart but casual night on the town in New York. Millie looked ravishing in a black maxi, with gold wedges and a large orange gerbera in her hair. Laney had gone with the copper shift dress that totally complimented her complexion and made her brown eyes pop.

Tash had opted for leather-look skinny jeans and a black shirt, with her leather biker jacket over her shoulders. The addition of a stack of bangles on one arm took the vibe from funereal to wild chick.

When they got downstairs, Todd was already waiting outside in the car.

"Well, well, well," Laney said in a sing-song voice when she spotted him through the window. "It's like a miracle. The very handsome Todd, who just happened to stir the hormones of our lovely Tash, has just appeared at our hotel exactly when we need him."

"Yep, a miracle sent by the Patron Saint of Lust," Tash confirmed with a grin. "Hey Todd, thanks for picking us up. I figured you were they guy to make our first night in New York interesting."

Todd bowed jokingly, before offering his hand, then sweeping open the car door with his other hand. As Tash moved past him, she realised he smelled great. Really, really great. Laney wasn't the only one who could effectively forward plan. Calling him and booking him for tonight had been a masterstroke. If there was anyone who was going to get her out of this inexplicable rut into which she'd slid, it was the man with the intoxicating whiff of Dolce and Gabbana's Light Blue.

At the restaurant, Laney jumped in first with the offer for him to join them and Tash mentally punched the air in triumph.

"It'll pass the time," Laney whispered to her, "and stop us talking all night about Cam." Tash's sentiments exactly, and in the end, that was exactly how it panned out. Over a dinner of incredible Asian food – Todd ordered, assuring them he knew all the best dishes in the restaurant he chose – they laughed, chatted and put the reason they were here to one side. Even Laney joined in, Tash noticed, marvelling at her friend's strength. But then, Lanes had always been the rock of the group, the reliable one, the steady force in the midst of chaos. Tash had always figured it was the trauma of her mum leaving when she was a teenager. Dealing with that had given her some kind of weird super-strength and God, she needed it now.

Todd regaled them with stories about his gigs as an extra, had them in stitches over his indiscreet tales of the goings on behind the scenes when he was in the chorus of a Broadway play, and admitted with mock shame, that his second biggest pay check – after the advert for the deodorant foot spray – had come when he got a bit part in a crime show playing a dead body in Central Park.

"My finest work," he assured them over post-dinner coffees, while Tash noticed that his arm was now loosely draped over the back of her chair.

Oh, she was liking this one. Was it really inappropriate to hook up with someone on the same weekend as your best friend's life fell apart? Laney would understand. After all, wasn't she just saying this nightmare with Cam had taught her to let loose a little, to stop being so responsible and start embracing spontaneity? Surely spontaneously shagging a gorgeous New Yorker fell into the category of acceptable endeavours? Live for the moment and all that.

They stopped at several bars on the way back to the hotel, throwing back shots in each one, keeping things on a purely superficial, upbeat level. By the time they got to the fourth bar, an Irish pub a couple of blocks from the hotel, Tash was so horny she could jump Todd at the slightest opportunity. Millie was completely pissed, which just meant that she got even more sweet and giggly.

Laney, however, was beginning to show signs of stress, repeatedly checking her watch. One a.m. One ten. One fifteen. They threw back another round of shots.

One thirty.

Cara and Cam would be heading to the airport now.

"Do you want to go back to the hotel?" Tash whispered to Laney. "We can wait there for Cara's text." Laney shook her head. "No. What's the point? I think I'd rather be here, surrounded by people. I'm less likely to crumble," she said, gesturing to the rambunctious crowd that had broken into a rowdy chorus of "The Wild Rover".

Tash wasn't objecting. Todd's hand had found hers at some point in the last hour, and when he'd stood to go to the gents, his lips had brushed her cheek.

But hey, much as it was rousing her libido to the point of near-orgasmic, she'd decided she wouldn't be taking it further tonight. God, it was horrible when decency took over and intercepted her dodgy moral judgments. The "spontaneity" argument she'd attempted earlier wasn't actually working. Was it inappropriate to hook up with someone on the same night that your pal's life fell apart? Absolutely. Damn. Being a good friend sucked sometimes.

As if reading her mind, Laney leaned in towards her, so that she could be heard over the deafening chorus of the rabble. "You know, honey, I really don't mind if you want to take off with him. I definitely would. He's lovely. And just because Cam's a prick, doesn't mean we should all suffer."

"Seriously? Wouldn't you think I was a crap pal?"

"Noooooo!" Laney was slurring a little. A few too many shots had passed their way. "It would cheer me up," Laney countered. "Show me that there's still hope for some kind of life after this is all over. If you can pull, so can I." Laney held up her glass, gin and tonic again now, and did a "cheers" gesture, slopping some of it over her hand. She either didn't notice or didn't care.

Todd was back from the gents now and slipped back into the booth next to Tash, the touch of their legs setting off fireworks in her pelvic area. Man, he was hot. This was excruciating. However despite Laney's assurances, Tash wasn't going there. At least not tonight. This was why she preferred a life with no moral code – it got in the way of damn fine sex.

She spotted Laney checking her watch again, so Tash did the same. Two a.m.

They both turned their gaze to Laney's phone, sitting perfectly still in the middle of the table. Nothing. No text, no call. But the anxiety level palpably rose. Over the next half an hour, an emotional pyramid formed. Anxiety rising on one side, enjoyment and hilarity plummeting on the other. Poor Todd noticed the shift in atmosphere and Tash could see it confused him.

"I'm sorry it's all gone a bit flat," she whispered into his ear, desperate to lick it while she did so. "It's because my friend is waiting for a really important text and we're just all getting a bit nervous for her."

It was time to make an executive decision. "Can you take us back to the hotel please?" His disappointment was obvious and it absolutely mirrored hers. "I know what you're thinking," she told him, this time adding a soft kiss to his lobe. "And usually, I'd be up for carrying on the party, but it's … complicated tonight."

He smiled softly. Cute. So cute.

"Can I see you again before you leave?"

Tash took in the earnest expression, the impeccable manners he'd shown all night, his charm, his humour and the fact that she'd wager her entire shoe collection on him having a six pack under that black shirt, and nodded.

"Perhaps. I hope so."

Leaning over the table to the other two, she said, "Come on, girls, let's head back to the hotel." Despite Laney's objections earlier, Tash saw the relief that crossed her face. Two fifteen. Still nothing. This must be excruciating. Suddenly, she just wanted to get back to the hotel and wrap Laney in a comfort blanket of love.

In minutes they were back in the car, and the hotel came into view ahead of them. Tash was busily trying to dissuade her inner workings from staging a full out protest at the prospect of saying goodbye to Todd, when a noise made them all jump.

The buzz of an incoming text.

Tash turned to see the colour drain out of Laney's face as she flipped open the leather cover on her phone, checked the screen and … puzzlement now. She turned the phone to show Tash and Millie. No text.

Millie rifled in her bag until she found her phone, checked it – nope, not hers.

So that left … Reluctantly, Tash removed Todd's hand from her thigh, and reached around into her back pocket.

Incoming text message, the screen advised.

Tash punched in her passcode and waited for it to load.

A new and quite inexplicable feeling came over her when she saw the name.

Sy.

She was tempted to ignore it but her thumb had other ideas, immediately jumping into action to open the full text.

"Hey, neighbourhood watch is reporting that you're

missing in action, last seen leaving with a suitcase. Shall I call Interpol?"

She quickly pressed the lock button, clearing his intrusion from the screen. What an arse. Why was he keeping tabs on her? What was he, her keeper?

Another text. Her thumb jumped the gun again.

"PS: Kinda miss you."

Aaargh, how bloody annoying. What a dick. Why was he going all heavy all of a sudden? Hadn't they existed for years on a solid foundation of casual sex and no further attachments? Didn't they often congratulate themselves on finding their perfect match – someone who had the same values (or lack of) and wanted exactly the same things? Why was he doing this? Another bloke having a mid-life crisis? Or did he just wake up one morning and decide to spoil it all?

And why did she now feel completely sober? The tosser had even killed her New York tequila buzz. Her teeth clenched with irritation. That was it. As soon as she got back she was calling a halt to everything. No more booty calls. No more flirtations. They were done. The limit of their relationship would now be discussing the weather if they happened to have the misfortune of sharing the lift.

That decided, she shoved her phone back in her pocket.

"Everything OK?" Millie asked, just as they slowed into the kerb.

"Fine," Tash replied. It would be. Just as soon as she put Mr Suave Next Door Neighbour straight about a few things.

Laney and Millie exited from the left and right back

doors, discreetly leaving Todd and Tash in the front. He leaned towards her, as she knew he would, and kissed her softly.

"So call me tomorrow, if you're free or just need a great driver to get you around."

"Why, do you know one?" Tash couldn't resist it, and it was worth it to see him do the crinkle eye laugh thing. The one that looked like … Bloody hell, why was he in her thoughts again when she was sitting here with this perfectly gorgeous, incredibly hot specimen of manhood?

She shook it off, reached for the door handle, putting her hand on his arm when she realised he was going to jump out, go around and open the door for her, the way he'd done at every previous stop that night. "It's OK, I can manage," she told him, adding "with perfect manners" to the hot and gorgeous list.

She leant over, kissed him again. "I'll call you tomorrow."

"Promise?"

"Promise," she told him, then stepped out and watched as the red lights at the back of the car pulled off into the New York night.

For a moment, she stood there in the deserted street, trying to analyse what was going on with her. Was she really drunk?

Earlier she had decided that Laney was the priority and sacrificing a sensational hook up had been a purely physiological decision, carried out against the wishes of several parts of her anatomy.

So how come now, after that text from Sy, there wasn't a single shred of her being that still wanted to have sex with the hot, gorgeous, well-mannered New York driver?

39

Millie pulled the fluffy robe across her body and walked a little unsteadily over to the bed, reaching it just as Tash burst in the door.

"You didn't stay out with him?" Over on one of the beds, Laney got the question in first.

Tash shook her head. "Nope. Would rather be here with you."

Laney was visibly moved. "I think that's the nicest thing anyone's ever done for me."

"Yeah, well, don't expect it to happen again. It's a one-time thing," Tash countered with faux-irritation.

Millie smiled. At least she did on the inside. She'd had so many drinks, she wasn't sure if her extremities were responding to commands. But she watched as Tash dropped her clothes where she stood, stepped out of them without picking them up, grabbed a robe from the wardrobe and joined them on the huge bed. Millie had known without a shadow of a doubt that Tash would come back. For all her brusque exterior, she'd never walk away when one of them needed support.

Like now.

All three of them were staring at Laney's phone, which was sitting in the middle of the duvet, absolutely still.

"Right, we have two choices." Tash pointed out the obvious. "Keep staring at it or text her. It's three a.m. – so that means eight o'clock at home. If they've gone with Cara's fucked up plan, they'll have checked in, gone through security and be waiting to board the flight. Text her, Lanes. I know it hurts, but let's get this over with and find out what's happening."

Laney didn't move. "I can't," she whispered. "I physically can't."

Millie picked up the phone. "Do you want me to do it for you?" Her stomach was churning and it wasn't caused by the excess of alcohol.

Laney shook her head, then her expression changed. "I know! Text Cam first. Yep, that's what to do. OK, can you say this?"

She got ready to dictate, and Millie prepared to type, glad that despite the slightly blurred vision she could still see the keys. There was no time to sober up or look for her glasses. She had a job to do.

"Say, 'Morning, darling'…"

Millie began to tap the keys. "'Hope Manchester is sunny today and can't wait to see you tomorrow morning'," Laney continued. "'Love you. Xxx.' Send."

Millie pressed the final button, then placed the phone back down on the middle of the bed. This was it. What happened in the next two minutes could change everything.

When the phone buzzed, all three of them jumped.

Laney covered her eyes. "Who is it? Him or her?"

Millie picked up the phone and checked. "Him."

She opened the text, read it out aloud. "Me too, babe, and yes, it's a sunny day here. Will be even sunnier tomorrow when I'm with you. Love you back."

"I fucking hate him," Tash spat, at exactly the same time as Laney said, "I don't get this." Then she continued, "I just don't. Is he really with her? Is he sitting there next to her, while he's texting me, telling me he loves me? Or is … is … Am I going mad?"

Millie shook her head. "No, because it doesn't make sense. Lanes, I really think this is a mix up. It's some other guy she's with."

"But I saw them in the restaurant that day and there's been all the other little things that don't add up," Tash interjected.

"I know, but none of those gave absolutely conclusive proof, did they?" Millie insisted. "It could all be a huge misunderstanding. Something completely outlandish and bizarre, but with a totally innocent explanation."

"Maybe you're right," Laney said, the desperation thick in every word.

The phone buzzed again, making them all jump for a second time.

Millie reached for it again. "It's from Cara," she announced. "Sorry, forgot to text. We're in the departure lounge, take off soon. All going exactly to plan."

Laney slumped back on to the bed. "Well it looks like we're about to find out if it's a big misunderstanding or not."

40

"God dammit, my head hurts," Laney groaned, as she squinted to prevent the death rays of daylight from permeating her brain. Wow, she felt like death. Head banging. Stomach churning. Hands shaking.

Although, as the realisation of what was ahead of her today dawned, she was fairly certain she'd have been feeling all of those things anyway. And if she hadn't been so pissed, she'd probably have been awake all night pacing the floor. At least, as it had played out, she'd had a few hours' sleep. Or a few hours in a self-induced coma might be more accurate.

After retrieving her phone from the bedside table, she checked the screen. One message. Her heart thudded until she opened it and realised it was from Matt. Very nice accountant guy, Matt.

"Hope you're OK. Will wait for your call to advise on next steps."

Somehow, his kindness made her feel even sadder. There were nice guys in this world. Just a shame she'd managed to pick one that wasn't.

Pushing herself up, she tried to ignore the head rush that increased with every inch. The movement made Millie, lying beside her, stir.

"Come on, sleepyhead. Time to go wreck my marriage."

Millie's eyes pinged open and then snapped shut gain. "Bollocks, that hurt. Why did we do that to ourselves? Why?" she wailed.

"We were blocking out the pain," Laney answered, deadpan, as she struggled to her feet. "Do you reckon we'll need medical intervention to rouse Tash?"

Millie shook her head, then winced as the pain permeated her nerve endings.

"No. Watch this." She nudged Tash. "Tash! Tash! Wake up. Channing Tatum is on the telly."

Tash's eyes sprang open and she flipped upright like a Z-bed coming to life.

"Morning!" she chirped, then stared at the TV. "Cow, you were lying! Oh well, how are we all this morning?" Not so chirpy now, but still disturbingly alive.

"Doesn't your head hurt?" Laney asked her.

"No, not at all."

"Dry throat, sore bones, nausea?"

"No."

"Jeez, you're a machine," Millie whistled.

"And I'm starving," Tash added, making the other two groan.

Tash called room service and ordered a pile of toast and bacon, before jumping in and out of the shower in a

316

lively ten minutes. Laney and Millie were still slumped on the sofa, waiting for the large dose of ibuprofen they'd each taken to kick in.

"So how are you feeling – other than the 'close to death' thing?" Millie asked her.

"I'm actually grateful for the pain," Laney told her. "Otherwise I'd be on my knees, thinking about the day ahead. I can't believe this is actually happening today. It still feels so surreal. Like I'm watching it on a screen or in a bubble in my imagination."

Millie nodded empathetically. "Whatever happens, you'll survive it, Lanes. Although you might want to start coming up with an explanation in case that's not Cam with Cara and you have to explain why you're not at home waiting for him when he arrives there tomorrow morning."

Laney smiled sadly. "Somehow, no matter how I wish that was true, I just can't see how it could be possible."

Tash came back into the room, towel drying her wet hair. "How what could be possible? That Cam Cochrane will still be in possession of his penis after today?"

"Tash," Laney replied quietly, so as not to break her head any further than it already was, "you reduce everything to some kind of base gutter level, do you realise that?"

"I do indeed. Yay, breakfast!" she added breezily when the doorbell interrupted them.

It took another hour, but at eleven a.m. they finally made their way to the Carlyle, choosing to walk the four blocks to clear their heads.

Walking into it was like entering another world, with its plush beige patterned carpet, and muted cream tones with gold inlaid embellishments on the walls. For a second, Laney's heart soared with the romantic beauty of it all, but then she remembered why they were there.

At reception she explained who she was and why she was there to an impeccably courteous young lady with a French accent. The booking had been made in the name of Personal Proposals and pre-paid, so that they'd get access to the room. However, there were strict instructions that when Miss Deacon arrived, the check in was to be processed as if it was her name on the reservation, so as not to alert Mr Cochrane to the planned surprise. Oh, and all extras were to be paid by Miss Deacon upon check out.

The receptionist took it all in her stride, as if strange requests were absolutely commonplace at the Carlyle. In a hotel that hosted some of the most famous names in the world, they probably were.

A concierge led them round to the lifts to their left, and then showed them to the room. On the sixteenth floor, the superior suite had an impressive king-sized bed, a separate lounge area decorated in similar elegant tones to the foyer, and a stunning view over a quaint internal courtyard below. Only when the concierge had retreated, did Laney realise she'd been holding her breath and allow herself to exhale. With the release, came two large tears, which rolled down her cheeks.

Tash put her arm around her. "Lanes, don't do this to yourself. On you go downstairs and Millie and I will take care of everything up here. Or we can just abandon the plans altogether and bail out. I know a great Irish bar we can drown our sorrows in."

Laney wiped the tears away with the sleeve of her

black polo neck and shook off the pain. "Thanks, Tash, but I need to do this."

"Sure?"

'Positive." She had to. Because if it really was Cam, then she had to know – and if it wasn't, she had a responsibility to her client to make this the proposal she'd always, like, totally, dreamt of.

They worked wordlessly for the next ten minutes, preparing the room as they'd done for many other proposals before this one.

Rose petals strewn across the sumptuous bedding. Bottles of Budweiser placed in the mini-bar. Music – Cara's iPod nano, featuring all her favourite songs – plugged in to the mp3 speakers. Laney experienced a small tug of satisfaction as the first song began. Cam bloody hated Mariah Carey. Finally, a knock at the door announced the arrival of the silver ice bucket they'd ordered at reception. A bottle of Cara's favourite Cristal champagne was placed inside.

Laney checked her watch. Two o'clock. If the flight was on time, they'd be here in the next hour or so, depending on the lines at immigration and the traffic on the way. She felt sick, her legs were trembling and she wanted nothing more than to go home to her own bed and crawl under the duvet.

Instead, with one last wordless gaze around the beautiful room, she left, and retreated to a coffee shop that sat fifty metres along the street, on the other side of the road. It wouldn't be easy to get a good look from that angle, but all she needed was a glimpse, the tiniest window of opportunity and she'd know if the man entering one of the grandest hotels in the city with his future fiancée was her very current husband.

Tash ordered a cinnamon bagel with a large cappuccino, Millie went for toast with a skinny latte and Laney ordered a coffee. Black, strong and potent.

The painkillers and the two bottles of water she'd consumed had taken the edge off the physical symptoms, but they didn't cover heartache and desolation.

The other diners must have been slightly curious about the three unhappy women who sat saying nothing, just staring intently out of the window.

Finally Tash cracked and pulled out her phone. "I've had an idea." She fired off a text. "It's a long shot, but I'm wondering if Todd has picked them up. You used the same car service for us too, didn't you?"

Laney nodded. "Yes, but they must have hundreds of drivers. What's the chance of ..."

Tash's phone buzzed and she turned to show them the screen. "Just picked up Scottish couple from Newark. Heading to Carlyle."

"ETA?" she asked.

"10-20," he replied.

"I'm going to have a heart attack," Laney whispered as her chest tightened.

They stared. Stared some more. Stared for longer. No limo. Just cars, vans and – for God's sake, why was that truck stopped there?

A massive juggernaut with a drinks logo on the side had stopped directly outside their window and now the driver was hanging out of his door, chatting to a cop on a bike. "Come on, come on. Oh, for Christ's sake, move along."

It was probably only five minutes, but it felt like an

hour before he finally waved goodbye to NYC's finest and drove off, allowing them to regain their partial view of the Carlyle entrance

"We haven't missed them," Millie said confidently. "No way. They'll be here in a minute. Any minute now. Definitely."

So once again they stared. And then they stared a little longer. And a bit longer.

"Oh, for fuck's sake, I can't stand this," Tash blurted, picking up her phone again.

"ETA?" she repeated.

The wait for a reply was interminable. The content, when it finally came, was excruciating.

Tash's voice was defeated as she read it out. "'Already dropped. On way to next job downtown. Drink later?' Shit," was Tash's final verdict.

Laney's eyes went back to the building in front of her and she mentally counted up sixteen floors, then let her eyes linger on the windows there. The room they'd booked for Cara was at the other side of the building, but it didn't matter. Was he there? Was she staring at the building in which her husband was right now drinking Budweiser and delighting in the surprise his girlfriend had delivered? Was he caressing his lover? Or – best option - was he looking at the rose petals and wondering where he could get a supply of anti-histamines?

41

"I almost want to just go and start drinking again. At least it makes the time pass quicker," Millie announced, only partly in jest. This afternoon had been interminable. They'd gone back to their hotel and tried to sleep. Only Tash succeeded. Millie and Laney ended up lying on the sofas staring at the TV. Now, Millie couldn't even remember what they'd watched. A soap. She couldn't remember the name. And then a quiz show, where they had to guess words or something like that. Her eyes were engaged but her brain wasn't – it was too busy trying to think of ways to minimise the catastrophe of tonight and coming up completely blank.

Laney came out of the bathroom and pulled a jacket from the wardrobe. "OK, I'm good to go," she said, her voice completely flat. Millie knew there was no point in trying to dissuade her – she'd tried so many times already.

"You look like a ninja wife," Tash volunteered when she spotted Laney's outfit. She had a point. Black trousers, black jumper, black boots, and a black jacket and matching scarf. "I'm in mourning," Laney replied, attempting a joke that fell flat because it was just too near the truth. Millie could see the pain etched into every one of the worry lines that seemed to have appeared on her face.

The three of them had spent their whole lives chatting up a storm and yet now, as they made their way back to the Carlyle, they were completely silent for the second time that day.

There were some occasions for which there were just no words.

At reception, Laney took the lead, waiting to speak to the same receptionist who had dealt with them earlier in the day.

"Did our client's check in go smoothly, Marianne?" she asked, quoting the name on the French girl's name tag.

"It did, Madame. They seemed very happy."

"Great. I believe Miss Deacon left an item here for me to collect?"

"Indeed." Marianne consulted a colleague, who disappeared into another room and then returned, carrying a small box and a sheet of paper. Laney signed as requested, before taking the box with thanks.

Tash only got one foot on to the pavement outside before she cracked. "Snap it open. Let's see it," she pleaded.

Millie saw the panic in Laney's eyes. "We don't have to, though," she countered, subtly thumping Tash's hip.

"We really don't, Lanes. There's no need."

"There is," Laney told them in a whispered, broken voice.

The three of them huddled around, as she pulled a navy blue velvet box out of the little bag and, with shaking hands, opened it.

It was so absurd, Millie felt a bizarre urge to laugh. A huge pink square stone, the size of an ice cube, bordered on all sides by diamonds.

"I'm sure my Barbie had a ring like that," Tash exclaimed, summing up what they were all thinking.

"Tash, you never had a Barbie," Laney argued.

"True, but if I did, she'd have a fuck off big pink ring like that one."

Despite the pain, or maybe because of it, Laney emitted a hysterical giggle that then spread like a virus to the rest of them. Before Millie could stop it, she was doubled over, gasping for breath, tears running down her cheeks. It was a full five minutes before they stopped, recovered, and regained the power of speech.

"I think I'm going crazy. Absolutely crazy," Laney spluttered.

If she was, Millie decided, then they were all going crazy together.

Ten minutes later they rounded the corner from East 81st Street onto Fifth Avenue and the Met was right there in front of them. Millie had been to Manhattan a few times before and now she chided herself for leaving it this long to visit this building. It was an architectural wonder. Majestic. Grand. Dignified. Absolutely stunning.

She'd always thought she wanted a windswept

proposal in the valleys of Glencoe or the on the banks of a beautiful loch – polystyrene Nessie not included – but she could see why this would be an incredible backdrop for the most important moment of someone's life. If Leo ever decided to ask her to be his wife, somewhere like this would be entirely acceptable – or was that just wishful thinking on her part?

On the street, the vendors in the wagons and vans selling hot dogs, French fries and donuts were packing up for the day, some of them already moving off, others still clearing up the debris around their patch. Laney in front, they headed up the steps to the closed doors of the building, where one lone man was standing, wearing a tuxedo, his distinguished grey hair swept back like a forties movie star.

"Clark?" Laney asked, holding out her hand to shake his.

"Yes, ma'am," he said, breaking into a perfect smile.

"I recognised you from your headshot. Pleased to meet you and thanks for helping us out tonight. So did the agency brief you on what we need you to do?"

"Sure did. A proposal, I believe? And I've to deliver the ring?"

Laney nodded, and pulled out the box. Millie could see how hard she was trying to keep it together, so she decided to step in and take over.

"Ok, so the couple will arrive by limo in …." she checked her watch, "about an hour. If you could be there ready to open the car door, that would be perfect. They'll then sweep up the stairs, and stop there," she pointed to the midway point, a terrace step that was wider than the others.

"At that moment, if you could come forward and hand the ring over to the gentleman, then retreat. The proposal will take place. The couple will return to the car. If you could be there to open the door again for them that would be perfect. And that's about it. Did I cover everything, Laney?"

"You did."

"Excuse me – I heard the accent. Are any of you fine ladies called Mrs Cochrane?"

"That's me," Laney answered, as they all turned to greet a very suave arrival. Millie felt the corners of her mouth rise as she mirrored the beaming smile of the African American man who stood there, perhaps in his early sixties, wearing a white suit with a multi-coloured shirt and a white fedora.

"I'm Lincoln. We spoke on the phone and I'm sure pleased to meet you."

"I'm sure pleased to meet you too, Lincoln."

It was the first genuine smile that had crossed Laney's lips all day, Millie noted.

Looking over his shoulder, she could see a group of men dressed in the same style, several of them carrying brass instruments. Millie counted two trumpets, two saxophones and a trombone.

"Where would you like us to perform? And can I just check that you definitely want the songs we discussed on the phone?"

"Absolutely," Laney answered, "and I think having you guys up here at the doors would be perfect. That way your sound will fill the air, but you won't be too close to the couple to drown out their words."

"Sounds like a fine plan to me," he confirmed, and

then beckoned his band members to join him.

"Thanks, Lincoln. And we'll be out of sight, but your cue to begin playing is when the limo draws up and you see Clark over there opening the door."

"We'll be right on it," he assured them, heading up the steps, chuckling. "It's a good night to fall in love."

"Laney," Millie asked suspiciously, as if questioning a child that had been caught red-handed in a prank, "weren't you supposed to arrange a string band and a harp?"

Laney's eyes were wide with innocence. "Perhaps."

"And is Lincoln the leader of a string band with a harp?"

"Perhaps not."

"And the reason for that is ..." Millie was loving the edge of pure mischief that was creeping in here.

"It's my new motto," Laney replied, succinct and matter of fact. "I've decided to break a few rules."

42

Band? Check. Butler? Check. Rose petals? Check. Videographer and photographer? Check. Fireworks? Forget it. Laney had researched it and setting off fireworks was illegal throughout the whole of New York State. Much as it was tempting to have Cam and Cara's moment interrupted by the NYPD, she'd decided against it. Instead, they'd had a hundred candles couriered up by motorbike from a handmade candle boutique in midtown. With them now positioned one at either end of each step, the whole way up, it looked beautiful. If Cara was going to complain about the lack of explosive colour, Laney would just point out that it came with the humiliating possibility of spending her first night as an engaged woman in jail. Especially as evidence of the arrest would be captured by the photographer and videographer that had just arrived and set up at a discreet distance, beside one of the pillars that dominated the façade of the building.

Now, as she surveyed the scene, the nerves kicked in again. Somehow it was easier when she was carrying out tasks, organising and checking. When she stood back and took a breath, that was when the pain flared.

"How you holding up there?" Tash asked her, coming up behind her and throwing her arm around Laney's shoulders.

"Crap," she answered honestly. "It's like watching a car crash in slow motion, and knowing that you're not going to escape it without being hurt. Really badly hurt."

"Laney …"

"Don't tell me to leave, because I can't."

Tash put her hands up in surrender. "Fine, but in that case, we really need to get out of sight because they're going to be here soon."

Laney nodded and took one last look at the scene they'd created. The uplighters that made the building seem like it was shimmering in the night. The romance of the candles and rose petals. The setting sun was the perfect backdrop, the sky a bruised mix of blues, oranges and blacks.

She had to hand it to Cara – when it came to taking possession of someone's husband, she planned to do it in style.

Laney felt her phone vibrate and checked it. Matt the Nice Accountant.

"Ready when you are," it said.

Right now it didn't feel like she would ever be ready.

"Thanks. Should be kicking off shortly. Will let you know."

Laney shoved her phone back in her pocket, gave a

thumbs up to Lincoln the band leader, then to Clark the butler, and watched as both of them returned the gesture. "OK, girls, let's get out of here."

Tash and Millie, one on each side of her, slipped their arms through hers as they retreated across the street. This was usually the exciting part – when you'd done everything possible to make the moment perfect and you just had to stand back and watch it play out. This time the excitement had been replaced by nausea, trembling hands and utter terror. Not since the moment her mother had walked out of the door had she felt this scared. If the girls weren't physically supporting her, there was a good chance her legs would buckle and she'd be sprawled on Fifth Avenue.

They positioned themselves in the deep doorway of a beautiful light sandstone building, partially obscured by black metal railings. Despite the fact that they were only thirty metres away, Laney was confident they wouldn't be noticed.

She wasn't sure if that was a good thing or a bad thing.

"Right, here you go," Tash said, producing three pairs of binoculars from her over-sized leather tote. They took them on every job to make sure that even from a distance they had a close up of the action.

"You OK?" Tash asked, slipping her free hand into hers.

Laney nodded. She had to be OK. For the next ten minutes she just had to be.

One last scan of the scene they'd created and she could see that everything was just perfect. Exactly as she'd envisaged it. There were a few tourists milling around, a couple of students sitting further along the steps, a few

natives out for a stroll with tiny dogs on leads, most of
them making curious glances at the candles, Clark, and
the band. Some even took a seat on a step to watch what
was about to unfold, but thankfully not within the
artificial boundary that had been created by the two
parallel rows of tiny flickering flames.

"There's the car," Millie said quietly.

Laney flipped her head to the side so quickly she was
sure she'd just given herself whiplash.

Was that it?

There were hundreds of limos in Manhattan and that
could be any of them.

What were the chances of this being the right one?
What were the chances of this car containing the two
people that were about to blow her life apart?

Except ... "Oh fuck, it's slowing down. It's them.
Fuck, I can't breathe." Laney didn't even know who she
was talking to and whether or not anyone could hear her
over the noise of her heart thumping in her chest. *Don't
faint. Don't faint. Do not faint*, she told herself, but her
shaking legs weren't necessarily listening.

The sleek black car drew to a halt at the bottom of the
steps and, right on cue, Clark stepped forward and
opened the back door. Laney could see him reaching
forward and then emerging from the cover of the car
holding a hand, followed by an arm, a bare shoulder,
blonde hair, a face ...

Laney gasped as she put the binoculars to her eyes.
Cara was utterly exquisite. Her flawless skin was lightly
tanned, her honey blonde hair pulled back and twisted
into a perfect chignon, with tendrils escaping at the front
to frame her beautiful face. Laney could see the red

dress, a breathtaking sheath with roses trailing across one shoulder. It was like watching an advert for haute couture, the vision of perfection come to life.

Laney felt a stab of sympathy for her. This girl deserved to have a good man. Someone who would love and cherish her. Someone who didn't have a wife waiting at home.

"Come on, come on, come on," Tash whispered under her breath beside her, while on the other side, Millie was so silent Laney wasn't sure she was breathing.

Cara paused, turned, looked back into the car, put her hand out and waited for her love to join her.

Up at the top of the stairs, Lincoln and his band gently eased into their first song, the undulating beauty of "Moon River". Millie's silence turned to a sob.

Suddenly thoughts went off like machine gun fire in Laney's head, each one ricocheting off her skull. It wasn't going to be him. It wasn't. It was a mix up. Someone else. A joke. A stunt for a TV show. Or a dream. Yep, that was it. This whole last three weeks had been a dream and any minute now she would wake up in her own bed with the man she was going to grow old with.

A hand. That was all. Just a hand. It reached out and took Cara's, the black of his jacket slipping back to reveal the white of his shirt cuff. Cara was stepping back now, allowing him to emerge fully from the vehicle, to move into view, to …

She could only see the back of him but it was enough.

The blonde hair, the wide shoulders, the slight swagger when he walked.

Cara didn't take her eyes off his face, as they glided

upwards, every step giving the trio in the doorway a better view.

"Fucker," Tash said, her voice weary.

Laney couldn't disagree.

It wasn't a mistake. Or a stunt or a practical joke. And no matter how much she desperately wanted it to be, it wasn't a bad dream.

It was real. Real life. And the end of everything she thought she had.

Laney couldn't scream and she couldn't cry. All she could do was watch as her husband climbed the steps of the Metropolitan Museum of Art with his lover.

43

The video captured every sublime moment.

The girl in the red dress led the way, but at the mid-point on the steps, where it plateaued for a few feet, the butler was now waiting for them. In his right hand, he carried a silver tray, held aloft, with a tiny blue velvet box in the centre.

The girl in the red dress, her eyes ablaze with love, her perfect white smile never leaving her, turned to her lover, then waited as he instinctively realised what he was to do.

He reached over, took the box, opened it so that only he could see the ring inside. A flicker of surprise, an almost indiscernible nod of the head, then he dropped to one knee.

Around them, candlelight dancing in their eyes, the bystanders watched, hands over mouths that were open in awe and wonder.

The man's voice, steady, warm, just loud enough for the microphone to pick up his words.

"Darling," he told her, taking her left hand in his. A hesitation. A catch in his throat. A deep breath. "Will you marry me?"

The girl in the red dress, no tears, just laughter, as she threw her head back and cried "Yes."

The band seamlessly moved from "Moon River" to a song that made the man pause, flinch. The slow bluesy version of a classic that Ray Charles did in the sixties. "Your Cheating Heart".

The lover stood there among the rose petals, as if frozen, until he realised that the beautiful woman's lips were coming closer, closer, closer …

The videographer had no idea how he was going to edit out the bit where the newly engaged bloke sneezed in his fiancée's face.

44

"I can't even cry any more." Laney, two hands around a huge coffee mug, stared straight ahead as she spoke, not even registering the other customers that were crammed into the Irish bar that had become their local haunt. "It was him, wasn't it? I mean, it wasn't just me who saw it?"

Repeatedly asking questions that she already knew the answers to – wasn't that one of the signs of madness?

"Do you want me to show you the video again?" Tash asked, picking up her mobile phone from the table. The videographer had yet to edit it, but at Tash's request, he'd already sent the raw footage and all three of them now had it on their phones. "I want to go to Asiate. I want to confront him. Come on, Lanes – we can't let him get away with this. We just can't. Aaargh, it's so wrong."

Laney took another sip from the steaming mug and

didn't even care that it burnt her top lip. For a moment she visualised how Tash's suggestion would play out. They'd enter the restaurant, push past the maître d', storm across the room and she'd slap Cam Cochrane across the face. Cara, confused, would scream, and someone would call security. Laney would announce that Cam was her husband, and Cara would cry, begging him to tell her it wasn't true. He'd put his head down, caught like a rat in a trap, and Cara would scream again. The other diners would all be watching now, equally aghast and intrigued. They'd be entranced by the beautiful girl in the red dress and they'd feel horror that these three women were causing her such distress. They'd pity the poor betrayed wife, while tutting with distaste that she chose to air her dirty laundry in public. Someone might even pull out their mobile phone and record it, posting it on YouTube, where the most painful moment of her life would go viral and be watched by six million people, culminating in an appearance on *Ellen*, where she'd share her trauma and be given a two week, all-expenses paid trip to Cabo to help heal the pain.

No. She wasn't going to track him down. There was nothing to be gained from it and Cara may be, like, *totally,* annoying, but she didn't deserve to find out her new fiancé was a cheating scumbag in a restaurant on what should be the happiest night of her life.

Let her have this. Let her have her dream for now.

There would be plenty of time for hurt, rage and suffering later. And if Cara still wanted him when the dream became a nightmare, that was up to her.

Laney had what she came for: unequivocal proof that Cam was leading some sort of fucked up double life.

Guilty, your honour.

"No." Laney said simply, and watched as Tash's face flushed with fury. Taking one hand off the coffee cup, she reached over, and placed it over Tash's fingers, currently drumming the crap out of the table in frustration.

"I know it's not how you would handle it, Tash, but if we go hunt them down now, it takes away my element of surprise and there are a few things I need to take care of before that happens. I need to do it my way. "

"Which is?" Tash challenged.

"I want to take back control of my life."

The statement triggered a memory.

Picking up the phone, she pressed redial on the last call. Matt the Accountant answered on the first ring, despite the fact that it was almost three o'clock in the morning. She made a mental note to buy him something nice in duty free to thank him.

"Hey. You sound like you're in a bar, so either it wasn't him and you're celebrating, or you're drowning your sorrows," he said, showing impressive perception skills.

"Sorrows," Laney replied, determined not to break down. The poor guy had already seen her in full-scale tears mode, and she didn't want to give him flashbacks.

"You're kidding! It was him? What a knob."

"He is indeed," Laney agreed. On a better day, she could come up with something witty or smart, but today she just had to get through the call without disintegrating into heaving sobs.

"Can you go ahead and do what we planned?"

"Of course. I'll get on it right now."

"And your mate – the joiner – he'll sort out the door?"

"Yes. I've already got him teed up, so we'll shoot over to your house in the morning and it'll be done by the time you get home."

"Thanks. I couldn't face being there when that was happening. Seems so … significant."

"No worries. And Laney … I'm sorry. This shouldn't have happened to you."

The sympathy in his words made her throat close and forced her to furiously blink back tears. So much for not crying.

"Thanks Matt. I'm going to go now before you've got a sobbing mess on your hands again." She hung up, knowing he'd understand.

Tash had one eyebrow up in suspicion. "What was that about?"

Laney took a moment and a couple of deep breaths to recover. No crying. She would not shed another tear over that bastard.

"Matt's changing the locks – I left him a spare key so he could go do it for me before I got home. He's got a few financial moves to make, too."

"Like?" Tash asked, suspicion turning to grudging respect.

Laney looked at her watch. "Let's just say, I hope Cam doesn't try to pay for dinner with his credit cards or debit cards from our accounts, because in about another five minutes they'll both be cancelled. Then his access to all our sources of finance will be blocked, so that he'll have nothing but the cash in his pocket. Of course, Cara will still have the credit card he gave her, but he's going to have to worry about how to settle that next month, because not another single penny is coming from me."

"And how is Matt accomplishing all this?" Millie asked, entering the conversation for the first time.

"Because I gave him the user names and passwords for all our accounts and a list of instructions on how to shut Cam out of all of them. I'm also fairly sure he has a secret account, which he's been syphoning cash off our joint accounts to finance. Matt's working on tracking that and if he finds it, he'll shut that down too. Or at least stop any payments going there from my accounts."

"Isn't some of that illegal? Like hacking?' Millie was biting her bottom lip now, a sure sign that this was concerning her. "I don't want you to end up in serious trouble."

"He won't challenge me – not if I'm right and he's been stealing money from me to pay for Cara all along. I want the house sorted, the finances sorted, and then I'll take care of Cam."

"And how do you plan to do that?" Tash this time, and there was no mistaking the glint of evil delight in her eyes.

Laney stared straight ahead, her voice low and deadly. "I just need to see him one more time."

45

"Is it there yet?" Tash asked, gesturing to Laney's laptop.

For the tenth time in the last hour, Laney checked her emails. "Nope. But hang on, there's an email from Matt. 'Just heading to house now', he says."

Tash checked her watch. "Ten past two. So that's just after seven a.m. in the UK. That's efficiency for you."

Tash had a flashback to the first time she'd seen Matt, in her flat, after he'd escorted her home from a drunken night out. Her instincts about him had been right. Too nice. Definitely too sweet, too nice, too laid back. Not attractive to her at all.

However, in the spirit of friendship and kindness, should he ever require anyone to stare at his abdominal area all day, she would definitely be up for the job.

Another ping. *Her* phone this time. The screen said HLD.

Hot Limo Driver.

Despite her promise to call him, she'd bailed out. Today wasn't the day for it. That's what was wrong with her, she'd decided. It was Laney's troubles that were throwing her equilibrium off. As soon as her friend got over her heartache – and Tash would help her every step of the way to forget the scumbag she was married to – Tash could then revert to young, free and religiously hedonistic.

The text she was opening now was in response to one she'd sent a couple of hours ago, asking that he take them back to the airport tomorrow.

His reply was late but agreeable. "Of course. See you then – unless my favourite client is still awake and would like a tour of the city?"

Must give him full marks for effort. She liked that kind of confidence and charm in a man.

On any given day, he'd be exactly her type. Gorgeous, edgy, direct, and unapologetically exuding male energy and sex appeal.

"Sorry. Almost asleep. Another time … x"

There wouldn't be another time. Bugger. Sometimes there were just too many fish in the hot, single sea.

A ping. Bloody hell, there were too many electronic communication devices in this room. Lying on the sofa, Tash looked to her right, to see who it belonged to. Millie didn't react, so either it wasn't her ringtone or she was too comfortable lying on the other sofa in a pale pink onesie to respond.

On the floor next to her, Laney sat crossed legged in soft grey shorts and a white T-shirt, with her laptop open on the coffee table. "It's there," she said, staring at the screen.

Tash knew what she was referring to.

They'd been waiting for some contact from Cam ever since he was last seen, approximately six hours ago, disappearing into the back of a car, having just got engaged at a New York landmark.

It was now Saturday morning in Glasgow, and he'd told Laney he'd be home to make a baby, so he was going to have to explain why he wasn't there. Macabre as it sounded, they'd all taken bets, with the losers to buy the lunches for the next week. Laney thought he'd say he had to go to head office in London for a meeting with the company chiefs. Millie thought he'd feign illness and say he was too sick to fly home. And Tash thought he'd claim that he was in hospital after a brutal mugging in the street. That may just have been wishful thinking, she decided.

"What does it say?" she asked Laney, the suspense excruciating.

"Hi darling, so sorry, not going to make it home. Been called to office to do urgent training for new recruits. Know it's ovulation weekend, so have taken Monday and Tues off. Hope not too late. Will make it up to you darling. Call you later. Love you xxx

"PS: Phone not working at moment, so going to take it to tech dept when I get a chance."

"Training? Shit, I should have said that," Tash sighed.

Laney didn't answer. Millie leaned over and hugged her and, as if affection forced her back to life, she eventually found her voice.

"He's fucking unbelievable." There was no anger. Just pure disbelief. "Who did I marry? I honestly have no

343

idea."

Tash stared at the ceiling, trying desperately to control her fury. How dare he? The guy was scum. Laney wanted to handle this in a mature and reasonable fashion and Tash found it incredibly frustrating that she had to honour that, despite wanting to repeatedly bounce a mallet off his genitals.

She lifted her head from the arm of the couch and raised herself up on one elbow. "And how sneaky to lie about the phone thing."

"What do you mean? How do you know it's a lie?" Millie's brow was furrowed with confusion.

"Because he's obviously saying that so he can switch his phone off. Otherwise Laney could call him and she would hear by his ringtone that he's abroad."

"You're right," Laney agreed, sadly. "The lying bastard."

Tash was heartened that there was a definite escalation of anger. Good. They were moving along the stages of grief: denial, pain, bargaining, anger and electric probes on nuts.

Tash rolled off the sofa, and bumped along until she was sitting next to Laney on the floor, put her arm around her shoulders, kissed her softly on the cheek.

"Lanes, we'll get through this," she told her softly. "Whatever it takes, and no matter what happens, you've got us, and life will get better. I promise."

Laney's head flopped down on to Tash's shoulder, and it stayed there until the tears stopped falling.

46

The sun was shining, streaming through the kitchen windows, and to Laney's credit, it didn't highlight a single speck of dust on the worktops. Oh, how she'd cleaned. Yep, she was a cliché. Since the moment the taxi had dropped her home, she'd been like a Stepford wife on crack. Without the "wife" part, obviously.

Cam's wardrobe had been the first stop.

Revenge had been tempting, but really, what was the point of cutting up his suits or sewing raw fish in his waistband? It was a waste of perfectly good clothes and she just couldn't do it. Instead, she'd put them all in suitcases and black bags, and they were currently lined up downstairs in the dining room, next to several cardboard boxes containing all his worldly goods.

His shit CD collection. His high-tech speakers. His fidelity gene. Nope, sorry – must be a mistake. That one didn't live here any more.

Fuelled by a sense of purpose and coffee from the flight deck coffee machine, she'd spent the rest of the day scouring, dusting, stripping beds, washing towels, removing every trace of his DNA from this house. She'd de-Camd her habitat.

He was gone.

When she found herself getting tired, she'd just pour another espresso and watch that damn video again. The moment of horrific truth. Now she knew every expression on his face, every rise and fall of his chest, every dart of his eyes.

A couple of times she'd wondered how he and Cara had spent their extra day in New York. Did they walk in Central Park? Make plans at the top of the Empire State Building? Stay in bed and do nothing but have sex and eat room service? From each other's buttocks?

Her wince was interrupted when the clock dinged on the hour. Eight a.m. If he came here straight from the New York flight, he'd be arriving in an hour or so.

How would he explain that one to Cara? *Sorry love, I know we just got engaged, but I just need to nip home and see my wife.*

Yet even as she thought that, she knew the truth. He'd say he had to go to work and Cara wouldn't question it – just like Laney had taken that at face value all these years.

He definitely worked at MindSoar, of that she was sure. She saw his salary go into one of their accounts every month. But obviously, he didn't work the long hours he'd led her to believe, given that he'd had time to stage an intense affair.

What a naïve fool she'd been.

Not any more.

The doorbell rang and her heart leapt. That was quick! He must have jogged through immigration and baggage reclaim.

Her legs suddenly felt weak, like they weren't capable of supporting her body, so she put her hand on the wall for support as she walked down the hall, turned the new key, opened the door and …

"Matt!"

He offered up a sympathetic smile. "Hi. I just wanted to drop this off. I didn't want to leave it with the new key under the plant pot …"

A brown envelope appeared between them and dangled in mid-air for a second, before Laney noticed it. The combination of no sleep and too many coffees had thrown off her powers of reaction.

"Come in," she offered.

Matt put his hands up. "No, it's fine. He must be due back soon?"

"In the next hour."

"Nervous?"

"I'm … something. Not even sure any more. Just feels … weird. Sorry, I'm not being very articulate. It's just all becoming a bit of a blur."

"I understand," he said, and Laney got a real sense that he meant it. God, how self-absorbed was she? She'd never even asked him about his relationships or his life outside of rugby and being a very nice accountant.

"You might want to sit down before you read that, though." He puffed, as he gestured to the envelope. "It's not pretty."

"How bad? Can you give me the bullet points?"

"I went through all your accounts like you asked me to. He's taken about twenty grand in the last three years, mostly cash withdrawals that then got deposited into another account he had in his name only. He did one bank transfer when he first set it up – that's how I found it. And the three hundred pounds a month? That went to a building society account, then it was moved right back out again to an account in Cara's name."

"I'm not even going to ask how you found all that out," Laney sighed.

Matt shrugged. "To be honest, as soon as I started really digging through all your accounts, it was fairly straightforward. He'd made loads of simple errors. And by the way, you're being charged far too much for your health insurance. I know an accountant who can help you with that."

Their smiles broke the discomfort of the conversation.

"Matt, thank you. I can't tell you how much I appreciate your help."

"No problem at all. You take care. And I'll call you next week about that health insurance."

Laney laughed and waved him off. Back inside, she shoved the envelope in a kitchen drawer. It was good to have it in black and white, but it didn't tell her anything she hadn't already suspected.

He'd lied. He'd cheated. He'd destroyed everything they had.

The doorbell rang again and this time, she knew it was him. She just knew.

Yet, strangely, she felt a sense of calm spread from her heart outwards.

The door was barely opened when he huffed in past

her, carrying a holdall and pulling a trolley case behind him. "What a fucking morning," he raged. "Bloody bank cards wouldn't work, credit cards are stuffed, too, and when I tried to phone the bank they said they'd all been bloody cancelled. Can you give me twenty quid for the taxi, darling?"

"Is it a Glasgow Ride Cab?" Before he could answer, she popped her head out of the door and saw that it was. Even better, it was a driver they used regularly and he recognised her. Laney made the "signing" hand gesture and he nodded in understanding that she was saying she wanted it to be put on her account. Personal Proposals was an account customer, as it was much easier than having to deal with cash when they were ferrying couples around the city.

The cab driver drove off and she turned, jumping when she saw he was still standing right behind her. Too close. Way too close. And now … touching!

One of his hands went around her neck and he leaned in to kiss her. Her internal alarms went off like sirens in a police chase.

She pulled back sharply, before the contact made her throw up, but managed to keep her voice as close to normal as it could be.

"So your phone's working again?"

"What?"

"You said your phone was broken, but then you said you'd called the bank. Did your tech guys fix it?"

Rabbit. Headlights. She could see he was trying to run through his memories to make sure he gave the correct response.

"Erm, yeah. They did."

Wow. So that's what it looked like when he lied to her face. A dart of the eyes. The pulse of the vein in the side of his neck. The tightness across his lips. So devious and – she realised – so familiar.

Turning, she headed down the hall and into the kitchen, desperate to escape the claustrophobic closeness. There, she lifted her mug of coffee and tried to act relaxed. She was glad she'd stayed casual - jeans, cuffs rolled up at the bottom, bare feet and a red T-shirt that fell off one shoulder.

In the last few days, a thousand scenarios had played through her head when she thought about this moment, a dozen speeches, a ton of emotions. But now it was here, she was perfectly calm, absolutely focused.

He had pushed a mug under the coffee machine, pressed a few buttons and left it to percolate while he turned to her, that young-Val-Kilmer-in-*Top-Gun* grin as suave as ever.

"I've missed you, darling. It's so good to be home."

No nervous dart of the eyes. No pulse in the neck. Maybe he actually meant that. This guy was a mess. A complete screw up.

"And I'm so looking forward to spending two days in bed with …"

To her horror, she realised he was about to move towards her again and she knew exactly what he would do. He would put his hands around her waist, he'd kiss her, then he'd slip his palms upwards, lift her up, placing her down on the kitchen worktop. He'd kiss her again, and his hands would go under her T-shirt and … Nope, wasn't happening.

As he took another step towards her, she cut him off

with, "So how was Manchester?" He halted, thrown off by the interruption.

'Yeah, great. London, too. Was chuffed to be asked to work with the new recruits. Shows where I am in the hierarchy and that's moving towards the top." He grinned. Had he always been this smug and obnoxious, or was it only because he was overcompensating in trying to cover up a lie?

Another one.

Enough.

"And how was New York?" she said quietly.

Silence.

Dart. Pulse.

Silence.

And an expression of utter horror on his face.

Laney turned to where her iPad sat on a stand, pressed play.

The New York street. The limo. Cara alighting, Then Cam. They glide up the steps. The butler. The tray. The ring. The …

"Stop it. Please, just stop it," he begged, panicking.

"It doesn't matter. I got to see it for real the first time around."

"You were there?"

"I was there. Across the street."

"Fuck."

"Nope, I didn't stay around for that bit."

It was a cheap shot but hey, she was dignified but she wasn't an angel. He had both arms out now, beseeching her to forgive him.

"Laney, I'm so …"

"Don't dare say sorry. Don't dare." Her voice switched

from steely and calm to low and dangerous, with an overtone of warning.

"Here's what I know." Laney told him, noticing that his face had completely drained of colour and was now a disturbing shade of grey that aged him ten years.

"I know you've been seeing Cara for a couple of years. I know you've been lying to me. That you stay with her, travel with her, holiday with her, and tell me you're working every time. I know you Skype her at midnight for sex."

He winced.

"I know you've been taking our money and paying for your life with her. I know that she has a credit card for her use and I know that you pay some of her rent."

"The bank cards…?" he said, realisation dawning.

"I cancelled them all," Laney confirmed.

"I also know that you spent the weekend in the Carlyle and that you're now engaged. And I know you were prepared to come here today and make love to me because you were still going to go along with our plans to have a baby."

That one stung and she almost lost it, fighting back a wave of grief and a flood of tears.

"I therefore know that you are scum."

He didn't argue.

"I know that everything you possess is boxed up in the other room and will be sent to whatever address you want within the next twenty-four hours. If you don't have somewhere for it to go by then, I'll burn it.

"I know …" She choked. This was getting too hard. "I know I trusted you and I thought we were for ever. I was wrong."

His body language told her he was about to speak. She decided to let him. "Lanes, I'm so …" he paused, noting the fury that flashed across her eyes, changed tack, switched from apology to explanation. "It wasn't meant to go this far. It was a fling. Casual. Nothing special. But she got way more into it than I did, and then it was too late and I didn't know how to get out of it. I was flattered, Lanes. A total dick and so fucking stupid, but she was just so gorgeous and …"

"Is this supposed to be making me feel better?" she asked archly.

There were tears in his eyes now as he frantically ran his fingers through his hair, before leaving both hands on top of his head in a surrender position. "Shit, sorry, but … It wasn't meant to last, Lanes. I don't want to be with her, I want to be here with you, but I just … couldn't … didn't want to stop. Not yet. And then the stunt at the weekend. Fuck. You've no idea how shocked …"

"Oh, I think I do."

"Of course you do. Sorry. But it was just … I had to go along with it. What could I do? I couldn't say no. There was a fucking butler there and everything."

Laney had no idea why that mattered, but clearly it did.

"I had to do it."

"You didn't." Her chest was starting to hurt now and she didn't know how much strength she had left in her. "Do you love her?"

Argh, she was so annoyed at herself for asking it but she wanted to know.

He exhaled. "No." No dart. No pulse. He was telling the truth. Yet hearing it didn't make her feel even a tiny bit better.

"I think she's great, but she's not you. I'm meant to be with you."

"You're not. Go now, Cam. Go to a mate's house, go to Cara's flat, go anywhere. I don't care. Just don't ever come back here."

"But …"

"Go." The aggression, the blaze in her eyes, the finality of her tone combined to make it indisputable.

He picked up his holdall and the case he'd come in with, turned, and headed to the door. There, he stopped. "Laney, I didn't plan any of this."

"I know," she told him. "Because *I* did. Now get out."

He still looked utterly bewildered as the door slammed behind him.

With a flurry and a tumble of bodies, Tash and Millie burst out of the utility room.

"Is he gone?" Tash blurted, eyes wild.

Laney exhaled properly for the first time all morning. "Yes."

"Thank God," Millie said. "I had to physically restrain her at one point. I'm sure I've dislocated my shoulder."

This was one of the worst moments of her life, yet strangely, Laney was smiling.

Tash and Millie. They'd come back with her from the airport, refused to leave her alone. They'd cleaned with her, packed with her and held her when it all got too much. Actually, Millie held her – Tash just tried to cajole her to come out into the back garden and start smoking. Apparently you were never too old to wreck your lungs.

Laney had lived through betrayal before and she knew

she'd get past this in time. She had absolutely no doubt that she was strong enough to cope. She had loved Cam with all her heart, but he broke it and she wasn't going to give him one more day of sadness or pain. Cam Cochrane was out of her life. But the really important people were still in it.

"Right, get your coats. One more task and then we're done."

"Cara?"

Laney nodded. "He'll probably walk to the pub at the end of the road and phone a cab from there. That'll take half an hour or so. If we get there fast, we'll beat him."

"We'll take the Beetle," Millie exclaimed, ignoring the roll of Tash's eyes.

"OK, but quick. I don't want her to hear his lying, cheating version. I owe it to her to explain. She did nothing to deserve this and she needs to know the truth."

47

Laney stood at the front, Tash and Millie behind her, as she pressed the button on the intercom.

"Hi baby," a sunny voice chirped through the speaker.

Not the greeting she expected, or the way she wanted this to start.

"Cara? It's Laney, from Personal Proposals."

For a moment there was complete silence, then a buzzer and the click of the door mechanism. Laney, Tash and Millie trotted up the stairs, Laney's stomach churning. Strangely, this was the part that she was dreading most. She had just had her future stamped over until it was dust, and now she was about to do the same thing to someone else.

To her surprise, Cara was already at her front door waiting for them.

"Hi, Cara."

"Hi," the younger woman replied warily, making no

move to invite them in. That suited Laney fine, especially as she could see Cara was dressed for more than just a cosy chat. Whoever designed the bodycon dress she was wearing should sign her up to front their next campaign because she was selling it! Low cut, revealing perfectly pert breasts, every curve and sinew of her figure oozing femininity and beauty. Her caramel hair fell in loose waves around her shoulders and her make-up was subtle but stunning. It wasn't hard to see what had attracted Cam. There was an involuntary wince as that thought permeated her heart.

"Sorry to land on you like this, but we just wanted to have a chat about … I mean, tell you that …" Her brain and her mouth refused to co-ordinate. This was so hard. The poor girl. She was about to have her future decimated and it was killing Laney to be the one who delivered the pain. 'I'm not sure where to start, but there are a few things I need to tell you. About Cam. Your … fiancé." Laney stuttered over the words again, as Cara's thick, impeccably shaped eyebrows raised.

"Cara, maybe it would be better to have this conversation inside," Millie suggested.

"No. It's, like, fine. Talk here."

Her voice had a hint of something that wasn't there before. Laney realised the only way to do this was quick and direct.

"Cara, I don't even know how to say this, and I'm so, so, sorry, but …"

"He's your husband."

Laney, Tash and Millie all visibly reeled backwards as Cara's words stunned them.

Tash was the first to recover. "You knew?"

Cara rolled her eyes. "Of course I knew. I found the card in his wallet, looked up your company …"

That piece of information rang a bell. Cara had told them that on her first visit to the office.

"Saw you on your website and realised you had the same surname. After that it was easy. Checked your Facebook page and the photos of your lives were there."

"And yet you still wanted him?"

"I did." Cara folded her arms and shifted her weight to one hip like a sullen child.

Laney was incredulous. "You did all this deliberately?"

"Look. We were meant to be together and it's me he wants to be with. He just needed a bit of a push along the way. Can't believe you let it go that far, though. I really thought you'd confront him the minute you found out."

"So that was your plan?" Laney wasn't getting this at all. She knew? She bloody knew all along?

Cara's glossy mane shimmered as she nodded. "Yeah. That first day, I just wanted to meet you and see what you were like. I was curious. Wanted to check out the competition and let you know about Cam and me. I was sure you'd blow it wide open that night. But you didn't. And then I thought when you asked me to come in for the next meeting to discuss the update on the plans, that you were going to tell me then that you were married to him. But again you didn't. Although you did look like you were about to collapse."

"You bitch," Millie interjected, and Laney and Tash spun their head to her in surprise. Confrontation wasn't normally Millie's style, but she was so rattled Laney experienced a tug of gratitude for the loyalty.

Cara wasn't similarly moved. "Maybe, I am," she agreed. "But you were the one that let it carry on, so I decided to see how far you'd take it. Didn't think you'd go all the way to New York. Kept waiting for you to ambush us at the airport. Or the hotel. But you didn't. You kept it going and hey, I got the most incredible weekend of my life out of it so I'm, like, totally grateful."

The edge of smug satisfaction too much for Tash. "You fucking …"

"Tash, leave it," Laney ordered, all at once icy calm as a new realisation dawned.

Cam was a lying, cheating, ruthless, self-obsessed prick. And he'd just found his perfect match.

To the surprise of everyone there, Laney laughed. Properly laughed, then delivered her final words on the matter.

"You know what, Cara? You two, like, *totally* deserve each other."

48

"You look like you've cried all night, not slept and would prefer to be anywhere else but here," Millie said, as she handed Laney one of the skinny lattes she'd picked up on the way into the office. She plumped down beside Laney on the sofa, the fringes of her shawl fluttering against the layers of her deep blue maxi dress.

Laney lifted the lid and took a sip of the white froth at the top of the cup. "You're right on the first two, but not on the third. I'm glad I'm here. It's a distraction. I'm surrounding myself with happy, excited people and hoping it rubs off."

"You might want to stay away from Tash then. Don't know what's up with her, but she's been a grumpy cow for weeks now."

"She's always been a grumpy cow." Laney laughed.
"True."

"Who's a grumpy cow?' Millie spun around to see

Tash marching in the door.

"You are."

Tash stopped, eyed them, exhaled, and then grinned. "That's not exactly a newsflash, is it?" She joined the others over at the sofa area. "Shit, Lanes, you look awful. Rough night?"

"I was just asking her the same thing," Millie said.

Laney took a moment to think through her answer. "It's really strange, but all the hurt is gone. It's like Cam Cochrane doesn't even exist any more and it's almost like he never did. I'm so used to him being away that I don't miss his physical presence. I hate him for what he did, but now I just feel like … I have no idea who I was married to. We've never spent more than a night or two a week in the same house, sometimes less. Last night I kept wondering what it would have been like if we'd actually lived together all the time. Would we have got married? Stayed together? Or would we have realised much sooner that it wasn't right? I think …" She stalled, then pressed on. "I think what I miss is our future. The one I thought we would have. But I'll get used to it. I'll find a new one," she finished, with a sad but determined nod of her head.

The door buzzer went and Tash picked up the pink phone and pressed the release button to let them in.

"Who is it?" Millie asked.

Tash shrugged dismissively. "No idea. Sometimes I just like to be surprised when they walk through the door."

Millie was still giggling when Fred and Mrs Crean burst in, desperate to share her news. "We've just been down at the station, dear, and everything is good to go.

Oh, all those dancers with those fit bodies have given me quite a hot flush."

"Hi, sweetheart." Fred reached down and kissed Laney on the cheek. "Everything is all organised along at the station. Tash had the set up going like a military operation."

"Brilliant. Thanks, Dad. We should really get going then," Laney decided, before turning to Millie. "What do you think?"

"Definitely." Millie checked her watch and felt the familiar flurry of excitement that she got right before every job – despite the fact that this train station flash mob wasn't her idea of the romantic pinnacle of someone's life. Still, it was a big event, it would get great publicity and it would hopefully earn them another happy client who would tell the world how great they were.

The five of them walked to the station, arriving twenty minutes before Maggie was due. If all went according to plan, Maggie would come here thinking that she was meeting Paul for a day in town shopping, only to leave the station with a big sparkly ring on her finger. This was why Millie loved her job. Loved it!

She cast her eye around the station and spotted nothing out of the ordinary, which was exactly how it should be. The dancers were blending in with the commuters, none of them obvious to her at all. Good. Tash had done an amazing job, as always.

Millie cast her eye upwards to one of the few higher windows inside the building, the office in which their videographer would be filming the event. Getting permission had been a struggle, but Tash had arranged it in the end. The glint of the camera lens told Millie that he was in position. So all they need now was a bloke with a ring and …

Her scan of the crowd stopped, reversed and settled on a familiar face.

"Tash," she said, puzzled. Beside her, Tash looked up from her clipboard.

"What?"

"Isn't that your next door neighbour with benefits?"

She watched as Tash followed her eyeline, until she saw…

"Fuck, what's he doing here? He's everywhere I go lately," she said, furious. Or at least, the words were furious but the tone behind them was surprisingly lacking in aggression.

A piercing noise rang through the air. "Whoah, what's that?" The sound morphed into harmonica and the first bars of "Be My Girl" boomed the station into life.

"Oh no! No!" Millie cried. "Too soon! It's not supposed to start until Maggie arrives. Tash! What's happening? We need to get this stopped and get everything back to the way it was before she gets here."

Millie was in full-scale panic mode now, heart racing, frantically looking around for some kind of explanation or help in getting this sorted. They'd never had a proposal disaster and they weren't going to bloody start now.

"Tash! Tash! Where's the music coming from?"

"From the speakers! The station agreed to put it through their PA system. Oh fuck, heads will roll for this. And noooooo, they're dancing! Dear God, stop them dancing!" Tash screeched.

Swivelling back round, Millie saw that she was right. The dancers had sprung to life. Four guys in suits swaggered to the central spot. Six "students" discarded their backpacks and joined them. Two ticket collectors cast off their jackets and hats, and shook out long blonde tresses. What looked on first inspection to be three old ladies and an elderly gent suddenly went from being hunched over a timetable to pirouetting across the floor to join the others. The rest of the commuters stopped to watch the action, eyes wide with surprise and anticipation, already reaching from their mobiles to video it so they could share it with everyone they met that day.

And then there was Paul, strutting dramatically through the centre towards them, his grin wide, coming closer, closer …

"Paul! What the hell are you doing? She's not here yet, you clown!" Tash yelled. "Get back to the start and …"

Millie stopped listening. Because out of the corner of her eye she saw someone else cutting across the concourse, his face covered by a hat and large glasses, his purposeful stride putting him on direct course to collide with Paul. "Excuse me! Excuse …" she cried, too late. He bumped into Paul, who staggered out of the way. Oh, dear God, this was chaos. Carnage! She had to do something. Stop the dancers. Stop the music. Stop this guy punching Paul's lights out. Stop the …

The new arrival, standing directly in front of the dancers now, started to tap his feet, then swing his hips, then …

Paul, still smiling, clambered to his feet and slipped into the middle of the pack of dancers.

Centre stage now, his replacement threw off his hat and glasses and Millie laughed – laughed and cried and screamed as Leo, her lovely Leo, burst into the choreographed movements, leading the dancers, his actions flawless. From the back, the two that had been dressed as ticket collectors moved forwards, and she recognised Deedee and Rianne, the two girls who had been at her house and … Millie's hands flew to her face, covering her mouth, chin dropped in surprise.

"Hey Baby Will You Be My Girl?" They all sang, Leo the loudest, his eyes locked with hers, as he strutted, he shimmied, he boogied and he begged her to be his, right through until the final bar of the song. That's when the dancers all fell on to one knee, and Leo took ten steps forward, dropped down, pulled out a red leather box, opened it and held it aloft.

"Millie Jones, I love you. Please, please marry me."

49

"Are you crying? You are, you're actually crying!" Laney exclaimed, forcing Tash to sniff loudly and wipe her face with the sleeves of her favourite Nicole Farhi cardi.

"Only because I thought we'd fucked up a job," Tash replied. She could see that she was fooling no one, least of all Laney, Millie and Leo, with whom she was standing in a huddle.

It was only ten minutes after the performance, but already the crowd had dispersed, the dancers were gone, and it was as if nothing had ever happened, except for the fact that one of her best friends looked like the happiest girl in the world.

Leo was next to speak. "Laney, I'm sorry about what happened and I'm sorry about the timing of this. I'd never have planned this to happen the day after … you know."

Laney shook her head, smiling. "Please don't say that. This is exactly what we all needed. Something wonderful to cheer us up and remind us there are some good guys out there."

"I wouldn't go that far," Tash joked dryly. "I mean, he obviously indulged in an inordinate amount of subterfuge to pull this off. And a train station flash mob proposal for Millie? Do you not know her at all?" she teased.

Leo rolled his eyes. "Don't even get me started. I sent Paul – he's an old mate from drama school …"

"So THAT'S why he never seemed emotionally invested," Laney cried, everything becoming clear.

"Yeah, I guess. Anyway, I'd explained to him who you all were, but he got totally flustered and messed it up. I told him to find out what Millie's ideal proposal would be and he reported back that she wanted this …"

"But the flash mob was *my* idea," Tash argued.

Leo nodded sheepishly. "I know that now. But I didn't realise it for ages. We only sussed it out when he said you wanted a simple band as an engagement ring and I realised that wasn't Millie's style. Actually, I'd forgotten about the ring up until then. I was so busy working on the proposal that I forgot the most important bit. Thank God you mentioned it to Paul."

"You really are hopeless," Tash teased.

"Indeed I am – and that was never clearer than at that moment, when I made him describe your appearance and realised he'd got you two mixed up. By that time he'd been teaching me the moves and I'd been working every spare moment with the dancers, so we just decided to go with it. Oh, and the dancers – they were a group we hung

367

SHARI LOW

out with at drama school, too. I had them email you right after Paul reported that you wanted a flash mob. I knew they'd help me out with extra rehearsal time so thank God you gave them the job. Paul would rehearse and then I'd meet him at night or early in the morning to go over the steps. Or the girls would come to the house."

Millie punched him playfully. "And I believed the stories about early morning runs and meeting the girls while you were out jogging. I'm so gullible. So who was the girl in the red car outside our house that day?"

"When?" He was genuinely puzzled.

"When I was coming home I saw her. I saw her again on Pollokshaws Road near Guy's travel shop."

Leo puts his hands up to proclaim innocence. "I genuinely have no idea."

"That's so weird. She was vaguely familiar but I couldn't place her. Maybe it was just a total coincidence that I spotted her twice in a couple of days. Wonder why she was sitting in our road, though."

Laney looked pensive, then, "Hang on - blonde? Red sports car?"

"Yes."

"Is that her?"

They all followed the direction in which Laney's finger was pointing. Over at the entrance, Guy from the travel agents was still taking pictures for his new brochure, the one that advertised Personal Proposals Worldwide."

"Yes!" Millie exclaimed, when she saw the woman that was standing next to him. Laney explained, "That's Jorja – Guy's girlfriend. I met her when I went to book the New York trip because she works in his office. He told me she's massively jealous. She must have been checking you out because he'd been over at your place?"

"Oh. Well after what happened to you, I can see her point," Millie admitted, before turning all her attention back to her new fiancé. "Honey, what you did today was incredible."

Leo adopted a sheepish expression. "I know now it wasn't the kind of proposal you dreamt of, but least it was memorable." He squeezed Millie and she reached up and kissed him.

"Urgh, stop that. You'll put people off their lunch," Tash moaned.

The four of them were still laughing when another body joined the party. Tash sensed him behind her, even before Laney said, "Sy, good to see you."

"And you," he agreed, before leaning over to kiss Millie's cheek and shake Leo's hand. "Congratulations. That was some show," he said warmly. "Tash, can I borrow you for a minute?"

Tash groaned inside, then reluctantly followed him. Just because he was so good looking in that beautifully cut suit, and smooth and smart and great in bed didn't mean she was always going to … What did he just say?

He'd pulled her into a quiet corner, just the two of them, and now his mouth was moving.

"What?"

"I love you," he repeated, with utter confidence. "And I think you love me."

"I don't," she argued. Who was he to tell her how she was feeling?

"Yes, you do. And it's pissing you off because you're starting to miss me when I'm not around."

SHARI LOW

"I'm … I'm … I'm … not!" Oh bugger, she was. He knew it. She knew it. She just refused to admit it. "OK, maybe a bit. But Sy, I can't do the relationship thing. I don't want it."

His hand was under her chin now, lifting it up so he could study her face, before he asked, "So what do you want?"

Tash closed her eyes and let her mind adjust to this new truth. She'd never wanted a full-time relationship. And no, it wasn't because she was damaged, or flawed in any way. In fact, it really irritated her when people assumed that to be the case. The truth was she liked her life. Liked her freedom and her space. The casual sex she could do without, but – at the risk of coming over all Mel Gibson – she couldn't live without her freedom.

"I just want what we've got," she finally admitted, "but maybe a bit more often. I'll never want to get married and I don't want to have children Sy. And I'm not giving up my flat because sometimes I like to do my own thing. I want to be with you – just not all the time. Are you sure you can live with that?

"I can live with that," he assured her, so convincingly that she actually believed him.

"And we could lose Giselle," she added with a smile.

"She's already gone."

"Really. When?"

"When I realised that I only wanted you." He traced a line along her cheek – it was beautiful, moving, poignant and …

"Right, let's get something else straight. We could be together for fifty years and it will still not be OK to touch me up or kiss me in public."

His laughter was loud and infectious. "You think we'll be together in fifty years?"

Tash decided that for one time only she'd break her own rules. She leaned over, kissed him. "Only if you're lucky."

50

Fred rested his head on the grey velvet back of the office sofa and exhaled. "It's like history repeating itself. I'm so sorry this happened to you, love."

Laney took his hand. "I'm so sorry it happened to you too, Dad. But you managed, didn't you? You got over it."

Fred nodded. "I did sweetheart – eventually – but I don't want you to do what I did. I don't want you to waste years of your life hoping he'll come back, praying for him to walk in the door and say he's made a terrible mistake."

Laney shook her head. "I won't, Dad. And it's different. You'd been with Mum for twenty years, you had a child together. Sometimes I'm not even sure if I ever knew him at all."

There was a loud pop in the kitchen and then a rousing cheer. The others were all in there pouring the champagne to celebrate Millie and Leo's engagement.

Laney had taken the opportunity to tell her dad about Cam before anyone else slipped up and blurted something out. Fred had reacted exactly as she expected – an initial burst of fury, a genuine threat that he'd have him arrested, deep frustration that it wouldn't solve the situation, and then finally sadness that his girl was having to deal with this. Now he was moving on to support and determination to help Laney prevail. Just as he had done.

Mrs Crean came bustling out of the kitchen carrying two glasses of champagne, looking resplendent and youthful in her bootcut jeans and smart, tailored white jacket, blonde hair swishing as she walked. Goldie Hawn was definitely missing a twin. She handed the bubbly over with a kiss to the top of Fred's head.

"Back in a mo! There's cake in there and I'm just going to pinch some for all of us. Life's too short to resist the odd indulgence," she told them with a twinkle in her eye.

She was barely out of earshot, when Laney said, "You should marry her, Dad."

"You wouldn't mind?"

"Absolutely not. And when you decide to pop the question, I know a great company that can help you with that."

Fred found that hilarious. He laughed a lot these days, Laney noticed. It suited him.

The door buzzer punctuated his sentence and Tash stuck her hand out of the kitchen, picked up one of the pink phones and pressed the entry button.

"Well, maybe I'll talk to you about that soon," he

admitted with a shy smile. "You know Laney, I really believe the right person is out there for everyone. You just need to find them."

Behind him the door opened; a new addition to the party. He crossed the room, a shy grin accessorising the genuine affection in his eyes.

When he reached the sofa, Laney returned the smile.

"Dad," she said, "have you met Matt? He's our very nice accountant."

THE END